SUGANDHI ALIAS
ANDAL DEVANAYAKI

T.D. Ramakrishnan is the author of three cult novels in Malayalam that blur the line between the popular and the highbrow – *Alpha*, *Francis Itty Cora* and *Sugandhi Alias Andal Devanayaki*. In 2017, he won the Vayalar Award and the Kerala Sahitya Akademi Award for *Sugandhi*.

Priya K. Nair teaches English in St. Teresa's College, Ernakulam. She has previously translated *Alpha* and *Francis Itty Cora* into English.

D1246194

SUGANDHI ALIAS ANDAL DEVANAYAKI

T.D. RAMAKRISHNAN

TRANSLATED FROM THE MALAYALAM BY
PRIYA K. NAIR

HARPER**PERENNIAL**

An Imprint of HarperCollins *Publishers*

First published in English in India in 2018 by Harper Perennial
An imprint of HarperCollins *Publishers*
A-75, Sector 57, Noida, Uttar Pradesh 201301, India
www.harpercollins.co.in

2 4 6 8 10 9 7 5 3 1

P-ISBN: 978-93-5277-765-5
E-ISBN: 978-93-5277-766-2

Typeset in 11/14 Adobe Jenson Pro (OTF) at
Manipal Digital Systems, Manipal

Printed and bound at
Thomson Press (India) Ltd

MIX
Paper
FSC FSC® C010615

for Dr Rajini Thiranagama
no more tears sister

1

When I arrived at Divine Pearl, a secret Sri Lankan military camp that lay ninety-five kilometres from Colombo, it was quite late in the evening. DP was a prison camp built by the British colonizers to house hardened criminals. Though the façade resembled the palace of a feudal overlord, it was a fully equipped jail designed to hold prisoners securely and to torture them in many ingenious ways. The main building had twenty-two cells spread across three floors, and three rooms called prayer rooms that were used for interrogation. In a small building adjacent to it were offices and rooms for the officials. DP stood atop a hill in the middle of a hundred-acre tea plantation. We were subjected to a thorough frisking before being allowed in, even though we had special sanction from the president himself.

We were there for pre-production work on a movie, *The Woman Behind the Fall of the Tigers*, that Transnational Pictures was producing in collaboration with the Sri Lankan government. The crew comprised of me – Peter Jeevanandam, the scriptwriter – the director Christie Alberto from Scotland, his girlfriend and cinematographer Mary Ann, Tony Bernard who was one of the producers and Charles Samaraveera, a top official in the cultural ministry and a close confidant of the president. The camp in-charge, Colonel D'Silva, and his entourage treated us with a great show of hospitality. This could be attributed to the typical fancy third-world citizens have for Hollywood, or perhaps it was because the government had shown special interest in this project. The movie was an effort by the Sri Lankan government to whitewash the atrocities that had been committed in brazen violation of human rights during the civil war. But we planned to use the opportunity to portray how anti-democratic stances within a movement can fragment and weaken the revolution itself. Christie had picked me to write the script since I had spent several years with the Tigers working on a movie project during Prabhakaran's time, but had been forced to flee for my life without completing it.

Colonel D'Silva explained the working of the camp in detail. The most dangerous of the Tigers were housed in this camp. They could not be rehabilitated or reintroduced into society, as neither liberty nor torture could change them. Many of them still believed that their dream of a Tamil Eelam could be realized. Some of them had even lost their mental balance. There were prisoners who thought that Prabhakaran was still alive and would come to rescue them. Some of them would suddenly turn violent or attempt to commit suicide. Each one of them had been charged with hundreds of crimes, including mass murder, terrorism and anti-national activities. The trials were prolonged endlessly.

'And until then?' Christie asked our guide anxiously.

'And until then, it's our responsibility to see that they don't make trouble. But it's not easy.'

'Torture?'

'Yes. That is often required. As the prisoners are not ordinary criminals, we have to resort to different methods. Torture without using weapons or inflicting wounds.'

'How is that done?'

'There is physical as well as mental torture. Prisoners are made to lie naked in a big steel box resembling a coffin. Then spiders are let loose into it. When the spiders crawl on their naked bodies, the prisoners writhe in pain. In another box, there are millipedes. There are also boxes filled with ants, scorpions, crabs and snakes. Because the prisoners are not allowed to die, we only use snakes that are not poisonous. Every day, the prisoners have to lie in one of these boxes for hours while they are interrogated. All these people have been questioned hundreds of times. Yet we continue to question them in the hope that they will talk. But they are Tigers, after all. They do not give in easily. All this happens in the prayer rooms upstairs. After the physical torture is over, we start torturing them mentally. We use the prayer room on the first floor for this. It is a mini-theatre that shows movie clips of the Sri Lankan army defeating the Tigers in battle and the victory celebrations that followed. They also show the Tamils suffering under the Tigers. These clips are played in the hope that they will make the prisoners feel guilty. We also have footage of the prisoners' relatives cursing the Tigers, confessions of people like Daya Master who surrendered, and the advice of people like Karuna who shifted loyalties. They are also shown clips where the Tigers are criticized on international platforms for their atrocities. When movies are not being shown, songs parodying Prabhakaran and his people are played loudly.

'The prayer room on the ground floor is a modern torture chamber. It houses torture machines of international standards. There are machines to pull out nails and crush bones, cots that administer electric shocks, machines that simulate drowning, electric sticks that can be used to penetrate anuses and vaginas, gas chambers that make you laugh or cry continually and weaken your body, whips studded with nails, chairs of thorns, and microscopic instruments used to administer shock to private parts. These machines are not used in ordinary circumstances. But the prisoners live in fear that they might be used at any time. Every day at eight in the morning, after roll call, the prisoners are shown these instruments and are given detailed descriptions of how they are used, before being taken to the second floor. But they are Tigers and are not easily fazed. And we still haven't received permission from the president to use these machines. It may be because the International Human Rights Association keeps a close watch nowadays.'

By the time the Colonel had finished explaining all this, Christie had become impatient. 'We want to see everything,' he said.

The Colonel and a couple of army officers began bombarding us with questions: When will the shooting begin? Who is playing Prabhakaran? Is Mary acting in the movie? Will you shoot here? Christie and Mary were inspecting the rooms without giving clear answers to the questions. But I wanted to meet Thamizholi. Unfortunately, I wasn't able to meet her or any other prisoner. The Colonel bid us farewell saying, 'As there are security issues, you will only be able to meet the prisoners tomorrow.'

My mind was in turmoil after the prison visit. I did not share Christie's and Mary's excitement. It was the first time they were visiting such a place. But when I recalled the torture chambers in Kilinochchi and Vanni, this one seemed to pale in comparison.

We were staying at the Taj Samudra in Colombo. Christie and Mary shared an executive suite. I had a room to myself. Being the producer, Tony had to conduct several business dealings, so he too had a room to himself.

'How do you feel now?' Samaraveera asked, slightly inebriated and eager to start a conversation.

'Full of confidence. Peter's story is so startling. We will make magic with it. Please see to it that all the necessary arrangements are made.'

'You can ask for anything you want. This is the president's pet project. The world needs to see the Tigers in their true colours. We have to silence those who are slandering the government with accusations of human rights violations and mass murder.'

'But Samaraveera, this is a movie.'

'I know. We will not interfere with any aspect of movie-making. You have complete freedom. All of us have read Peter's story … even the president. When it is made into a movie, the world will undoubtedly see the truth.'

'Thank you, Samaraveera. I didn't know that your president was so broad-minded.'

'Well, that is why he has asked the cultural department to pay your remuneration as well as finance the movie.'

'He is indeed great. But if we speak about his greatness in the movie, we will lose credibility.'

'An intelligent artist will find a way – and you are very intelligent.'

The cultural department had arranged a grand dinner for us. The who's who of the film world were in attendance, including Vimukthi Jayasundara who had won the Caméra d'Or at the 2005 Cannes Film Festival, Chandran Rutnam, the director of

The Road from Elephant Pass and a notable Sri Lankan presence in Hollywood, and Malini Fonseka who had starred in *Akasa Kusum*. The glamorous Anusha Rajapaksha clung to Christie in her revealing outfit, fanning flames of gossip that she was our heroine. After the formal introductions, Christie spoke about the project.

'I met Peter, quite unexpectedly, in Berlin. It is only because of his good fortune that Peter, who had attempted to make a movie on the revolution during Prabhakaran's time, is still alive. This movie is Peter's story. An amalgam of the story he wrote and the life he lived. When Peter narrated the story, I realized we would have to approach the story from a different angle than *The Road from Elephant Pass*. My focus was on the violence and anti-democratic traits that lead a movement – and the people it claims to represent – to utter destruction. I am an outsider looking at this subject. Peter was looking at it from the inside. This movie was born out of the tension created by our differing perspectives. Mary is my friend and the cinematographer. We feel that Mary's experience in Hollywood will be an added advantage for our movie. Everything else will be decided after Peter's script is completed. We hope that all our Sri Lankan friends will help us in our endeavour.'

They all wished us luck. Chandran Rutnam asked us to approach him if we needed anything. Anushka whispered to Christie, 'I am eagerly waiting for your call.'

After the sumptuous dinner, Samaraveera bid goodbye, saying that he would arrange for us to meet the prisoners.

Not just any prisoner – Thamizholi. It was her that I wanted to meet.

Yes, I would meet her.

Colonel D'Silva led us to Thamizholi's cell with a warning: 'She becomes violent suddenly. Don't ask too many questions. Just listen to her if she talks.' Thamizholi had been the commander of the women's wing of the Viduthalai Tigers, and one of the leaders that the Sri Lankan military had captured alive after the last battle in Mullaitivu. The official version was that she had surrendered. But nobody who was familiar with the Iyakkam or who knew Thamizholi personally could believe this. The enquiries about her and her trial were being prolonged endlessly. The torture she had endured in Sri Lankan prisons had exhausted her mentally as well as physically. But her flaming eyes had lost none of their earlier vitality and determination. She looked at me with the contempt and loathing of a caged tiger. To be honest, I was shocked by the way she looked at me. It was clear that she had not recognized me. It wasn't possible for her to recognize me. We had met only once, nine years ago, in Daya Master's room. Daya Master, the media chief of the Iyakkam in Kilinochchi. I had gone to meet Prabhakaran to propose a movie about the freedom struggle. I had a movie like *The Battle of Algiers*, which had been shot against the racist war of 1983, in mind. But it was difficult to convince them. They viewed cinema as they viewed all other art forms – propaganda intended to dismantle the false perception about the Iyakkam created by movies like Mani Ratnam's *Kannathil Muthamittal*. Neither Daya Master nor his accomplices had enough knowledge about the medium to be able to understand my vision. They did not even permit me to meet Prabhakaran.

The only relief came in the form of Sugandhi, a fighter who accompanied Thamizholi. She was able to understand what I was trying to do.

'I am Peter Jeevanandam. We met a few years ago in Daya Master's office in Kilinochchi.'

She looked at me carefully.

'Daya Master? It is a mistake to address that Sinhala shit with respect. You tell me, why have you come here? Did he send you?'

'Please don't misunderstand me. I have no connection with him. The movie project I was forced to give up has now been taken up by a Hollywood production unit. The Sri Lankan government has also given consent. I need your help.'

'My help?'

'Yes. I want to know where Sugandhi is.'

'Sugandhi?'

'Yes.'

'I don't know. How would I know? She left the Iyakkam. Who knows if she is still alive.'

'Who would know that better than you?'

'Inside the Iyakkam, Prabhakaran did not tolerate insubordination. Nobody who questioned him was left alive. But Sugandhi was spared. I don't know why. I don't know what happened to her.'

'Is there any way of finding out?'

She fell silent, then spoke in a low voice as if remembering something.

'The Sri Lankan refugees in Paris have a group called Karupu. They published a magazine of the same name. During the war, they criticized both the government as well as the Iyakkam. Sugandhi used to write in that magazine under the pseudonym Eezhathachi. I think the editor of *The Sunday Leader*, Lasantha Wickrematunge, who was later killed, put her up to this. If you meet anyone connected with them, you might get information about Sugandhi.'

2

I had heard about the magazine *Karupu* even before Thamizholi told me about it. Nallur Sivachidambaram, the leader of the Sri Lankan refugees in Paris, used to publish it online. Siva lived in Little Jaffna, a refugee ghetto near St. Denis. He was friends with the novelist Antony Shobasakthi who was also my friend.

When I reached the hotel, I immediately called up Antony and enquired about Siva. He only said, 'Please don't ask me about him. He died before his time.' But when I explained my need, he agreed to mail me the details. On 18 May 2009, the same day Prabhakaran was killed in Mullaitivu, unidentified assailants murdered Sivachidambaram inside the Manikka Vinayagar temple that had been built by the Tigers. And with that, the publication of the magazine stopped. Everyone believed that the magazine had been stopped because the last issue had carried an interview with the famous journalist Sonali Wickrematunge, who was Lasantha Wickrematunge's wife. But that wasn't the real reason. The issue had also carried an announcement that Sugandhi's autobiography, titled *Notes on the Life of a Female Soldier*, would be published from the next issue onwards.

Notes on the Life of a Female Soldier
By Eezhathachi

He was Ananda – Peter Jeevanandam, my lover. Thoughts of love had never crossed my mind until I met him. But I fell into a sea of love from the moment I saw him. If I hadn't seen him, my life wouldn't have turned out like this. I would have died a martyr to the Iyakkam. I can begin my story only after bowing to him.

I am Sugandhi. That is the name the Iyakkam gave me. My parents had named me Andal Devanayaki. I was born in Colombo and lived there until I was three. My father, Ratnasabapathy, was a Professor of Tamil in Colombo University. My mother, Kanakavalli, was a gynaecologist in Castle Street Hospital. Both of them had been born and brought up in Nallur, Jaffna. My brother's name was Soorya Jyothy. I don't remember their faces any more. My memories begin with their murder.

24 July 1983, Sunday night. I was barely three. We were in a car on our way home. When we reached the city limits, we felt something was amiss. There was fire and smoke everywhere. The shops were burning. When we reached Borella bus stand, a huge mob came charging at us with swords. They stopped our car and dragged my father out. They were not willing to listen. Shouting, 'Tiger! Tiger!' they stabbed him. Blood flowed. I don't know whether they did it on purpose, but they set fire to the car with me inside. My parents and brother were writhing in the throes of death. I was surrounded by fire, smoke and horrifying screams. One of the assailants, a bit more humane than the rest, opened the door and pulled me out of the car. Caught among the dead and the dying, I lost consciousness.

I grew up in refugee camps in and around Colombo. I have never wept more than I did during my time there. A thin rice gruel poured twice a day into an aluminium pan was my diet. I had to sleep on the bare cement floor. The camp resounded with the abuses of the Sinhalese soldiers. Every time I fell asleep, I would see the faces of my parents and brother and wake up. By the time my mother's brother, Kumaravel, who was doing research at the London School of Economics, could locate me and take me away, I was six years old.

It was my unfortunate childhood that led me to become a freedom fighter. Unlike many of the other women soldiers, I was neither forced into joining the Iyakkam nor were my family members threatened by them. It was because I had some misconceptions about it. When, at the age of twenty, I joined the Iyakkam in Anton Balasingham's London home with the half-hearted consent of my uncle, I thought that it was a revolutionary movement, an armed leftist revolt to attain the dream of Tamil Eelam. That is how Anton Balasingham's wife, Adele, convinced me. And it was that conviction which prompted me to give up my graduate studies at the London Film School to join them.

My uncle's house was in Holland Park in west London. His Bangladeshi wife, Neelambari Chatterji, was a newsreader at the BBC. Perhaps because they had no children of their own, they saw me as their own daughter. The mental wounds I had sustained as a young child had begun to heal slowly with their love and tenderness. By the time I was ten years old, I would laugh, sing and play like any other child. It was then that I started taking pictures with my aunt's Kodak camera. Later, this became my passion.

My uncle and aunt were very broad-minded. They gave me the freedom to decide what I wanted to do with my life. They encouraged my interest in films. That is how I enrolled in the London Film School. They had a realistic approach towards life. When I grew up, they told me who I was and didn't conceal anything. My uncle didn't agree with the ideology of the Iyakkam. It was his personal opinion. But when I decided to join the Iyakkam after being brainwashed by Adele, he did not stop me. He just said gently, 'Your hands are not meant for carrying weapons.' On the day I joined the Iyakkam, he said, 'I knew you would join them one day. I won't stop you.' But his eyes were full of tears. It was the first time I saw him weep. 'Call whenever you need me. Don't do anything that goes against your conscience.' Those were his last words to me. I never called him after joining the Iyakkam.

What happened in my life wasn't something I could share with him. I have never seen him since.

My aunt Neelambari was born in Chittagong into a family with communist leanings, and she had close associations with the British Communist Party. The party members would often come home and hold lengthy discussions with her. But my uncle stayed away from their debates. He was only interested in research in his chosen field – economics. Still, both of them closely followed freedom movements across the world. They used to subscribe to several magazines and journals connected with those movements. I was inspired by their awareness of the multiple dimensions of freedom, their courage and their ideological clarity. But in those days I didn't know of Rosa Luxemburg's stand on nationalism, and it was only much later that I realized the Eelam movement was not a class struggle of the proletariat against the bourgeoisie. I was only led by a thirst for revenge against the Sinhalese nationalists who had massacred my family.

Like other leftist intellectuals in London, my uncle also had connections with the Eelam Revolutionary Organization of Students (EROS) established by V. Balakumaran and Arul Pragasam. It was he who put forward the idea that Sri Lankan Muslims should also be included in the Iyakkam. He was willing to use his connections with the economic wing of the Palestinian Liberation Organization to help EROS. It was his association with the PLO that gave several Tamil Liberation outfits an opportunity to train at PLO centres. But when the Iyakkam drifted away from Marxist philosophy and shrunk to Tamil Hindu nationalism, my uncle distanced himself from the movement. Even when ideological fissures sprung up in EROS and people like Balakumaran joined the Tigers, my uncle continued his friendship with them while still maintaining that they had not chosen the right path.

I was a high achiever in Holland Park School – in studies, sports and music. I was not bad looking. I was dusky and had inherited a regal grace from my mother who belonged to the Jaffna royal family. I was trying to drown my sorrow in a sea of friends, romances, petty squabbles, Britpop, martinis and film school, when Adele Balasingham came looking for me. She fanned the dying embers of revenge within me. And then everything was lost.

I didn't understand most of Antony's mail. It was a letter Sugandhi had sent four years ago. It made no mention of where she was now. The only solace came from the knowledge that she was still alive.

I realized that I couldn't expect any help towards making my movie from these quarters. Reading the disappointment etched on my face, Christie poured me a drink.

'Don't worry, Peter … Sugandhi is still alive. Now we can make enquiries.'

'But where will we look for her?'

'Everywhere possible. But we can't prolong this project endlessly. We leave for Jaffna in the morning.'

'I know meeting Sugandhi and this project are not connected, but if we do meet her, our movie will have a greater impact on the audience.'

'How so?'

'We are making this movie based on what we have read, seen or heard. To a certain extent, even I have no first-hand experience. But Sugandhi has been through it all. That is the difference.'

'We will try. I will ask Samaraveera to find her, whether she is in England or in Sri Lanka.'

I did not believe that Samaraveera would find Sugandhi. She wouldn't be anywhere Samaraveera's military connection could reach. But we could try to find the source of Sivachidaṃbaram's email.

3

When I was scrolling through the *Karupu* website looking for Sugandhi's writings, quite unexpectedly I came across *The Story of Devanayaki* by a Meenakshi Rajarathinam. It wasn't clear whether it was a fictional or factual piece. But the picture that was posted along with the text seemed very familiar, and I suspected that it was a photograph of the painting in Sigiriya.

The Story of Devanayaki
By Meenakshi Rajarathinam

Let's go back a millennium in time. It is AD 992 in Kanthalur Salai, located in the southern part of the Kulasekhara empire. It was established in the ninth century by Emperor Karunandadakkan, and during the period of Vikramaditya Varaguna, it grew to become an intellectual centre of world renown. When the Ay dynasty came to control the Kulasekhara empire, the repute of Kanthalur Salai soared. The main reason for this was that the Cheras converted it into a military camp, taking into consideration its strategic location at the southern tip of the empire. Soldiers were trained and weapons were manufactured here. But according to local legend, the place became famous for the liquor, called kantha, brewed from a plant which was found only in the Agasthyakoodam forest. In his Kanthalur songs, Vikramaditya Varaguna's grandson, Poomani Pananaar, who was the court poet during Mahendravarman's reign, sung about the magical properties of this plant which lured husbands away from their wives and pushed them into the arms of other women.

By the final decade of the tenth century, Kanthalur had become as famous as Nalanda. It had also become a centre for manufacturing weapons that were sold to neighbouring countries. Teachers of martial arts were recruited from Mahodayapuram and the northern territories. Soldiers from all over the world came to train in kalaripayattu. There was an unwritten rule in many countries that only a man who had trained in Kanthalur could become the ruler or the head of the army. That's why the young princes of Kalinga, Sinhala, Srivijaya and Kambuja came to train themselves here. Those who could not come invited teachers from Kanthalur to their native lands. That's how the fighting techniques used in Kanthalur came to be known by different names in different parts of the world. This influence can be discerned clearly in bokator which is practised in Kambuja and in pencak silat which is practised in Srivijaya. The swords, shields and fences made by the blacksmiths of Kanthalur too were exported on a large scale. The Nair warriors trained in Kanthalur offered their services to armies in different parts of the world. The training offered to soldiers and spies and the export of weapons made Kanthalur different from other princely states.

Kanthalur was a beautiful harbour town, located in the area that extends from the present-day harbour of Vizhinjam to Trivandrum in Kerala. It was the second most important trading centre of the Kulasekhara empire, where ships from Greece, China and Arabia dropped anchor. The streets were filled with Arab and Chinese merchants who came to sell silk, precious stones and gold and to buy pepper, spices, sandalwood and ivory. In Kanthalur were merchants who could bargain in six or seven languages, thousands of soldiers from foreign lands who had come for training, and beautiful women. Comfortable guest-houses were provided to foreign travellers, and maids whose skin was the colour of sandalwood would serve them venison and liquor. The king's men maintained law and order assiduously and collected a meagre tax of 1 per cent. The royals rode in colourfully decorated ox carts with their entourage. For entertainment, there were taverns, theatres and dance halls. Kanthalur Salai was prosperous and boasted of comforts comparable to any other city in the world. Traders from foreign lands envied this place which offered wine and beautiful women.

The fort of Mahendravarman, a dependant chieftain of the Chera emperor Bhaskara Ravi Varman I, was situated on a small hill overlooking the sea not far from the harbour. To the left was a lighthouse with a 120-foot tower from which one could see ships approaching. A white flag with a deer, the insignia of the Kanthalur rulers, fluttered aloft the flag post in front of the palace. The luxurious palace boasted of twenty-seven bedrooms spread across three storeys. A large family – that included Mahendravarman's queen Parvathy Thampuratty, his other wives, several of his concubines and their children – lived here. Around it were buildings and outhouses for ministers, generals and servants. The fort also contained a lovely lotus pond and two temples dedicated to the goddesses Lakshmi and Durga, who presided over prosperity and war respectively. The royal court was decked with elephant tusks on either side and the king's throne was made of gold. The court assembled every day. As the king gave great importance to overseas trade, the royal court had special seats for foreign traders. Though agriculture prospered, the main source of revenue was foreign trade. Mahendravarman paid obeisance and tax to the Chera emperor in Mahodayapuram but, for all purposes, he ruled like a king.

Four kilometres to the northeast of the fort, beyond the main streets, beyond the dense forests, was the largest military training centre in the Chera empire – Kanthalur Kalarikal. It was built in such a way that the traders and foreign nationals who alighted from the ships at the harbour could not tell that there was an important military camp in the vicinity. It had twenty-four kalaris equipped to train forty people each, and rooms where more than a hundred blacksmiths forged weapons. Stables for horses and elephants lay scattered around the area. In the centre, near the armoury, was the house of Periya Koyikkan – Kanthalur's army general. A veteran of many wars, he had travelled all over the world to learn and teach martial arts and the use of weapons, and his knowledge was immense. His fourth daughter, Devanayaki, is the heroine of this story.

Beyond the kalaris was an open ground – Kanthalur Kalam – where novice soldiers practised. It was equipped to simulate battle scenes. There was no place anywhere that could compete with Kanthalur's resources in this field.

A small river, the Thiruvaiga, cut across the Kalarikal. On the other side of the river lived acharyas who imparted Vedic and other knowledge to students. Periya Salai, as it was called, was the brain of Kanthalur. There were raised platforms on the streets where intellectuals and artists met. Students from all over the world came here to study the Vedas, medicine, astronomy, politics, economics, music, literature, dance and art. Beyond this were the holy Padmatheertham pond and the Sree Padmanabhaswamy temple.

Every day, Mahendravarman would bathe in the lotus pond, offer prayers to Lakshmi and Durga, and cross the Thiruvaiga in the royal boat to pay obeisance to Lord Padmanabha before ascending the throne. There was a law that forbade anyone from being in the temple when Mahendravarman arrived. But the law was broken once.

Devanayaki stood rapt before Lord Padmanabha, singing Andal's Thiruppavai, completely unaware of Mahendravarman's presence. Though his guards went to push her away, he stopped them. He stood silently near her, his hands folded in prayer. As he was immersed in prayer, he did not notice her beauty, but her mellifluous voice remained with him. He had never seen her dance or sing in public. When he made enquiries, he came to know that she only sang before Lord Padmanabha. When he heard this, he felt a deep respect for her.

There was not a single person in Kanthalur who was not bewitched by Devanayaki's beauty. It was as if her narrow waist, rounded breasts, beautiful wide eyes and long black hair were in a race towards perfection. Her figure was not like that of the Chera women. She resembled the tall, slim, wheat-complexioned damsels of Kambuja. But she was stronger and more elegant than them. She was the daughter of Periya Koyikkan's third wife, Chamba, who hailed from Kambuja. It was when Periya Koyikkan had gone to train the young sons of Kambuja king Jayavarman V, that he married the court dancer Chamba. Unfortunately, she died within three months of arriving in Kanthalur, struck down by an unknown disease. Devanayaki was nurtured by Periya Koyikkan's first wife, Madhavi, a devotee of Lord Vishnu. Periamma, as Madhavi was called, taught her Andal's devotional songs and the traditional dance form of Dasiattam.

Devanayaki was quite unaware of how powerfully enticing her eyes and smile were. All the young men in Kanthalur wanted to marry her, while she remained unwed at the age of twenty. Paying scant heed to them, she - unlike her peers - did not confine her interests to dance and music, but busied herself in learning science and politics. The stories her father would tell her about the women who occupied exalted positions at the royal court in Kambuja had inspired her. She wanted to take an active part in court politics and did not wish to remain confined merely to song and dance. As well as studying the *Arthashastra*, a political treatise, she secretly received training from her father in the art of using weapons. Singing Andal's songs and dancing before Lord Padmanabha's idol were merely ways of expressing her devotion. That is why she never performed for the public.

Devanayaki first entered the royal court as an assistant to Srinivasa Shasthri after completing her studies in political science under his tutelage. However, Mahendravarman was completely enraptured by her beauty and adjourned the royal court after ordering her to present herself in the royal chamber. Shasthri, filled with pride and joy, placed both his hands over her head and blessed her. But she didn't feel any happiness. She felt ashamed of herself as she realized that the king had not seen her knowledge or abilities but was merely attracted to her physical beauty. As if she was nothing more than her body. But what if the body was the only reality and everything else was a myth? She could have asked Lord Padmanabha who had, as usual, appeared in her dreams the previous night. Perhaps the Lord had known that it was the right time for her purple-hued nipples to turn black...

'You cannot defy the wishes of the king. Consider him to be Lord Padmanabha and accept him. The king is like God for us. This is the first time he is giving such an order. Consider yourself blessed.'

'But without asking for my consent?'

'Don't say that. I pray that you will realize it is God's grace. He gives and takes away without asking for permission. The king is our earthly God. He can decide which field to sow and which one to harvest.'

Though Devanayaki appreciated Shasthri's use of the field as a metaphor, she remained impassive. She remembered studying political treatises that advised one not to embark on a war in which failure was certain, and that the best ploy was diplomacy if it ensured a dignified result. He was the ruler. It was futile to resist him. Her intelligence persuaded her to utilize the opportunity, but she faced Shasthri like a question mark.

'The king is disappointed because none of the seeds he planted has taken root. If you give birth to a boy, he will be the next ruler of Kanthalur.'

Before he could complete his words, Queen Parvathy and her maids arrived to escort Devanayaki to the palace. The queen arrived to the accompaniment of drums. She was carrying a lit lamp and the traditional eight auspicious objects in her hands. Her maids followed her with laden trays. The queen adorned Devanayaki's forehead with sandalwood and vermilion, decorated her hair with jasmine and frangipani and led her to the inner chambers. Devanayaki hesitated.

'Don't worry, my child. All of us came here in much the same manner.'

'But all this is happening without my parents' knowledge.'

'They were informed earlier. Now a messenger has gone to give them the details. Periya Koyikkan and Madhavi will be delighted. Don't walk any further, get inside the palanquin. It is our responsibility to get you there without a scratch.' Another queen, who looked as if she were next in command, said as she helped Devanayaki into the palanquin, 'From now on, it is the king who will make the scratch marks.'

The queens and their entourage followed the palanquin. Devanayaki was astounded by the interior. It was like a moving palace. The seat was covered with satin-smooth deer skin. One could sit back or recline as desired. The fragrance of roses permeated the space. An exquisite mirror was placed in front of the seat. Maids walked on either side, fanning her. She gazed at her reflection in the mirror. What was the expression on her face, she wondered. Was it happiness, anxiety or an unknown fear? Was it a mixture of all three? The innocence and mischief in her dimples had not yet deserted her. Nobody could guess that she was twenty. The king had always seen her from a distance. It was only today that he saw her in relative proximity. Was the king forty years old or fifty? He must be twice her age at the very least, she thought. Is it for this that I sang devotional songs in the Sree Padmanabhaswamy temple? Clad in his royal robes, with a crown on his head, she could not picture him clearly. Now the time to see him at close quarters had arrived. He seems like an impatient man, she thought, or he would have called her after the assembly and issued his commands in private. But he had adjourned the assembly in haste and had summoned her to his chambers in public. Am I a celestial beauty that he was bewitched like the sage Vishwamitra the moment he set his eyes on me, she wondered.

After Devanayaki alighted from the palanquin, Queen Parvathy led her to a large chamber. Its walls were decorated with portraits of Karunandadakkan, Vikramaditya Varaguna and Bhaskara Ravi Varman. The queen spoke about each portrait at length and asked her to offer flowers as a sign of respect. Then she prayed to the Devi idol in the southern part of the palace, circumambulated around the tulsi plant and placed a tulsi leaf in her hair. She felt as if she too had become part of the royal family.

'Devanayaki, you are beautiful. It is rare to find someone like you, who has learnt singing, dancing and martial arts along with other disciplines. Shasthri told us everything. Your mother Madhavi said that outspokenness is your only fault. She is worried that you might speak without thinking before the Royal Highness. She requested us to advise you as your elder sisters. We were worried whether the king would agree, because as one's age increases, one's desire usually decreases. Thankfully, just a glimpse of you set things right. When he stopped the assembly and ordered you to meet him, we were more surprised than you were. I hope that you will be blessed with a son who will continue the lineage. The king will come to his bedchamber half an hour after dinner. Bathe and bedeck yourself before you go to him.'

'I am scared, elder sister. I have never thought about a man besides Lord Padmanabha.'

'Don't worry. Until the king married me, I too had only thought about the deity in Thiruvanchikulam. It was as a gift for my singing and dancing in the temple precincts that I got the king for my husband. But I was not fortunate enough to give him a son. You have got the king for your husband as a result of singing devotional songs in the Sree Padmanabhaswamy temple. What can be more fortunate than the deity appearing in the guise of the king? You have been blessed by Lord Padmanabha. Come, let's go upstairs. The third chamber on the second floor is the most important bedroom in this palace. The king hasn't come here for a long time. It's as if he had tired of these things. But today, something seems to have changed. Perhaps he'll decide to start using the room here again instead of staying back in his own palace. It all depends on your abilities and your luck. Your clothes and ornaments are in your room. The maids will help you.'

The queen did not enter Devanayaki's bedchamber. No other queen had the right to enter this room now. There were four or five young maids to help her dress. Laughing and narrating stories about the lionhearted ruler, they removed Devanayaki's robes and made her wear the light yellow fabric worn by the queens when they bathed. Then they massaged her luxuriant hair and body using oil brewed with medicinal herbs from Agasthyakoodam. Paying no heed to their chatter, she hummed a song from *Nachiyar Thirumozhi*. She was preparing in case he asked her to sing. Though the maids did not understand the words, they understood the fever that gripped Devanayaki when she hummed 'for you my breasts rise'. They burst into laughter. But instead of feeling shy, Devanayaki sang, 'Last night, Lord Padmanabha told me that it was time for my nipples to darken.' They were startled. This was a queen unlike any they had seen before.

4

By the time she had finished bathing in the lotus pond, smearing her body with vaka flowers and turmeric, had draped a length of green silk from China around her waist and a similar one across her breasts, and adorned her hair with fragrant jasmine and frangipani, it was noon. Her fear evaporated as she stood, decked in emeralds and pearls, gazing at her reflection. A belt studded with the famed nine precious gems was around her waist, a diamond ring sparkled on her nose, elegant anklets adorned her feet and beautiful bangles jangled around her wrists. She felt that there might be some truth in what Madhavi said: that she had descended from the celestial beauties. Accompanied by her maids, she prayed at the temples of Lakshmi and Durga before partaking of the meal served to her. She then rested for a while, before Parvathy and the other queens arrived to escort her to the royal bedchamber.

Not completely satisfied with the way the maids had dressed her, the queens made minor adjustments to her hair and garments. They tightened the silk around her breasts while asking, 'Are your breasts throbbing as you dream about the royal highness?'

'Oh no! She didn't tie it tightly enough, and I don't know about the king's preferences.'

'There is nothing to know. Your ignorance is your greatest strength. Just obey him. Try to please him. Give back more than you receive. The Royal Highness will teach you everything you need to know.'

But Devanayaki's heart raced as she climbed the steps to the royal bedchamber. The queens did not accompany her. She prayed for Lord Padmanabha's guidance to behave with propriety towards her royal husband. As she silently entered the veranda that led to the chamber, she heard his deep voice, 'Come inside.' She pushed open the door and entered. He was lying in bed. He was still wearing his crown and royal garments. He didn't look as old as he was purported to be. Extremely handsome, he seemed to be enveloped by a divine aura. Though he gestured to her to sit by his side, she remained standing as though she hadn't noticed. In reality, she was looking at him to her heart's content.

'I've heard that you perform only in front of Lord Padmanabha.'

'I hope you are not offended, but that is true.'

'Why?'

'He is the only man I've liked.'

'Like Andal?'

'Andal's devotion was confined to prayer. I prefer political science and economics.'

'So have you come to help me in matters of the state?'

'Until I entered the royal court, that was my only intention. I had looked upon you only as a king. But the moment you commanded me to your bedchamber, you became my Lord Padmanabha.'

'So now you can sing and dance for me?'

'If you so command.'

'Well, I command. A song first.'

She sang 'Margazhi Thingal' mellifluously. As he got up in appreciation, she touched his feet in reverence. When he pulled her up and seated her on the bed, she blushed. He said, 'You sang beautifully,' and kissed her on either cheek, as if giving her a gift for her singing. The first gift she would receive from him. She felt a pleasurable chill creeping up from her feet. It was the first time she was experiencing a man's heat and kisses, that too from the ruler of the realm. Her eyes shone like stars with pride and happiness. She returned his gifts with twice the passion. Though Mahendravarman's royal garments and crown were impediments, she knew that he liked her.

'Will I incur your displeasure if I say something, Your Highness?'

'No, tell me.'

'Don't your royal garments and the crown belong to the court? Why should you wear them here?'

'Clothes are unnecessary for the bedchamber. Do you feel these clothes are barriers?'

'No. I just wanted to see you properly. Not the king, but Lord Padmanabha who was attracted to me and invited me here.'

He agreed. He got up to remove his robes. She took off all her ornaments except the aimbadathali and her pearl waist-chain. The silk cloth around her breasts had loosened. She didn't bother with it. Divested of his royal garments, the king looked much younger. He was balding, but physically fit. His complexion was dusky. His chest sported a few marks of war and was adorned by a tiger-claw pendant. 'A very tall man with well-proportioned limbs. Will I reach up to his shoulders? He is not as I feared he would be. He seems to be very decent in his approach towards me. He doesn't display the hurry he seemed to be in at the royal court. He is behaving in a very calm manner. Not even looking at my body.' As she stood hesitating, wondering whether to go to him or wait for him to approach, her gaze fell on a table laden with fruits and drinks. There were berries, fruit juice, tender coconut water, grapes and bananas. As she stood confused about what to offer him, he said,

'Those who have studied political science should not hesitate...'

'I'm sorry, I don't know your preferences.'

'From now onwards, your tastes are mine too.'

'I like to drink kantha, eat bananas and the venison of doe.'

'Why only doe?'

'I am a woman after all, Your Highness.'

'You are mischievous, aren't you? And what are your other preferences?'

'Among gods Krishna, among devotees Andal, in songs the Thiruppavai, in jewellery anklets, in dance Apsarayattam, in clothes the breast-cloth, in ornaments the aimbadathali, among months Margazhi, among kings Mahendravarman, and among lovers En Peruman.'

'Who is En Peruman?'

'That is how Andal addresses Lord Krishna. From today, My Royal Highness, you are my En Peruman.'

'Now don't you want to know my preferences? Some of them are your own.'

'I am indeed lucky.'

'I too like kantha, the juice of berries and venison, but I am not particular about having doe.'

'Oh, that was a joke.'

'Lord Padmanabha among gods, among devotees the Azhwars, in jewellery anklets, in dance Dasiattam, headgear in attire, among weapons the sword, and to ride horses.'

'And?'

'Among women my lovers, among lovers my wives – among wives Devanayaki.'

As the king tried to gather her in his arms, she deftly slipped away. She decided not to make it too easy for him. She asked, 'Can I pour you some kantha?'

'Not today. This is a special occasion. There is a drink from Simhapura – it's amruth.'

He took a bottle from the cupboard and poured it into two silver glasses. She sipped hesitantly. It was sour.

'Is this what amruth tastes like?'

'This is like our kantha, but far superior and a hundred times more expensive. It should be sipped slowly. But if you can't, then drink it in one gulp. Don't let the sour taste put you off. The intoxication comes very slowly and lasts the whole day, but does not cause any problems. And if you eat something sweet, the intoxication doubles.'

As Periya Koyikkan had often given her kantha to help her relax after strenuous practice sessions, she gulped down the drink without much difficulty.

Mahendravarman leaned back in his royal chair, glass in hand. She looked at him as if to ask what she should do next.

'Since the song is over, you may now dance. This attire is sufficient, and we will make do without musical instruments. Just imagine that you are in the presence of Lord Padmanabha.'

It was a royal command. Immediately, she closed her eyes, bowed to mother earth and began to dance. The king sipped the amruth. She danced to the fourth and fifth stanzas of *Nachiyar Thirumozhi* as she had practised earlier. As she danced oblivious to her surroundings, he gazed at her. The intoxication of dance and liquor spread slowly. By the time she had finished dancing to 'Vaaranamaiyiram', she fell upon his chest. Exhausted from the dance, she unthinkingly gulped down more amruth. After long kisses and tight embraces, they finally reached the royal bed. Whispering, 'Let me see you properly,' he freed her from her cumbersome garments. As she was intoxicated, she felt no embarrassment. Offering the beauty of her naked body to him, Devanayaki lay on the bed. Mahendravarman stood mesmerized, looking at her Grecian perfection. He knew that if he touched her, the vision would be spoilt. Finally, unable to control himself any longer, he crushed her in his embrace. He murmured 'En Paapa,' she whispered 'En Peruman,' and tears fell upon his chest. From that moment, Mahendravarman started calling her 'Paapa' and she addressed him as 'En Peruman'.

Everything happened so quickly that one couldn't say whether Devanayaki had permitted him to enter the sanctum sanctorum to worship or he had pushed open the door. As twilight approached, Devanayaki lay on Mahendravarman's chest, fatigued from her first intercourse. When she woke up, the first thing she noticed was a couple of grey hairs on his chest and the grey in his moustache. 'Oh! The poor man is growing old. Maybe I am mistaken. I didn't think he was fatigued when he was ploughing the field or sowing the seeds.' As the thought struck her, she laughed out loud. Luckily, it didn't wake him up. He was in a deep sleep. 'I failed only in one thing,' she thought. Though she had determined to think only of Lord Padmanabha, her decision evaporated before Mahendravarman's endearments, and when she reached the zenith of pleasure, only Mahendravarman remained in her mind.

After all, he was her Lord Padmanabha now. It was twilight, but she didn't know if it would be proper to wake him up. But if people didn't see the king, who had gone for his siesta, they would start wondering. Should she inform them that he was still sleeping? But she was caught in his long arms. Suddenly, she became aware of her nudity, and for the first time she felt shy. As she tried to move his hand to get up, he awoke, just as she had feared.

'Paapa, are you in a hurry to leave?'

'It's twilight. What will the queens think?'

'They won't worry. They know that if I like you, we will be going downstairs only for dinner.'

Though she felt happy, she did not show it. She tied up her hair and leaned on his chest. As he remained silent, she asked him with a lowered gaze, 'Did you like me?'

'Why do you doubt that? Amruth needs to be sipped only once to gauge its quality. Now I am truly intoxicated.'

'So am I.'

He took off his ruby signet ring and put it on her finger. Her eyes filled with joy.

'En Peruman, I am indeed fortunate.'

On the eighth day of meeting her, Mahendravarman made Devanayaki his eighth wife with all royal ceremonies. It was the biggest celebration in the history of Kanthalur. The Chera emperor, Bhaskara Ravi Varman, arrived to preside over the ceremonies. Ships sporting flags of far-flung countries dropped anchor at the harbour. Many warriors who had learnt martial arts from the kalaris here returned to witness the ceremony, the most prominent among them being Mahinda, the Sinhala king, and Jayavarman, the ruler of Kambuja. They were Periya Koyikkan's disciples and it was a special occasion for them as the bride was their guru's daughter. All of them knew Devanayaki.

Mahinda, the ruler of Sinhala, had wanted to marry her. They came bearing precious gifts. Even Mahendravarman could not tell whether Jayavarman's gift of the apsara crown or Mahinda's gift, a gold chain studded with the nine precious gems, was more valuable. But Devanayaki liked the grey Arab steed gifted by Iqbal Muhammad, an Arab trader, best.

The whole city celebrated the wedding for seven days. The guests were led to the palace on decorated elephants and horses, to the accompaniment of music. The streets were filled with flags and other decorations. There were special guest-houses built for the guests, and three kitchens catered to their needs. Liquor flowed freely. The warriors displayed their skills. There were special prayers at the Sree Padmanabhaswamy temple on all seven days. Boat races, exhibition sword fights and Vedic recitals – the celebrations were varied. The royal guests as well as the commoners agreed that it was the greatest celebration Kanthalur had ever witnessed.

Along with the wedding ceremonies, special prayers were conducted to please the gods so that the royal couple would be blessed with a son. As they were immersed in the rituals, neither Mahendravarman nor Devanayaki could see or participate in the celebrations. They were surrounded by smoke from the holy fires and the chanting of the Vedas. It lasted until the seventh day when, in the southern chamber, a chain was put around Devanayaki's waist before the idol of the goddess. Then she was led to the royal bedchamber. She was made to stand naked and, with the highly guarded tantric rituals of the yoni puja, Queen Parvathy presented her with a talisman to ensure pregnancy.

It was then that Devanayaki noticed the chain that all the queens of Kanthalur wore around their waists. It was an oval-shaped gold leaf, held tight with two gold clasps around the hips, just below the pearl waist-chain – and it covered her genitalia completely. It had the insignia of a deer, which was the emblem of the Kanthalur king. The inside was covered with velvet. Every action except sex could be carried out without hindrance. It had a lock near the navel which the wearer could never open. The keyhole could be found only on close scrutiny, and the key was with the king. She found it a bit difficult to walk while wearing it.

The queen comforted her, saying that she would get used to it.

Devanayaki asked, 'Why doesn't he trust us?'

'It is not because he doesn't trust us. It is more like the great wall around a fort – for protection. He does not want any intruder to force himself upon his queens.'

'What should I do next?'

'Sit with him when he eats, and serve him with your own hands. Haven't you heard that the best way to a man's heart is through his stomach? After that, both of you should pray before Emperor Vikramaditya Varaguna's portrait. Pray for a son as strong and handsome as him. The best moment for intercourse has been calculated. The king will lead you to the bedchamber when it is time.'

When they were alone, Devanayaki asked the king to remove the chastity belt. He refused, saying that there would be enough time to do it later. 'We have important matters to talk about now,' he said.

She feared that she had angered him. But he told her that she should help him in matters of the state.

She asked him, 'Is it because a woman is expected to be as wise as a minister when she gives advice, as loving as a mother in her affection, and as sensual as a whore in bed?'

Mahendravarman replied that he did not believe the old adage applied to a queen. He added that, for him, a wife's love was not the same as maternal affection. He said, 'Some Sanskrit scholar who had no knowledge about these matters must have written it. The greatest virtue a queen needs is to be loyal to the king.'

'Is that why you have tied a chastity belt around my waist?'

'That is a ritual, centuries old. It is to ensure that nobody enters your body or mind using powers of persuasion, threat or force. And according to political treatises, the queen is among those people a king should fear.'

'Don't trust Chanakya's words blindly. You should interpret them in context. Science is supposed to free one from fear, not inculcate fear. Pardon me if I'm wrong.'

Mahendravarman looked at her in surprise.

'You are clever. I'm lucky to have a wife who can help me in matters of administration. But this is not the time to talk about such things. The auspicious hour is at hand.'

By the time Mahendravarman got the key to the chastity belt, she had taken off her garments. He held her close and ran the small gold key from the back of her neck down the length of her spine. She felt ticklish. But the key unerringly reached the right spot and the lock fell open. He entered her at the appointed hour.

Giving more than she received, and engaging in matters of politics, Devanayaki quickly become the king's most beloved queen. When the royal court assembled on the fourteenth day after the wedding celebrations, she accompanied the king. A seat was arranged for her next to the throne.

In the royal assembly, the king often paid heed to Devanayaki's opinion. Naturally, a large number people did not like this. They worried that the king was being henpecked. But overcoming all their misgivings, Devanayaki became the king's principal advisor within six months of their marriage.

One day, she proposed that elephants should not be used in the army. When she said that the elephant brigade would be a burden in future wars, everyone including the ministers laughed. Even Mahendravarman laughed at the absurdity of fighting a war without elephants. Unable to bear their mockery, Devanayaki left the assembly earlier than usual.

When the other queens told her that she should focus on giving the king a son instead of interfering in matters of state, Devanayaki felt terrible. She didn't know why she hadn't conceived even after seven months of marriage. Why were the seeds that were being sowed refusing to take root? As it would be treasonous to blame the seed, everyone was blaming the field.

Mahendravarman too was upset when he entered the bedchamber at night. He wondered whether he should follow Devanayaki's advice or accept the words of those whom he considered his gurus. He didn't show any interest in unlocking the chastity belt that night.

'If Peruman was troubled by my words, I won't come to the royal court again.'

'No, don't take such a decision. But be careful about your words. It is not easy to change military strategies that are centuries old.'

'But I am concerned about your safety and the security of the country. The spies informed you just two days ago about a substance the Chinese traders have with them. It can explode like thunder. It is said to be made with coal and sulphur. If someone attacks us using such things, won't the elephants run amok? Our fort is also not very secure. Proximity to the sea has advantages as well as disadvantages. We welcome visitors who dock at our harbour with open arms. An enemy can reach and even enter the fort without any trouble.'

He pretended not to hear her. Suddenly, he got up to fetch the gold key and Devanayaki forgot everything else. They became En Peruman and En Paapa. When she asked why everyone blamed the field for remaining fallow, he did not respond. But when his eyes filled up, so did hers.

The next day, he compelled her to go with him to the royal assembly. He explained to the court why Devanayaki had proposed removing elephants from the army. Everyone listened in surprise. But Devanayaki remained silent. Finally, yielding to compulsion, she spoke about her anxieties regarding security.

'But Kanthalur doesn't have any known enemies. Most of the neighbouring kings have trained at our kalaris. In places like Sinhala, most of the guards have been trained here.'

'That is the biggest problem, Your Highness. Most of the neighbouring kings and their soldiers know where our kalaris and weapon storehouses are. They also know the locations of trade centres and the treasury. This is not an issue when these countries are on friendly terms with us. But if they turn into foes, then this will certainly become a problem. The Sinhala king, Mahinda, wasn't very happy when he left after the wedding.'

'En Paapa, how did you know this?'

'After I started attending the royal court, I formed a small covert group of seven members. I speak here on the basis of what they have told me. Mahinda had wanted to buy five thousand of our soldiers. You, My Highness, refused and demanded that they be paid on a monthly basis. This irked him. Moreover, Mahinda is also displeased because my father refused his proposal for my hand three times. He presented us the necklace studded with nine gems only to display his wealth and power. When he entered the ship, Mahinda whispered that he would crush Kanthalur under his foot.'

'Is this the truth?'

'Yes.'

The assembly was in shock. They discussed defence strategies in case the Sinhala king attacked. Arrangements were made to move the wealth of the country to the Sree Padmanabhaswamy temple. It was decided to call back all the Kanthalur warriors from Sinhala and to stop selling weapons to the kingdom.

But they fought over a trivial issue that night. When she looked at a betel leaf after dinner, she had a vision: Rajaraja Chola from Thanjavur was moving towards Kanthalur.

'Periya Koyikkan has also informed me about this. We have made arrangements to send four hundred cavalrymen and one thousand soldiers to Aruvamozhi. We have also sent messages to the Pandya king who is in hiding,' Mahendravarman said.

'Please don't misunderstand me, Your Highness, but the Pandya king withdrew after being defeated in Madhura and sought refuge in Agasthyakoodam. How can he, who could not help himself, help us?'

'Then whom can we turn to for help?'

'I think it would be wise to attack the Cholas at Kongu Point after informing the emperor. When there is trouble in the north, they will be forced to move away from Aruvamozhi. We can keep sending men and ammunition to Kongu Point.'

'You are right. Mahodayapuram is more secure than Kanthalur anyway. The enemy cannot reach it from Kongu Point easily. But our emperor isn't that open-minded. He will say that we are burdening the empire with our internal problems. He only shows interest in collecting taxes every year.'

'Kanthalur is a province in the Chera empire and you, My Highness, and the emperor are good friends. He even presided over our wedding ceremony.'

'I had to pay him ten thousand gold coins and three baby elephants to ensure his presence. He even had an eye on your Arab steed, but I ignored it.'

'So what is your decision?'

'I am not going to beg for help. Kanthalur will face the enemy boldly – whether it is the Chola or the Sinhala.'

'I don't think it is an intelligent move. The Cholas have more men in their army and are better equipped. Their foot soldiers are strong. It will be difficult to win a war against them.'

'Then what do you suggest we do?'

'Why not a treaty? Isn't it better to pay taxes to the valorous Cholas than to the cowardly, selfish Chera emperor?'

'Devanayaki!'

The sound of his voice sent shock waves over Kanthalur. She trembled in front of Mahendravarman when she saw the usually soft-spoken king burning with rage. It was the first time that he had addressed her as Devanayaki.

'The kings of Kanthalur may lose wars. They may die on the battlefield. But they will never beg the enemy for peace when they have declared war. Any woman will compare her husband unfavourably with a warrior braver than him and may even want to sleep with him. That is the reason why I have locked you up in a chastity belt.'

Consumed by anger, Mahendravarman swept out like a hurricane from the bedchamber. Devanayaki spent a sleepless night weeping. None of the queens came to offer solace. The king came to her room just before dawn. Devanayaki fell at his feet. She was so full of sorrow that she couldn't find the words to ask forgiveness. At that time, the Chola army was approaching Aruvamozhi like a turbulent sea.

The next morning, immediately after the court had assembled, a messenger from Rajaraja Chola arrived. When Mahendravarman read the missive written on deer skin, he trembled with rage. The message said that the Chola empire would annex Kanthalur and that they would take care of everything without collecting taxes for a period of three years. They would also rename the harbour Rajaraja Cholapattanam.

Mahendravarman ordered the messenger's head to be cut off. He shouted, 'Who gave them the right to do this?' But Devanayaki stopped him. She reminded him that messengers should not be killed, punished or humiliated. Still, the messenger was stripped naked, tonsured and pushed into Agasthyakoodam.

That was Mahendravarman's greatest folly. Accusing Kanthalur of humiliating their messenger, the Chola army attacked Kanthalur on the fourth day.

It was the bloodiest attack in the Chera–Chola war. Over twenty-one days of battle, the Chola army succeeded in destroying Kanthalur's defences step by step. By the afternoon of the twenty-first day, they had besieged the city from all sides. The surviving Kanthalur army was trapped. Mahendravarman, who was riding an elephant, was captured alive. They refused to end the war, and killed soldiers and civilians indiscriminately. They set fire to trade centres, houses and ships anchored in the harbour. They looted the city and raped the women, not sparing young or old. The Cholas used fire as a major weapon in the battle. As their spies knew exactly where the army chieftain's house and the kalaris were located, they burnt them all down. They only spared the Sree Padmanabhaswamy temple and the Vedic schools that lay beyond the Thiruvaiga. Finally, when they broke down the entrance to the fortress, fewer than a hundred women and children remained alive.

5

Later, different stories were narrated about the aftermath of the battle. The most popular one is attributed to Periya Salai, where it was firmly believed that Devanayaki had divine powers.

On the twenty-first day of the war, when it was certain that Mahendravarman would lose, she made her way to the Sree Padmanabhaswamy temple using secret underground passages. Praying to the Lord to save her husband, she sang the Thiruppavai and danced until dusk. When, at last, she finally fell before the deity, a divine glow enveloped the temple and she became one with Lord Padmanabha. It was then that the marauding Chola army reached there, after having hanged Mahendravarman. But seeing the bright glow that surrounded the temple, they turned back without crossing the Thiruvaiga. Even her body was not seen after that. It was believed that this was how Devanayaki became Goddess Devanayaki.

They worshipped Devanayaki, who was as proficient as Goddess Saraswathi in music, dance and the scriptures. A beautiful temple was built for her at the point where the Thiruvaiga emptied itself into the ocean. All the idols in this temple were in the female form. Even Lord Ganapathi was in the female form of Vigneshwari. During the Panguni festival, the idols of both Lord Padmanabha and Saraswathi were bathed in the sea. In the fourteenth century, due to some natural disaster, the Thiruvaiga changed its course and, as a result, the Saraswathi temple was submerged. For a long time, the people of Periya Salai conducted music festivals and scholarly meetings in Devanayaki's memory, which later came to be known by different names. Slowly, Devanayaki, like Kannaki, became a part of the Arya Devi myth.

Another story was that the temple guards mistakenly assumed that Devanayaki had died. They took her unconscious body in a carriage and discarded it in the forests near Malayam. They planned to rob her jewels and bury her in the forest. As they were removing her ornaments, they felt a great lust rising within them and decided to violate her corpse. As they were cutting through her chastity belt, she woke up and cried out loud. Hearing her cries, a sanyasi called Thanumalayan came there. The soldiers panicked when they saw him and, gathering her ornaments, got into the carriage and fled.

Though he belonged to the marginalized community of Kuravas, the sage hailed from the family of the great Agasthya. Thanumalayan, who had prayed to the trinity of Brahma, Vishnu and Siva and gained miraculous powers, had foresworn marriage. Thinking that the naked body belonged to a nymph who had come to distract him from meditation, he cursed Devanayaki with losing her memory. Though his curse wiped out her past, Thanumalayan found that he still could not meditate. Unable to control his lust, he took her to his ashram. His celibacy ended that day. On her body, he tried out practices of tantric sex he had only read about. Though she was disgusted by the ageing body of the short-tempered sanyasi, his expertise in bed gave her so much pleasure that his physical appearance became unimportant. As Thanumalayan emerged from the river after his bath with mixed feelings of pleasure and guilt swirling within him, he heard a disembodied voice:

'Don't be upset. Your divine powers are intact. Goddess Parvathy has blessed you. The position of a grihastha-ashrami or householder is higher than that of a bachelor. The rituals of a wedding are irrelevant now. Bathe in the holy waters of Suchindram, pray to Lord Siva and assume the role of a husband. You will be blessed with prosperity and happiness.'

Devanayaki too heard the divine voice. Her guilt at having disrupted the sage's austerities disappeared. She took a dip in the Thiruvaiga, adorned her hair with flowers and touched the sage's feet. She was upset that she couldn't remember her past. But for the sage, she was Goddess Parvathy incarnate. He chanted a shloka:

The earth placed in the muladhara, water in the manipura,
Fire in the svadhishthana, air in the heart, and space above.
Placing the mind between the brows and breaking
    through the kula-path,
You sport with your Lord secretly in the thousand-
    petalled lotus.

Unable to complete it, he gathered her in his arms. Though she didn't understand the meaning, she stood in his embrace with piety.

'I don't understand,' she said.

'It is the *Soundarya Lahari* – Shankaracharya's verses in praise of the goddess. I will teach you all this later. What is your name, my beauty?'

'I don't know. You erased my memories.'

'That was a grave error. I cannot return what I have taken away.'

'It is not anger alone that you can't control. What about last night?' She smiled knowingly, disarming him.

'Yes, I lost control. Pardon me if I hurt you.'

'Please don't say that. You gave a hundred times more pleasure than pain.'

'You too gave back more than what I gave you.'

She lowered her head, feeling shy. He too felt embarrassed. As they rested after prayer and lunch, he advised her on how a sage's wife should behave. She listened attentively. 'If I meditate, will I too be able to speak to the gods like you?'

'Chastity is the best form of prayer for a woman. If you are chaste, the gods will bless you. If you call them in your hour of need, they will come to your rescue. Tomorrow morning, we will leave for Suchindram. As the country is at war, we have to be very careful. We must disguise ourselves. Wear clothes that will conceal your beauty. If anyone asks, tell them we are sages from the Himalayas. From today, your name is Anasuya - she who is without envy - that is the quality most desirable in a woman. May the trinity bless you.'

She liked her new name. They started on the journey early next morning. Covering her head with a tattered garment, resembling an aged sanyasin, she followed Thanumalayan. During the course of the journey, he spoke about himself. She listened in wonder to his story. Though Thanumalayan had been born in the Kurava community, he had attained knowledge from gurus who meditated on the Himalayas. And after three years of meditation in Agasthyakoodam, the trinity finally appeared before him.

'What was the boon they granted you?'

'Though it is a secret, I will tell you about it, as a man is not supposed to keep anything from his wife - I can wish for anything to happen, but I cannot reverse it.'

'Why didn't you wish for us to reach Suchindram without undergoing this arduous journey?'

'That is the difference between a sanyasi and an ordinary mortal. A sanyasi will never use his abilities for himself. The fact that I cursed you and erased your memory is unpardonable. I have married you as penance.'

'Oh! I thought it was because you liked me.'

'Of course, I liked you. But this was the reason why I married you.'

'I can't understand what you are saying.'

'If you live with me for a while, you will begin to understand.'

The journey, which took four days, passed without any mishap. Though the Chola soldiers returning with their loot stopped them, they were allowed to move on. They heard stories that Mahendravarman had been hanged and that the Chola army could only lay their hands on one-tenth of the wealth of Kanthalur. Anasuya, who had lost her memory, had no interest in these matters. She didn't even realize that it was her they were talking about when they spoke of how seven of Mahendravarman's queens had committed suicide by jumping into the fire, and how the soldiers had searched in vain for the beauteous eighth queen who had somehow managed to escape. When Thanumalayan jokingly asked, 'Are you the eighth queen?' she laughed and said, 'You have high hopes.'

But she was shocked when, after she had a bath in the temple pond in Koteshwara, the women there remarked upon how beautiful she was.

They bathed in the holy waters of Suchindram, cleansed body and mind, and entered the state of marriage. Obeying someone's orders, the village elders had arranged an ashram for them. The people welcomed the couple who were graced with divine blessings. They happily started their life together at the ashram. Soon, the ashram became a nerve centre for intellectuals. Anasuya welcomed everyone with respect and served food to the guests. She was the perfect wife. After bathing at dawn, she would wake the sage by touching his feet. She took care of his needs all day long. She accepted his opinions without question. She would not venture out without him, whether it was to the temple or to the street outside the house. She always walked behind him. She never looked at another man. Before lunch, she would wash his feet and drink the water. She waited for him to eat and would eat only what was left over. When he fell asleep after pleasuring her, she would touch his feet before sleeping. It is said that Lord Siva told his wife to emulate Anasuya in order to become the perfect wife.

But Thanumalayan's transition from a state of renunciation to one of material pleasures was quick. When he started teaching language, grammar and medicine to children, his fame as a teacher spread far and wide. The students gave him money and jewels in return for his knowledge. He accepted everything for Anasuya and their unborn son. He had to build rooms nearby for his disciples to stay in. The ashram turned into a small palace. They became prosperous. But the sage did not become vain, because he attributed all his prosperity to Anasuya's luck. Soon, she gave birth to a baby boy.

Through his disciples, the world came to know that Thanumalayan's wife was beautiful and that she had recently given birth to a child. After months of effort, the spies of the Chola emperor discovered that Anasuya was none other than Devanayaki. The emperor commanded Thanumalayan to come to the royal court and, at the same time, he reached the ashram disguised as a sage. Thanumalayan had told Devanayaki that her chastity would protect her. When the emperor reached their ashram in the guise of a sage, Devanayaki was breastfeeding her baby. She welcomed the sage and began preparing food for him.

'Don't make food for me. I only drink breast milk. I heard that there is breast milk in this house, that is why I'm here.'

Devanayaki sensed that it was a trap. But she squeezed some milk into a glass and gave it to him.

'This is foolishness. Does anyone drink breast milk from a tumbler? Your breasts are brimming with milk. You should come to me naked and allow me to drink. That is how I receive alms.'

Devanayaki grew red with anger.

'You are not a sage but a trickster. Please leave. I am a chaste wife. Do not harm me.'

'I have come because I know that you are not a chaste wife. You are Devanayaki, the youngest wife of the king of Kanthalur. When the king was killed, you ran away with this sage.'

'Don't to be absurd. I am Anasuya. I am Thanumalayan's wife. Please don't trouble me.'

'No. I will not leave without receiving alms.'

Shutting her eyes, she prayed to the trinity. They advised her to sprinkle the water with which she had washed the sage's feet on the visitor. When she did so, the Chola emperor became a six-month-old baby. She took the child in her arms and suckled him. Thanumalayan, who saw all this with his divine vision, rushed home to find the gods blessing Devanayaki. The gods restored the emperor to his real form after he begged for mercy. Humiliated, he ran away from the place.

The temple Thanumalayan and Devanayaki built on the spot where the gods appeared later came to be known as the Thanumalayan temple. Devanayaki gave birth to two more sons and a daughter, and they all lived happily together for a long time. This was the Kurava dynasty that later ruled Nanjinad. After the rule of the Konangi Kuravas and the Nanji Kuravas who ruled in the twelfth century, the Kurava dynasty slowly declined. Brahmins took control of the temple. The high-born Brahmins, who had only contempt for the Kuravas, transformed Devanayaki's story into the legend of Atri and his wife Anasuya. The story of Devanayaki was successfully Aryanized. Their version was that the gods wanted to test Anasuya's chastity and so they came in the guise of sages and asked her to serve food to them naked. She sprinkled the water with which she had washed her husband's feet on them, transforming them into babies.

The third story is the diametrical opposite, and goes like this:

When the Chola army forced its way into Kanthalur fort, the queens jumped into a funeral pyre in the courtyard. It was when the seventh queen jumped into the fire that the army reached the courtyard. Devanayaki, wearing a white garment and only her thali and waist-chain as jewels, was waiting for her turn to give herself up to the flames. They dragged her out, tied her up and brought her to King Mahendravarman. Unable to summon the courage to look at her, he bowed his head. The commander of the Chola army tied her hands behind her back, broke open her chastity belt and raped her brutally in the presence of the king.

As she wailed helplessly, the musicians from Thanjavur played their instruments loudly to drown out her cries. The guards whipped Mahendravarman who stood paralysed. When, at midnight, they were butchering the king and throwing the remains of his body into the sea, the commander of the Chola emperor was raping her again.

In the morning, only the hair and bones of the commander remained. In the next few days, the same fate overtook the rest of the war chieftains. Concluding that Devanayaki had become a bloodsucking monster, they set fire to the palace and its surroundings, and left. When the humans deserted the place, the vampire also left. Later, she came to be known as the fearsome Neeli.

These three stories, which give different versions of Devanayaki's life after the war, belong to different geographic territories. The people who made up these stories manipulated the details to suit themselves. Why this story has so many versions is a big question in cultural history. But in a 900-year-old manuscript written in the Pali script discovered in Sigiriya, Sri Lanka, in 2001, Devanayaki's story is told accurately. It was when I read an article in English about this text that I realized the historical importance of the wall paintings in Sigiriya, and the Gnana Saraswathi idol in Gangaikonda Cholapuram. I would like to read the text before I write in detail about Devanayaki.

Comments

1. *Thamizh Selvan*: Meenakshi Rajarathinam shows us a hitherto unknown part of history. It is not clear whether it is history, or imagination mixed with history. Anyway, it is a good story. Congratulations.

2. *Karpoora Nayaki*: History texts tell us very little about Kanthalur. I had recently read a newspaper report claiming that a historian from Chennai had discovered evidence that the ships anchored in Rajaraja Chola harbour as well as the town had been set on fire. Where did Meenakshi get the rest of the information from? It's a shame that it stopped abruptly, just when it was getting interesting. Anyway, it is a good effort. Congratulations.

3. *Nallur Gopal*: I read that report too, Karpoora Nayaki. The ruins of a fort without cannonball holes have been discovered near Vizhinjam. Is this Meenakshi Rajarathinam a Malayali from Trivandrum? How did she get into Karupu?

4. *Charles Murukesh*: If the Chola king that Meenakshi mentions is Rajaraja of Kanthalur, it's a shame.

5. *Dr D'Silva*: Meenakshi is looking for new ways to humiliate the Sinhalese.

6. *Kovai Kuveni*: I doubt that Meenakshi Rajarathinam is a woman. I perceive a male gaze throughout the narrative.

7. *Karpoora Nayaki*: That is the innate female characteristic of fault-finding. Kuveni, I urge you to emulate Anasuya.

8. *Nanchil Gouthaman*: I was surprised when I read about the temple of Suchindram. Nobody knows of these things.

9. *Kovai Kuveni*: It is not jealousy. I was merely sharing my anguish at seeing a woman portrayed in a negative light. I felt ashamed when I read about a woman like Devanayaki, who had studied the *Arthashastra* and political science, obeying Mahendravarman's commands without a murmur. And she actually sings on her way to the palace! She drinks the water after washing Thanumalayan's feet! Meenakshi is conveying a message that women should bow before authority – it's not right.

10. *Karpoora Nayaki*: Kuveni, Meenakshi was writing about what happened a thousand years ago. That might have been how people lived during those times.

11. *Kovai Kuveni*: Can't you smell the stench of Brahmanism in the Thiruppavai and the *Soundarya Lahari*?

12. *Karpoora Nayaki*: Kuveni, that's your olfactory problem. Also, stench is not a bad thing. Listen to the song Andal sings in the Thiruppavai. She asks Krishna's conch whether camphor stinks.

I didn't feel like reading any more comments. I shut the laptop. Should I call Manju? It's past midnight. She might be in a casino with some rich guy. Or in his bed. Though she had promised to ask the rap singers about Devanayaki, she hadn't called back.

I quite liked Meenakshi's story. It would be nice to read the book they claimed was discovered in Sigiriya. I decided to send an email to Meenakshi. But, as someone commented, is

Meenakshi Rajarathinam a man? Or is it Eezhathachi writing under a pseudonym?

6

I am sad sad
I am mad mad

I had just gone to bed when Manju rang. I had been waiting for her call since morning. She had texted yesterday, telling me that she was coming to Colombo and would like to meet me. Her job was to entertain rich men. Her luck turned when some gamblers, mostly from Kerala, felt that her presence at the gambling table brought them good fortune. She used to fly from Kochi to Colombo two or three times a week.

When she had entered the film world eight years ago, she was considered a promising actress. But when her movies flopped, she was labelled an unlucky one – even though the failures could not be attributed to her. Succumbing to the temptations of money and luxury, she lost everything. She used to joke cruelly about herself – 'Wrong pictures, wrong roles, wrong company.' When I asked her whether I was also on the list of people she thought of as 'wrong company', she would laugh. I knew the meaning of her laughter. She used to often accuse me of being her first pimp. The world behind commercial cinema is a strange one. It is very much like a casino. Very few people win at gambling. It's the same in the world of cinema. It was ironic that one who was labelled 'unlucky' in movies was considered lucky in casinos. As she still took good care of her appearance, there were men who considered it prestigious to be escorted by her to Bally's or MGM.

'Were you sleeping?'

'No. Where are you?'

'Very close to you. On the fifth floor. Right below your room. The hero who brought me here flew to Singapore after a good harvest at Bally's. I'm returning by the morning flight to Kochi. We were celebrating his winning four lakhs in three hours.'

'Did the celebration stop with drinking?'

'Are you mad? Will they bring me here just to look at me? Today, there were no problems. But usually, they go mad when they win. He was so happy that he just lifted me up right there in the casino and gave me one-fourth of his takings.'

'No wonder the gamblers vie for your company. You are a lucky star. You want to come up or…?'

'I'll come up. That's better.'

She reached my room within minutes. The scent of her expensive perfume wafted in with her. She was wearing a light yellow gown and a black hat. Her face was heavily made up. She came and kissed me before falling upon the bed and taking off her hat.

'What's up with your movie? Have you found Sugandhi?'

'No. What about your enquiries?'

'No use. Don't waste your time looking for her. Do the movie. Cast Janet Jackson or Cathy Graham in Rajini Thiranagama's role.'

'That's the plan now. Even if we find Sugandhi, I don't think she will be able to act. But I would like to meet her if she is alive.'

I shut off the light and lay down beside her.

'A man like you shouldn't be so sentimental,' Manju said.

'You will not understand.'

'I do understand, but keep your emotions separate from your professional life.'

'I am not mixing both.'

'Then why are you looking for her so anxiously? Talking about her?'

'Manju, we are rewriting the entire script. Sugandhi and I, who were going to make a movie about Rajini Thiranagama, are now characters in this movie. It is a movie about a movie that was not made.'

'Somehow I think you'll really go mad if you carry on like this.'

She didn't accept my explanation. I too decided not to waste time arguing. I gathered her towards myself.

'Did that gambler tire you out?'

'He was a cold fish. I was bored. That's why I called you right after he left.'

'Do you enjoy all this? Or is it merely work?'

'I try to enjoy it, but somehow I can't.'

'Let's have a drink.'

'No. We can drink any time. But I don't get you often.'

I tried not to disappoint her. Finally, as she was slipping into slumber, she asked, 'Peter, how long has it been since you went home?'

'Twelve years.'

'Didn't your mother pass away last year?'

'My mother died long ago. Then she died again last year.'

'It's not wise to hold a grudge for so long.'

'I will not go home before making a movie on Rajini Thiranagama.'

'It's been twelve years since you graduated from the institute. You have not been able to complete a single project. You are gambling away your career with this Tiger game.'

'Yes, you're right. But I cannot do another movie before I complete my project on Rajini Thiranagama. I will not do it in a slapdash manner. Wasn't it you who told me that it is better to do one good film than a hundred crappy ones?'

'I don't want to argue with you. I want you to win, at least this time. Don't be foolish and spoil this opportunity.'

'No, I won't. It's a Hollywood production and we have full support from the government. I expect everything to go off well.'

'Good luck to you.'

She woke up early to leave and, as usual, she took a hundred dollars from my wallet. She left me a note: *There is a music video on YouTube called SAD. I think that it is your Sugandhi.*

My god!

I located SAD on YouTube. The video began with loud sounds. The visuals showed a large crowd begging the UN observers not to leave. They were the same visuals used in *Sri Lanka's Killing Fields*. A singer came to the stage from the crowd. Slowly, reaching a high point of ecstasy, she discarded her clothing. The audience cried and averted their eyes. All this happened between visuals of rape carried out at gunpoint. When the singer fell unconscious, everything ended. The words 'I am Sugandhi alias Devanayaki' filled the screen.

I am sad sad
I am mad mad
Kill me kill me kill me
I am one who has lost her dreams
I am one who has forgotten love
Sad – mad

Though I'd watched the song that criticized the Sri Lankan army harshly, using crude expletives, I couldn't believe that it was

Sugandhi. It was not the Sugandhi I knew, neither her physical appearance nor her voice. She could never dance dressed in scanty clothes. But SAD was the abbreviation of 'Sugandhi alias Devanayaki'. I searched online and found SAD's website.

SAD

The Sri Lankans in Canada created an album titled *SAD* in memory of Sugandhi alias Devanayaki, the Eezham Tamil fighter. The album was produced by an Afro-American company called United Records Inc. The album had ten songs, of which Sugandhi had penned the lyrics for three. It was believed that Sugandhi, who was reported missing from 27 November 2002, had been abducted by a high-ranking official in the Sri Lankan army who had sexually abused her for months before shooting and killing her. Sugandhi had worked in the media section of the Iyakkam with Isai Priya, who was killed in May 2009 when the struggle was nearing its end. Sugandhi was a good rapper, like Mathangi Arulpragasam (MIA). After her parents were killed in the genocide of 1983, she had gone to live in London with her relatives.

Arulmozhi Nangai and Yamuna Sridhar had sung all the songs in the album. They were both Tamil Eezham girls who had grown up in Canada. The first song written by Sugandhi, which they recorded on 21 June 2009, was 'We hate lions'. The rest of the songs were recorded sporadically over the next one and a half years. 'SAD SAD SAD' was the last song to be recorded. Sugandhi had written the lyrics for 'SAD SAD SAD', 'We hate lions' and 'Burn! Your history'. The rest of the songs were written by Arulmozhi Nangai. 'SAD SAD SAD' was released in November 2012 and got a place in the top hundred in the US and France within three months of its release. By 2013, it was among the top ten in most European countries and number three in Australia.

We expect 'SAD SAD SAD' to win many music awards, including the Grammy, this year.

All of this was unbelievable. When arrangements were made to help her escape on 27 November 2002, during the bustle of the Hero's Day celebrations, Sugandhi was under protection and safe. It was impossible for a Sinhalese military general to abduct her from there. Moreover, as she was working at the media centre, she didn't need to travel. If Sugandhi had been killed, it had to be the Tigers who were responsible. This could be a clever ruse to hide it. Though I tried to call Manju, her phone was switched off. It was when I was about to leave for the airport that she returned my call.

'Was that Sugandhi?'

'No. It's a singer called Arulmozhi Nangai. She is singing Sugandhi's lyrics. Do you have friends in Canada?'

'My uncle Vinod Menon works at the High Commission there.'

'Good. Mail him immediately. Two Canadian singers, Arulmozhi Nangai and Yamuna Sridhar, have sung in SAD. It will be good if you contact them. Find out where they got Sugandhi's lyrics from. They have written on the SAD website that Sugandhi is dead. I want to know where they got that information from.'

'I'll email my uncle today and let you know if I get any information.'

'When are you leaving?'

'Right now. Bye.'

'Have a nice trip to Jaffna.'

I felt a twinge in my heart as I boarded the flight to Jaffna. I could not forget how I had escaped from there eight years ago. Even when I pretended to laugh at Christie's and Mary's jokes, my mind was besieged by the memories. Rajini Thiranagama, Thambimuthu, Sugandhi alias Devanayaki. The initial days of love, karthika flowers, betrayal, trial – exodus. Jesus! What an event-filled eight months.

For the initial work on the movie based on Rajini Thiranagama, I had stayed in a house arranged by the Iyakkam near the Jaffna Medical College with my classmate from the Institute, Bhuvana Chandra Chatterji, and Thambimuthu from the 'Voice of Tigers'. Bhuvana was the cameraman. He had assisted a famous director, Balu Mahendra, before he joined me. Though his parents were from Calcutta, he was born and brought up in Matunga in Mumbai. With his long hair and beard, the fair and handsome Bhuvana looked like an intellectual. He was taciturn, but his ability to visually conceive any idea gave a great boost to the script. He could understand the complexities of the emotional and political dimensions of the Iyakkam.

Thambimuthu, who had been in the military section of the LTTE, joined the media wing after he lost his left leg below the knee. Though he was experienced in camera work, editing and sound recording, he did not know much about cinematic aesthetics. He was a dark, stocky man, nearly twice our age. He was grey and balding. The energetic way in which he moved despite his artificial limb surprised me. We had a maid, Amudam, who cooked and cleaned for us. She would come to work in the morning and then again in the afternoon.

It was Thambimuthu whom I had first approached with the proposal about a movie on Rajini. I met him quite accidentally as I was coming out of the Alliance Française in Chennai, after watching a documentary he had directed that celebrated the Eezham after the ceasefire treaty. It seemed like a commercial movie with songs and dance – a paean to the Thalaivar. When we asked Thambimuthu why he had made such a documentary, he asked us, 'Why not?' That was how Thambimuthu, a videographer in the media section of the Tigers, conceived of a documentary. That night at the hotel, we spoke at length. I think that I was able to convince him about the endless possibilities of the cinematic medium. When I told him that I too was a student of the Film Institute like Balu Mahendra, he was quite impressed. We met a couple of times after that. It was he who put forward the proposal about a movie based on Rajini Thiranagama's life. But the leader of the Tigers and Thambimuthu had political motivations. For them, the movie was an effort to answer the accusation that the Tigers had been responsible for Rajini's death, and to establish that Rajini, who had been on their side to begin with, had never shifted loyalties. It was an attempt to whitewash their anti-human-rights activities.

When I joined them, I was quite ignorant about their hidden agenda. I only thought of it as an opportunity to do a movie within one year of passing out of film school. When Bhuvana joined hands with us, saying that this movie had international potential and we could work magic with it, my confidence doubled. Neither of us knew then that the Tigers were responsible for Rajini's murder. Bhuvana and I believed that it was either the Indian Peace Keeping Force or the Sri Lankan army. We planned the movie so that Rajini would be portrayed as the prey of both the government and the military. Both parties hated human rights activists. That is what Thambimuthu led us to believe. But when we made more enquiries during the writing of our script,

we realized that Thambimuthu had not been entirely honest
with us.

It was in the third week of my arrival in Jaffna that I met
Sugandhi. Thambimuthu brought her home, introducing her
as the ideal person to play Rajini. His choice was perfect. Apart
from the fact that she was more good-looking than Rajini, there
were no other problems. Perhaps Rajini had been as beautiful in
her youth too. Her front teeth were not as big as Rajini's. Her
eyes had a regal grace. She was as beautiful as a karthika flower
about to bloom. Just as she had written in *Karupu*, Sugandhi and
I were thrown into a sea of love. It was then that I realized that
love was something one had to experience, it was not something
that could be explained.

'Have you acted before?'

'No.'

'Have you heard about Rajini Thiranagama?'

'I've heard my uncle in London speak about her. But I don't
really know her.'

The announcement that we were about to land in Jaffna
awakened me from my thoughts.

7

Who was Rajini Thiranagama? The answer to this question is
not very simple. But the Sri Lankan government was trying to
manipulate the answer in a way that suited them. It was as part
of this agenda that a huge conference titled 'Who was Rajini
Thiranagama?' had been organized with the secret support of
the Northern Provincial Council. They were able to convince
the majority of the people who attended that it was a meeting

organized by the staff, students and alumni of the Jaffna Medical College. It was for the first time since her death in 1989 that such a huge meeting was being organized in her memory.

Immediately after checking into Tilko Jaffna City Hotel, we made our way to Veerasingam Hall.

By 10 a.m., the hall, one of the largest convention centres in Jaffna, was packed. Many couldn't find seats inside and gathered outside the venue. Perhaps the organizers were acting on Samaraveera's orders, but the three of us were given front-row seats. The organizers gave us a special welcome as we were the team from Hollywood who had come to make a movie on Rajini. There were a couple of Sinhalese men in the crowd scrutinizing everything around them. Perhaps they were Sri Lankan secret service officers in mufti. Four or five speakers were sitting quite impatiently onstage, in front of a garlanded photograph of Rajini. It felt like they had been waiting for us. The moment we reached our seats, the meeting began with a silent prayer in memory of Rajini. Marathakam Shanmugananthan, a professor at the Jaffna Medical College, rose to address the gathering.

'Good morning, everyone. I welcome all of you to this conference titled "Who was Rajini Thiranagama?" Rajini Thiranagama is the name of a martyr who lost her life in the Iyakkam – a name that ought to be written in letters of gold. She was a martyr who fought without weapons against the violence of the Iyakkam, the Sri Lankan military and the Indian Peace Keeping Force. She died twenty-five years ago. In the history of Sri Lanka, one cannot find another person like her. Unfortunately, the anxieties she shared through her activism, before she was killed in September 1989, have become the tragic history of the Eelam. But I doubt that the new generation has understood

Rajini Thiranagama properly. The aim of this conference is to create awareness about her life and her activism. In this meeting, Rajini's friend, Dr Valarmathi Kalyanasundaram, an oncology professor in the National University of Singapore, Reverend Father Alfred Chelladurai, secretary of the Jaffna Human Rights Watch, and Amina El Abidi, the famous Egyptian human rights activist and chairperson of the international agency, Women Against War, will speak about Rajini Thiranagama. These three dignitaries know three different dimensions of Rajini. First, we will have Dr Valarmathi Kalyanasundaram.'

The audience waited expectantly as Valarmathi stood up, bowed before Rajini's picture and walked towards the microphone. She held back her tears and began. 'I knew Rajini from a very young age. We were neighbours. Our childhood, like anybody else's, was filled with songs, laughter and stories. Often, her elder sister, Nirmala, would join us. When we grew up a bit, the bicycle came into our lives. Among us, it was Rajini who learnt to cycle first. There was a time when we flew around these lanes on our bicycles like butterflies. What a lovely time that was! Both of us were born in 1954, she in February and I in March. To be exact, she on 23 February and I on 23 March. Though she was just a month older, she behaved like an elder sister towards me. Not just me, she treated her elder sister Nirmala too in the same way. She displayed a maturity far exceeding her age. Her father, Rajasingham, a mathematics professor, brought up his children with a deep consciousness about the concept of freedom rather than as devout Christians. This child who used to giggle at jokes became quite serious when she reached high school. But she had always been a high achiever – in studies and in sports. Both of us joined medical college together. The majority of the students there were Sinhalese. But Rajini was able to adjust to the new language and customs quite easily. She was a topper there too. It was then that Rajini evolved into a woman who fought for freedom and human rights. The impact of communism sweeping across the globe in the 1970s did not fail to influence her. But she did not accept revolutions as dogmatic. She was wary about the violence inherent in any revolt. Her sense of freedom was rooted in democracy. That is why she was able to create political awareness among the usually apolitical medical students. We medical students, under Rajini's leadership, protested against the first student murder in Sri Lankan history in 1976 – the death of Veerasurya, a student of Peradeniya College.

'She believed in a world humanity that went beyond narrow cultural identities. It was then that she met and fell in love with a revolutionary, Dayapala Thiranagama. Though they came from different backgrounds, the purity of their love brought them together. I would joke with her, saying that she should insert a sentence into her Bible: "Those who are in love are indeed blessed, for this world is heaven to them." But for Rajini and Dayapala, the world was not heaven. After they got married in 1977, Dayapala often had to go into hiding. Two lovely girls were born to them: Narmada in 1978 and Sharika in 1980. Dayapala Thiranagama and Narmada live in England now. Sharika teaches Anthropology at Stanford University.

'Rajini did her internship at Jaffna Teaching Hospital. Unfortunately, I had to continue in Colombo. After completing my internship, I got married and went to Singapore. At that time, she was working in a village called Haldummulla. Before she completed a year there, she was appointed as faculty of anatomy at the Jaffna Medical College. Her colleagues and students remember her as an excellent teacher. She always tried to learn more about her subject and follow the latest research activities in her area. By the end of 1983, she got a Commonwealth Fellowship to pursue higher studies at Middlesex University Hospital in the UK. She did her research in comparative anatomy at Liverpool University. Her articles were published in leading medical journals. The paper, "Valves in Superficial Limb Veins of Humans and Non-human Primates" that she wrote in collaboration with A.T. Chamberlain and B.T. Wood which was published in 1989 in the *Anatomy Journal*, deserves special mention.

'Though she could have advanced her career in the UK, she came back home and taught at Jaffna Medical College. Our eyes fill with tears when we remember that it was during a period when most professionals were leaving the country to escape the raging civil war that Rajini came back. When she was in London, she supported the Iyakkam. Like her sister Nirmala, she too believed in it. But she soon realized that the Iyakkam was not democratic in nature. This realization and her understanding of the concept of freedom influenced her later actions. But, unfortunately, those who did not understand her courageous stand for peace killed her on World Peace Day. On 21 September 1989, they shot Rajini. I wind up my speech offering my tears as a tribute to her memory. Reverend Father Alfred Chelladurai, who stood with her in her struggle for human rights, will be able to shed more light on her activism. He will speak to you next.'

Father Alfred Chelladurai looked like he was more than eighty years old. When he got up with great difficulty and addressed the gathering in a quavering voice, a strange silence fell upon the audience.

'Greetings to all! Like Valarmathi said, I worked with Rajini in the late 1980s. It is not entirely correct to say that I worked with her. It would be proper to say that I gave her support, advice and the confidence to pursue her actions. As a notorious military officer had used all his strength on my body in the riot-stricken year of 1983, I was not able to walk or even stand up. Rajini was my friend Rajasingham's daughter. They were smart, intelligent people who loved this country and its people. They came to me in 1988 to speak about establishing a group called University Teachers for Human Rights in Jaffna University. I asked her whether she had given sufficient thought before deciding on this course of action. She smiled in response. Sridhar Rajan Hoole and Daya Somasundaram, who were her colleagues, had come with her to meet me. They were committed people. They had realized that the Iyakkam, the Sri Lankan army and the Indian Peace Keeping Force were all crushing the lives of the ordinary people. They wanted to expose this and sensitize the public against violence.

'I explained the concepts of human rights activism to them in detail. Human rights activists fight armed enemies without weapons. As individuals we might lose, but ultimately society will win. Most often, victory is attained after we die. That is the path Christ has shown us. The path Gandhi has shown us. That was the route the UTHR activists took.

'The reports published by UTHR were a mirror that reflected our society. Rajini and her team marked each violent incident that took place here. They announced to the world the names of those who caused violence. They tried to help the victims in every possible way, giving them protection, food, medicine and treatment. They started institutions like the Poorani Women's Centre to rehabilitate female victims. It was not activism carried out from safe bungalows in Colombo with aid from foreign agencies. They gambled with their lives to establish peace. When

UTHR started publishing reports about the violent activities of the Iyakkam, trouble began.

'The Sri Lankan military and the Indian Peace Keeping Force were able to justify themselves saying that they were military activities. But the Iyakkam, which claimed that it was acting for the people, was unable to justify its misdeeds. By this time, they had moved away from democratic principles and were trying to silence their critics through torture and murder. As Rajini chose to ignore their threats, she was killed. I have only one answer to the question – Who was Rajini Thiranagama? – posed by this new generation. She was the purest woman born on this soil. An epitome of tolerance and peace. A star of dignity. Thank you.'

He was tired by the end of his speech. Valarmathi and Marathakam helped him to his chair. When Amina El Abidi rose and started speaking in fluent English, those who were standing outside the hall pushed their way in.

'Dear friends, I first met Rajini when I went to London in 1986 to speak at a convention organized by Women Against War. Feminists and pacifists all over the world remember her with passionate zeal. She had eyes that brimmed with hope. Her voice was confident. On my way here, I read speeches made by famous human rights activists like Radhika Kumaraswamy and Nandita Haksar commemorating Rajini Thiranagama. I don't think a speech like that is relevant today. I think I should read the last part of the speech Dayapala Thiranagama made about her in 2009. When I spoke to Rajini's daughter Narmada, she too said that it was a good idea. Now, to Dayapala's words:

'It is also necessary to reflect upon the validity of Rajini's ideas in relation to the current political situation. To use Rajini's phrase, we are still walking through a dark valley and inhumanity is everywhere. One of the fundamental issues today is the fear of speaking out or

the right to dissent. The dark shadow of the ethnic war has not entirely disappeared. Unless the democratic space is expanded, with devolution of power to the Tamil community, peace will be as elusive as ever.

'It is possible that there will be more and more people like Rajini in both the Tamil and Sinhalese communities, since the political barriers for which she – as a revolutionary in support of the fundamental democratic right of dissent – had to give her life are still very much in place. Those who follow Rajini's path will make our world a better place.

'For twenty long years, I have been coming to terms with the terrible pain and anguish Rajini must have felt a few seconds before her death, and my inability to share it with her. I know how she would have felt. Once, she wrote to me saying, "If anyone knows me in this world like the pages of a book, it is you." I owe so much to her, for the depth of her love for me, and for a true understanding of the beauty of human love that our relationship taught me.

'Rajini and I loved Bob Marley's music. She liked one song in particular, and I would like to end by quoting from it: Get up, stand up, stand up for your rights.

'I have nothing more to add to Dayapala's words.

'Get up, stand up … stand up for your rights.'

The meeting ended earlier than we thought it would.

8

It was indeed strange that nobody at the meeting spoke about the mystery surrounding Rajini Thiranagama's death. Perhaps there were strict orders that it should not be mentioned. If not, at least Father Chelladurai would have said something. If people like

Daya Somasundaram or Sridhar who had worked with Rajini in UTHR had been invited, they would have spoken openly. Maybe the organizers did not invite them, knowing that they could not be controlled. Nobody elaborated on Rajini's changed political stance during the later days of the movement and her reasons for changing. So the question – Who was Rajini Thiranagama? – remained unanswered at the convention, which was clearly a state sponsored meeting. The only outcome of this meeting was that it brought Rajini into public memory once more.

When we sat down to discuss the script after lunch, this was the first question Mary raised.

'Peter, I feel that this meeting was a waste. They only spoke about matters which we already know. We want to know about the mystery surrounding her death. The audience kept mum like obedient students.'

'You are right, Mary. All of them spoke with fear in their hearts. The audience too were victims of fear. This is today's Sri Lanka. Clouds of fear surround us. Nothing is democratic. Everyone is under surveillance. We too are definitely being watched. Both the government that is celebrating freedom from terrorism, and the Iyakkam that is searching for a way to climb out of the abyss of complete failure, are afraid of the common people. And the hapless people of this country? They fear everyone. It's quite a paradox.'

'Peter, I completely agree with Mary,' said Christie. 'Nothing is going to come out of such meetings. We will just be wasting our time. Our aim is to unravel the mystery surrounding Rajini's murder and to portray it realistically.'

'So? Samaraveera?'

'Well, if the truth is as he says, there will be no problems.'

'Reality, to a certain extent, is in accordance with what he says.'

'Peter, reality does not have limits to it.'

By then, it was time for Christie to meet the NCP Governor, Chandrasiri. Though Samaraveera had told us that he would give us all the help we needed to shoot in Jaffna, Christie went to meet him formally. Amina El Abidi, who was staying in the same hotel, also went along. Mary who, like Christie, was not aware of my first project with Sugandhi, listened eagerly.

'Mary, we know a lot of facts, but there are certain things that we need to find out. When Sugandhi and I were working together, we made many shocking discoveries that led us into danger. The most important discovery was that Rajini and VP, as Prabhakaran was known, had met a few weeks before she was killed. He requested Rajini to stop her activism that criticized the Iyakkam and go abroad. During that meeting, Rajini realized that she could be murdered. That affected her later activities.'

'I can't believe this.'

'Neither could we. Initially, we found it difficult to believe that a man like VP would agree to such a meeting. Due to security reasons, such a meeting was almost impossible. But it was true. They spoke for almost fifteen minutes at a secret place in Kilinochchi. VP and Rajini were alone. But, unknown to VP, their entire conversation was recorded.'

'Have you heard this recording, Peter?'

'Yes. A leader high up in the Iyakkam hierarchy had recorded it. When the Iyakkam floated a political party in 1989, Mahattaya was its leader for a short while. Rajini had given medical assistance to some of the wounded activists of the Iyakkam. Differences of opinion with VP had led to Mahattaya's death in 1994. By then, this recording had reached the person who gave me the cassette. Sugandhi and I listened to it several times and she transcribed the entire conversation. Based on that conversation, Sugandhi and I wrote a script portraying Rajini as a victim of the Peace Keeping Force's atrocities.'

'Then?'

'That was a great blunder. The production of the movie was completely controlled by Thambimuthu. I never got the opportunity to meet VP or any other prominent leader. I gave the full script to Thambimuthu for final approval. As VP himself was acting in the movie, the media wing sent him the script for consent. When he saw the transcript of his secret conversation with Rajini, he was shocked. He shook with rage. More than the fact that the conversation was part of the script, it was the fact that people knew about this highly guarded meeting that enraged him. He summoned Thambimuthu and two others who were connected with the movie. Sugandhi was also called. VP firmly believed that Thambimuthu was responsible and did not suspect Sugandhi at all. He had always treated her in a special manner since she joined the Iyakkam. Maybe it was because she spoke English fluently and was very smart. Luckily, Bhuvana and I were location-hunting on the Jaffna Medical College campus at the time. Acting upon information that the situation was becoming tense, some teachers helped us go into hiding.

'By evening, Thambimuthu was dragged to meet VP. Within minutes, Thambimuthu was shot dead after being accused of revealing highly guarded secrets of the Iyakkam. He didn't get the opportunity to speak one word in defence. Thambimuthu struggled in the throes of death, unaware of what his crime was or why he was being punished. He kept trying to say something until his last breath. Seeing Thambimuthu struggle, Sugandhi lost her mental balance.

'She felt that her parents and brother were lying there gasping for breath. Forgetting all the rules of the Iyakkam, she rushed at

VP screaming, "Are you mad?" Several guns were aimed at her immediately, but VP stopped them from firing. She put the tape recorder on the table and switched it on. When the conversation between VP and Rajini flooded the room, silence fell upon the listeners. VP shouted, "Switch it off.'"

'Was she shot dead as well?'

'No. If that were the case, I wouldn't be wandering around looking for her. Switching off the tape recorder, she asked VP, "Does the king of the Iyakkam fear the truth?" Fearing that Thambimuthu's fate would be hers as well, she shut her eyes. But nothing happened. For the first time, VP pardoned someone. Who knows why? Sugandhi continued to work for the media wing for a while. Eight days later, on 27 November 2002, during the celebrations of Hero's Day, she made the arrangements for our escape.'

'Do you have a copy of the recording?'

'I lost the cassette. Only Sugandhi knows where the transcript she had written is now. I have a copy that I wrote down from memory. It may have errors.'

I gave Mary a copy of the transcript. She read it with surprise.

The Last Meeting

VP: You must forgive me, Rajini. I wanted to discuss some important issues. That is why I brought you here.

Rajini: Prabha, what is there to discuss? You are not interested in hearing names like Arulmozhi or Sivapadam.

VP: We are speaking from different perspectives. To attain a free land, we will have to sacrifice a lot. The Iyakkam is nearing victory. We can ensure it only if the ordinary people support the freedom fighters. It is certain that V.P. Singh's new government will withdraw the Peace Keeping Force. The number of countries supporting us is also on the rise.

Rajini: I'm not really interested in politics. These are topics dear to people like you who thirst for power. I only think of ways to bring peace to this land.

VP: When did you lose interest in politics? It was you who explained politics to me when we met at the age of seventeen. Why don't you realize that unquestioned authority is necessary to maintain peace and order?

Rajini: I don't trust you there, Prabha. You always have some excuse whenever a possibility for peace arises. Why are we wasting our time talking about this?

VP: I called you here to congratulate you as well as to request a favour. I really appreciate the fact that you chose to come back here rather than become a refugee in Europe. You could have lived comfortably abroad, satisfied with your degrees and pursuing your research activities. Instead, you came back and reopened the Jaffna Medical College after the Peace Keeping Force had destroyed it.

Rajini: Thank you. But I don't think it's a great sacrifice. I came with the kids you sent to fetch me to discuss some unpleasant issues. You were absolutely wrong to kill all the leaders of the Iyakkam and other freedom movements in order to secure your position. How could you act like that, despite having read the works of Gandhi and Subhash Chandra Bose? It was wrong to forcibly recruit women and children to the Iyakkam. And to enlist anyone in the military before they become mature is a crime.

VP: I cannot win this argument with you. It was necessary to build up the movement. You must understand that I was not working with selfish motives. I have only one aim – a free land. Once I attain that I will, like Gandhi, renounce power.

Rajini: Somehow, I don't believe you. You behave as if you are intoxicated with power. Tell me, how can I help you?

VP: You may be surprised when I ask you the first favour. You must go back abroad to continue your medical research. You must take up full-time research at some university in the UK or the US. That is the best option for you and your daughter.

Rajini: This is indeed hilarious. First you appreciate my decision to return, then you request me to go back. Are you in your senses?

VP: Yes, I am conscious of what I'm saying. You are a personality of international renown. Your words are given great importance. You criticize the activities of the Iyakkam, the Sri Lankan military and the Peace Keeping Force. Neither you nor your friends pay any attention to the good intentions of our struggle. When you talk about the women in the Iyakkam, you forget the fact that we respect each and every member, especially women. Not a single crime against women has been committed by our members – nor will any violence be committed in the future.

Rajini: Prabha, this is nothing great. Any government should function in this manner. But the Iyakkam lacks freedom and democracy, the most essential concepts for the success of any movement. Now, what is the second favour you want?

VP: You might think that this is a joke. I need this second favour only if you reject the first one. You must develop the infrastructure of Jaffna Medical College and raise it to international standards. Channel your energy into medical research. Don't waste your time and energy in human rights activism.

Rajini: Prabha, things are very clear. You are not in the least bit concerned about whether I do any research or not. You just want me to stop my activism, particularly my criticism of the Iyakkam. That is impossible. My student days are definitely over. I have decided to spend the rest of my life as a full-time human rights activist.

VP: If you criticize the Iyakkam, we may have to intervene. Then I might not be able to think of you as my friend or remember that our fathers were friends.

Rajini: Are you trying to scare me? I may not be able to think of you when I expose the human rights violations of the Iyakkam.

VP: So, we need not speak any further.

Rajini: I don't think so. I still expect you to give up violence, though.

VP: And I still hope that you will consider my requests. The first option is the best for you.

After reading through it, Mary asked me in wonder, 'Is all this true?'

'I'm not sure. I have my doubts. But they were of the same age and very conscious about their rights and freedom. They fought for their rights. It was during this time that Rajini's sister joined the Iyakkam and became an active member. When she was in London, Rajini too was an active member of the London committee of the Iyakkam.'

9

In the evening, the female students of the Jaffna Medical College organized an informal meeting of Women Against War. The venue was the conference hall in Tilko Jaffna City Hotel where we were staying. Nearly fifty people participated in the meeting organized by the student union's secretary, Poomani Selvanayagam, and her friends. They had initially planned to screen *No More Tears Sister: Anatomy of Hope and Betrayal*, directed by Helene Klodawsky and based on Rajini Thiranagama's life, and to follow it up with a discussion. Amina El Abidi was to be the moderator. But they altered the programme slightly after inviting us. They wanted Christie to introduce the documentary before its screening. While I was scripting *The Woman Behind the Fall of the Tigers*, I had watched *No More Tears Sister* several times. This was the most authentic documentary made on Rajini Thiranagama. Helena was able to successfully portray Rajini's personal life as well as accurately describe the political ideology she believed in. This documentary was widely shown in Europe, Canada and the US with the support of international human rights agencies, and pacifists, both Sri Lankans and Tamils who had settled abroad, lent their support. It had won several international awards, including awards for best documentary and photography, and had first been screened in 2005, which was the golden age of the Iyakkam. Though the Iyakkam intellectuals criticized *No More Tears Sister* produced by the Canadian Film School, they did not take a stand against it publicly. Fearing the Iyakkam, nobody dared screen the documentary in many public venues. But when it was uploaded on YouTube, both supporters and detractors watched and spoke about it.

Helene presented Rajini through the words of her sisters Nirmala and Vasuki, her husband Dayapala Thiranagama, and her children Narmada and Sharika. As original footage of Rajini was unavailable, Helena tried to recreate some scenes using Rajini's second daughter Sharika, but I felt that Sugandhi would have done a much better job. Sharika could become Rajini only in physical appearance. Her respect for her mother was an obstacle to embracing the role wholeheartedly. But Helene had to be applauded for creating in the audience a sense of having actually seen Rajini. The narration by the Booker-prize-winning Michael Ondaatje was touching. Yet, I felt that the documentary had not explored all the possibilities of the cinematic medium. Maybe it had to do with issues of authenticity in making a documentary.

The meeting began with Christie's speech.

'Ladies and gentlemen, good evening to you all. I feel that my introductory speech to the documentary is unnecessary. My colleagues and I are here to watch *No More Tears Sister* once more and to listen to your discussion. I am standing before you as Poomani compelled me to speak. *No More Tears Sister* altered my life in every possible way. Three years ago, before I watched this documentary in London, I had no idea who Rajini Thiranagama was. But after watching this documentary, she became the person I most admire. The more I learned about her, the more my respect increased. Rajini and Dayapala belonged to different races and different religious backgrounds. Their love story amazed me. Later, when I met Peter in Berlin, Rajini's story became a possibility for a big movie. As we progressed with the project, Mary Ann, the cinematographer in this project, became part of my life. These are my personal details.

'I feel that, as far as the organization Women Against War is concerned, Rajini Thiranagama is an icon of resistance and martyrdom. Rajini said, "I want to prove that ordinary women like me too have enormous courage and the will to fight alone and hold our inner selves together." We need such icons in these times, because all wars are essentially wars against women. They are cruelly exploited, emotionally, physically and sexually. For men clad in battledress, whether they come with swords or guns, on horseback or in armoured cars, the value of their conquest seems heightened by the violation of women. This is a reality that Rajini showed us, which we must recognize. There need to be resistance movements against wars.

'But often, we have to pay a very dear price for this. Rajini was willing to make that sacrifice. That is why she was able to write a few months before her death that, "One day, a gun will silence me and it will not be held by an outsider, but by a son born in the womb of this very society, from a woman with whom I share a history." I bow before Rajini's memory. Thank you all.'

A deep silence filled the hall when the eighty-minute documentary ended. For a while, nobody spoke. Then, one or two people walked out, wiping their tears. Though tea was served, not many people wanted it. After some time, Amina El Abidi stood up to initiate the discussion.

'Good evening, friends. This is an important day for those of us who belong to the organization, Women Against War. Though Rajini was not a member of our organization, she believed in this movement. She reacted against war with a hundred times more force than we did. I believe that the meeting held in Veerasingam Hall this morning will be of great help in re-establishing Rajini in our minds. That meeting, as you all know, was under the strict control of the government. Everyone who spoke at that meeting was under tremendous pressure. I don't think that this meeting is controlled to that extent. Nobody has told us what we can or cannot speak about. Yet, I must be careful. One of you might be a government spy. The moment you start speaking of peace and freedom, you become an enemy of the government. Because your president, like many other rulers in the world, fears the people and fears democracy. That is why hundreds of journalists and human rights activists in your country are kidnapped, go missing or are killed. I don't intend to prolong my words. Those of you who wish to speak are requested to come up to the stage and introduce yourselves before speaking.'

'Greetings, everyone! I am Karpooram. A final-year medical student. I write a blog on human rights issues within the Iyakkam under the name Karpoora Nayaki. I have certain points to raise against this movie. It is not proper that the director has only hinted at and not openly told us how Rajini madam was killed, who her assassins were and who wanted her dead. There are many people in this country who know the answers to these questions. More important than to find out who committed the murder is to find out who put them up to it.'

'Greetings! I am Maria Arputham. I echo what Karpooram said. More enquiries should be made into Rajini Madam's death. Enquiries should also be made about other such murders that were part of the war for the past twenty-five years.'

'Hello! I am Srikanthamalar. I cannot completely agree with Karpooram and Maria. After twenty-five years of war, our country is slowly moving towards peace. I think that we should not create fresh trouble by dredging up old issues. All of them, whether it is the Iyakkam or human rights activists like Rajini, fought for the freedom of the Tamils. Their chosen paths may have been different. There might have been quarrels and skirmishes in the midst of the war. Some may have been killed. None of that happened for personal gain. It was an effort to prevent the weakening of the Iyakkam. It was for the magnificent dream of a free land. We failed. If we had won, Iyakkam's flag would have been fluttering from Jaffna Fort. That is something we should never forget.'

'Greetings! I'm Anbu Chezhiyan. I know that it is not proper for me to speak at a women's meeting. But there is something to what my friend Srikanthamalar said. It would be wonderful if we could find a medicine to help us to forget everything that happened in this country. We will forget Selvanayagam. We will forget Ponnambalam. Let's forget Kuttimani, Dileep and Rajini Madam. Let's forget Annan, Balachandra and Isaipriya. Let's forget everyone. What will be left is peace ... Nonsense!'

Anbu Chezhiyan staggered out. He was drunk, but he hadn't seemed so when he spoke. Everyone stared at him in surprise. By then, a woman had started speaking.

'Good evening. I'm Susanthika. I'm Sinhalese. I was a fan of Rajini Madam from my childhood because, through her life, she showed us how Sri Lankan people can overcome barriers of race and language. The greatest revolution in her life was her marriage to Dayapala Thiranagama. Through that marriage, we witnessed how love becomes a synonym for revolt. Only love can overcome religion, race, language and colour. Women should be able to defeat war with love. Naturally, this also means that music, poetry and other creative arts will flourish. Violence will have to fail when faced with love.'

Karpooram could not contain herself.

'Susanthika, you are very romantic. Those who haven't had to personally experience the devastation of war can afford to be romantic. But we, who have lost everything in war, cannot. Rajini Madam and her friends started an institution called Poorani for the rehabilitation and empowerment of women who had to face the devastation of war. Some girls in Poorani tried to resist war with song and poetry. When they started to sensitize women against violence and encourage them to be independent and demand their rights, the Iyakkam turned against them. They did so because if women were oriented in this manner, they would find it difficult to forcibly recruit women to the Iyakkam and to brainwash rape victims into becoming suicide bombers. So they portrayed Poorani and its workers as anarchic feminists. According to the Iyakkam, all feminists were bad and so was the emancipation of women.'

This time, Srikanthamalar stood up.

'Karpooram, it is not right to speak like this. Iyakkam was a movement that treated women with utmost respect. No one has ever reported women activists being raped.'

'Maybe. But on the whole, the Iyakkam promotes a patriarchal power structure. They have never accepted that a woman has complete control over her body. They assumed extremely reactionary stances regarding morality. Why were Selvi, a Poorani member, and her friend Manohar killed? Selvi was a poet who won the 1992 PEN International Freedom to Write Award. No woman in the history of the Eelam had written such strong political poems as her. Sivaramani, who was a more vociferous poet, burnt all the poems she had written and committed suicide in 1991 at the age of twenty-three. There are more such instances that prove how brutally the Iyakkam treated female intellectuals.'

'Karpooram, you are only speaking of elite women. Ask any ordinary woman. They will never speak against VP or the Iyakkam. It was the Iyakkam that protected them from the Sinhalese army until the war ended. When the Peace Keeping Force came in like eagles to tear women apart, the Iyakkam protected them.'

'Okay. I'm not going to argue with you. I only spoke out because I want the truth behind Rajini Madam's murder to come to light. I hope that the truth will be uncovered when Christie and his crew make the movie.'

'I am Vaidyalingam Shanmuganathan. I was running a canteen in the Teaching Hospital when Rajini was killed.

I know certain details about the murder. The murderer was Bosco. Rajini's students pointed her out to him. Those students are now practising abroad. Bosco is dead. He had close connections with the Iyakkam. Four or five days before the murder, Bosco started visiting the hospital. I used to see him speaking to those students I told you about. He found out Rajini's routine at the hospital. He also made a note of the route she took daily. On the day of the murder, one of the students stood near the gate, another near the canteen, and signalled to Bosco as Rajini came out. I never saw Bosco near the hospital again.'

Everyone listened to Shanmuganathan's words in shock. Before they could recover from the impact of his words, a gunshot was heard. The bullet flew past me, just inches from my nose. Shanmuganathan, who had been shot below the left ear, writhed in pain on the floor. Blood spurted from his neck on to Mary's face. Many people fainted around us. Shanmuganathan, who seemed to have much more to disclose, died within minutes.

The police shifted us from the hotel to the Sri Lankan military base. Mary, who was admitted to the ICU in the military hospital, only regained consciousness the next morning. Though the doctor said there was nothing to worry about, Christie was anxious. The first thing she said when she woke up was that she wanted to watch *No More Tears Sister* again.

10

Shanmuganathan's murder was a setback for the Sri Lankan military. For the first time, since their total failure in 2009, the Iyakkam had managed to shock Jaffna. That too, by shooting a man speaking at a women's meeting in one of the better hotels.

The murderer cleverly escaped. The bullet was aimed not merely at Shanmuganathan, but also at the conviction that a second coming was impossible for the Iyakkam. That bullet sent shock waves throughout the Sri Lankan administrative system, alarming even the president. Within minutes of the murder, several meetings were held at the military and administrative headquarters of Sri Lanka, steps were taken to energize the activities of the Terrorist Investigation Division and to strengthen the secret service wing.

The cabinet decided that this was clear evidence that the Iyakkam feared Christie's movie, so they directed Samaraveera to hasten its completion. Though Samaraveera instructed Christie to wind up the research and rewrite the script following his directions, Christie refused. He argued that the government could not direct his movie. Finally, the president himself spoke to Christie and they reached an agreement. Samaraveera did not issue any more instructions regarding the script.

The international media reported the shooting incident extensively. The BBC and CNN telecast Amina El Abidi's interviews. She always spoke about upholding Rajini's martyrdom and the necessity of women raising their voices against war. Naturally, the Hollywood production based on Rajini's life became part of the news. Veering away from this trend, Al Jazeera telecast *Return of the Tigers*. Their Colombo reporter stressed that the Iyakkam was about to come back with redoubled vigour. It was as if the global media was waiting for its return. Channels in India and Sri Lanka discussed this issue. But as there were no further developments, this wave soon subsided.

Even after a week had passed, the TID was not able to identify Shanmuganathan's murderer, nor were they able to pinpoint the organization behind the crime. The only progress in the enquiry was that they were able to locate a white Toyota car, used by the assailant to escape, abandoned on the A9 highway near Chavakachcheri. Though eyewitnesses swore that a woman had been with the killer and that a man had sat in the car with the engine running to help them get away, the police could not arrest anyone. Shanmuganathan's relatives did not lodge a police complaint. What is more, they did not even claim his body after the post-mortem. No organization came forward claiming responsibility for the murder. But on the tenth day of the murder, someone placed an effigy of Shanmuganathan in front of Veerasingam Hall with a placard that read: 'The Fate of a Traitor'. This was a slogan used repeatedly during the heyday of the Iyakkam. Hearing this, many of the students who had organized the screening of *No More Tears Sister* left the hostel to stay with their relatives in Colombo. But Poomani Selvanayagam was forcibly pulled out of the hospital and taken to an unknown destination in a white car. This was a time when white cars were feared, and her friends became extremely anxious.

Due to security concerns, we stayed in Colonel Chaminda Mendez's quarters at the headquarters of the security forces. This was much more comfortable than the hotel. The colonel's beautiful wife, Anuradha, was a movie aficionado as well as a marvellous hostess. We never felt that we were staying at a military base. Anuradha's mesmerizing Sinhalese beauty, good food and wine were excellent catalysts, and work on the script progressed apace. Even the colonel made time to have dinner with us despite his busy schedule. One night, as we were having after-dinner drinks on the terrace, he shared new information about Rajini's murder.

'Christie, Rajini was not murdered by an ordinary killer but by one of the Iyakkam's professional assassins. They had trained

these assassins from the very beginning, and had given them
many privileges denied to the other cadres, like women, drugs
and alcohol. Their only duty was to murder those whom the
Iyakkam wanted dead. The rest of the time, they were free to
do whatever they wished. Sivarasan, Rajiv Gandhi's assassin, was
one of them. It was because he was a professional that Rajini's
assassin was able to shoot his target through the forehead even
though she was on a moving bicycle, and to fire enough bullets
to ensure her death after she fell down. To be honest, no one in
the military could pull this off. The pain of the victim does not
bother these hardened killers.'

'Was Bosco one of them?'

'He could have been. But I'm not sure. Because Rajini's
murder has another peculiar dimension. It might be connected
to her human rights activism or the Iyakkam. It could have been
her marriage to Dayapala Thiranagama. You must know of
Dayapala's connection with the Janatha Vimukthi Peramuna.
The JVP had close ties with the UTHR that Rajini and her
friends had established. It was to conceal this connection that
Daya Somasundaram changed the name of the organization
to UTHR Jaffna. That was a time when the government and
the Buddhists were hunting down the JVP. On the fifty-
second day of Rajini's murder, 13 November 1989, Rohana
Wijeweera, the founder-leader of the JVP, was killed in an
encounter with the army. The military intelligence reported
that Rajini had been working in the inner circles of the JVP.
The government suspected that UTHR Jaffna was a façade
for such activities. Surely the Iyakkam too might have had the
same suspicions.'

'But, Colonel, do you feel that such suspicions would lead to
murder?'

'Maybe not. But these are all reasons that could have led to it. It was the same in the case of the feminists that Karpooram was speaking about.'

'Yes. I was about to remark upon that. This is something that Christie can use in the movie. There was an undercurrent of western feminism in Rajini's activism.'

'The Iyakkam was never able to accept this. They were extremely patriarchal in their outlook. Under the pretext of protecting the chastity of women, they took a stance that denied women any sort of freedom. That is why they viewed outfits like Poorani with suspicion.'

'Madam, are you trying to make Rajini a feminist?'

'Why? Do you doubt it? Wasn't she a feminist?'

I looked at her without speaking. She was voluptuous and I couldn't avert my eyes from the visual feast her forty-year-old body was providing me. She understood immediately. But, unperturbed, she poured me another peg of whiskey. It was then that Mary got a text message from Karpooram saying that Poomani Selvanayagam had been abducted.

'Wasn't that the girl who went to so much trouble to screen *No More Tears Sister?*'

The colonel smiled in reply, then said helplessly, 'There is no use. She is the Lion's newest prey.'

Nobody asked who the Lion was. Everyone at the military headquarters seemed to know. Anuradha left abruptly. The colonel too departed after wishing us goodnight.

When the Lion came into the room, it was past midnight. He really resembled a lion. A middle-aged man with greying hair parted on both sides. He sported a dark moustache. Though he was wearing pyjamas, he had a military bearing and physique.

He had a way of staring at you with his eyebrows furrowed. Poomani, exhausted from fear and humiliation, stood up to greet him. The enraged Lion did not look at her. He brushed past her and sat on the sofa. Then he asked, 'Didn't they tell you how to come before me?' It was like the roar of a beast and she trembled in fear.

They had told her how to behave. She was to wear a light green or yellow sari well below the navel, and wish him ayubowan with lotus blooms in her hand. After the initial formalities, she was to change into a sarong. A light green sarong with yellow flowers had to be tied around her waist, then twisted through a filigreed silver ring several times and tied around the neck. He did not like women to use perfume, powder or any sort of cream. Sweat was the best perfume as it aroused him. So she was supposed to make an effort to perspire. As pregnancy was the first stage of punishment, she was to try and conceive as quickly as possible. She was to join him in smoking, eating and drinking – whatever he did, she had to emulate, obey unquestioningly.

She had been given all these instructions. But because she was exhausted from weeping, she had forgotten all of it.

Poomani asked for pardon and went to the washroom to change. There was a cupboard fully stocked with clothes. A beautiful lotus flower smiled at her from the blue water in a crystal bowl. The flower did not know her plight. Poomani took off her jeans and wondered whether she should bathe, then she remembered his penchant for the smell of sweat. She wore a sari and went to him carrying a silver tray. The expression of fear on her face, like a rabbit in the moonlight, enhanced her beauty. Unmoved, the Lion pulled her next to him.

'You are in the last year of medicine, aren't you?'

She sobbed as she nodded.

'Why are you crying? Don't you want to become a great doctor like Rajini and study abroad? Don't you want to become a human rights activist of international repute?'

Recognizing the sarcasm in his voice, she wept. She knew that escape from this fort, the most guarded place in Jaffna, was impossible.

'Intelligent girls like you are the pride of the nation. You shouldn't waste your life interfering unnecessarily in political issues. You are about to be punished for just that.'

'But I didn't do anything.'

'Didn't you organize a meeting of Women Against War? How did you get the courage to organize such a meeting when the whole world is after our country, accusing us of war crimes and human rights violations? Don't you know that what you have done is treason? Unfortunately, this country lacks the laws to punish such misdeeds. Moreover, the courts are filled with human rights activists, so laws would be futile anyway. That is why I have to punish people like you. War is the dominion of men. Why do women need to interfere?'

She bowed her head in silence. The Lion pulled her up. 'Do you know what your punishment is?'

She knew. It was the first thing the leader of her abductors had told her. 'If you resist, you will be thrown into the sea. If you obey, your life will be spared. But you will have to give birth to a Sinhalese baby.' Scared of death, she had agreed. But she hadn't realized that it was such an important person's baby that she had to conceive.

'Pattavesi! Why don't you smile? They brought you here alive because you agreed to give birth to a Sinhalese child.'

She did not want to aggravate the Lion further, so she tried to summon some confidence.

'I had agreed, but somehow I can't feel happy.'

He laughed. 'Be happy that you escaped death!'

She too felt it was true and a slight smile appeared on her face. He gathered her to himself greedily. She was tiny in his huge arms. Unable to feel happiness or to resist him, she cried out, 'Ayyo Amma.' He paid no attention to her cries. He held her tight to make sure that she was completely under his control. Fearing what was about to come, she stood still. But, as if to remind her of what was to follow, he ordered her to serve him food when the clock struck one.

The Lion loved food and alcohol. He insisted that she share everything with him. When she refused liquor, the Lion became furious, so she sipped a little. It helped her feel more confident. She had lost the life she was leading in any case, so it was better to accept what she had been given.

When the Lion finished dinner hurriedly, she understood what was needed and quickly changed into a sarong. As it took her a while to tie it neatly around her, he had to wait.

'Pattavesi! You look pretty, you don't look like a Tamil girl. Was your father Sinhalese?'

Though the term 'pattavesi' irritated her, she didn't say anything. She felt that it applied to her. She wasn't a virgin anyway. But only a woman who sold her body could be called a whore. Well, from today she was a whore, exchanging her body in return for her life. As she stood thinking, he said, 'Pattavesi! Come closer.' She realized that the profanity aroused him.

As he undid the first twist of her sarong, the Lion lost control. He led her to bed. Removing her sarong twist by twist, he took possession of her body. When the final twist was undone, she became part of his body.

'Is this the first time for you?'

'No. You are my fourth.'

He was surprised. He had imagined that the worst punishment for a woman was to be robbed of her chastity.

'Is it necessary to be a virgin to be punished like this?'

'No. But it is not very comfortable to become pregnant. And to deliver a baby is even more difficult. That is your real punishment.'

'Who started this strange system of punishment?'

'I started it. It began fifteen years ago. I have punished eight so far. You are the ninth. All of them, like you, were suffering from diseases like human rights or feminism. Three of them were cured. They are living with their babies and working in minor jobs for the government. Four are pregnant. Only one committed suicide. You are the first non-virgin to be punished. That is why you are not crying about your lost chastity – quite unlike the others.'

She made a decision and covered the Lion with kisses. Then she asked him, 'Can I dress you up in a sarong?' She took her sarong and put it around his neck. As he lay back enjoying her nudity, she pulled both ends of the sarong through the silver ring and pulled hard. The Lion died within minutes.

The next day was a public holiday in Jaffna. The dead body of the Lion, who had succumbed to a heart attack, was taken in an air force helicopter to his home town in Ratnapura with all official ceremonies.

Though Poomani's dead body washed ashore and was recognized, nobody claimed it. She was laid to rest in the public crematorium.

11

I received a very strange email on the third day of Poomani's death. I was shocked when I read the email address: poomaniselvanayagam@gmail.com. How could a dead person be sending me an email? Or had she sent it before dying? But she didn't know me well enough to write to me. On reading it, though, I understood that it was not from Poomani.

> *Dear Peter,*
> *This email will shock you, I am sure. I am not Poomani Selvanayagam. I cannot reveal who I am now as my official position doesn't allow me to do so. But I respect and admire Poomani. It was due to her courage that the marks made on the Lion's neck, because of the tightening of a sarong, had to be hidden under wreaths of flowers. These are now jokes in the corridors of power in Colombo. I too had gone to Ratnapura to put a wreath on his body. I didn't want to miss any opportunity for revenge. I saw other women like me put wreaths on him with hatred writ clear upon their faces. By then, the president had arrived to pay his last respects. When the police cordoned off the area, I left without waiting for the cremation. I am like Poomani and several other women: a prey. The Lion was not a racist when it came to searching for prey. He did not insist on Tamil women. That is why he trapped me thirteen years ago, by sending my husband to Israel for training just six months after our marriage. Though I was working as a researcher in the Sri Lankan archaeological department, I was also part of a group that opposed violence against women. We conducted a*

campaign about the problems women had to face during the civil war. My crime was that I had said in a public meeting that the Sri Lankan army could learn from the Tigers when it came to the treatment of women. Neither the media nor society paid heed to my words. But the military intelligence did. And the one-man court of justice, the Lion, punished me. As my husband was a captain working under him, and as I was not as courageous as Poomani, I had to submit to his will.

Within hours of my husband leaving for Israel, a gang came in a white car and dragged me out from my home. They broke me by threatening to kill my parents. The main accusation against me was that I was an Iyakkam spy. They used my speech at the Women's Day rally as evidence. All my resistance ended when they led me naked to the prayer room in Divine Pearl, where the Lion was waiting, pistol in hand.

I felt humiliated when he grabbed me, growling, 'Pattavesi!' No man other than my husband had touched me before that. I felt nauseated when I smelled his foul body odour. He looked at me with rage, shouting, 'Pattavesi!' That was the only way in which he addressed me until I left DP. Everything he did was nauseating. If you didn't join in those games, he would torture you. Despite his busy schedule, he would come to DP once a week, itching to mete out punishment. Before my husband came back from Israel, I became pregnant. When the Lion sent my husband straight to Elephant Pass, preventing him from even coming home, my punishment was complete. In the third month of my pregnancy, I was shifted from DP to another place. By this time, he had another prey – a student leader, not yet eighteen. Like me, she too had criticized the army. Because she resisted him, she was killed on the third or fourth day. But carrying the child of a man you hate is a punishment worse than death. The Lion had taken all precautions to ensure the safe birth of the child. I delivered a healthy baby boy. I feared that the baby would be taken away from me or killed. But nothing of that sort happened. Two weeks after my delivery, he sent me home – threatening to kill me if I dared to speak about this.

When I reached home, my parents behaved as if they didn't know me at all. They said they no longer had a daughter and asked me to leave. Even my mother, who had begged my abductors for mercy, had changed. My activist friends refused to help me because they were scared. After my experience, many of them gave up their activism. I later found out that the Lion had either misled or threatened them. Finally, I had to go back to the Lion with my two-month-old baby to beg for help. I was comforted by the thought that my baby was his. He took great pleasure in my pain and helplessness. 'Pattavesi! This is your punishment. You must never open your mouth against the military or the government.'

I begged for pardon. He didn't say that he had forgiven me. But his henchmen took me to a small house. A woman was living there with her two-year-old child. She, who had lost her ability to speak for a while during the torture, understood everything as soon as she saw me. She looked after me and my baby, giving him to me only when it was time for me to feed him. I called her Akka and she addressed me as Nanki. Though the Lion never came to meet us, he took care of all our financial needs. But I felt revolted because I was living off a man whom I despised. I wanted to resume work and continue with my research in the department of archaeology. But they had dismissed me from service for being absent without notice.

Only the Lion could help me in this predicament as he had placed severe restraints on me, forbidding me from going out or meeting people. I told the Lion's henchmen that I wanted to meet him. Luckily, he agreed to meet me in a secret place. He told me that I shouldn't bring my son. I had to wait for hours in the room. When he finally arrived, nothing had changed: the word 'pattavesi', his fat ugly arms around me and the stench of his sweat. I only smiled when he said, 'I think you see now that rape and impregnation are the best ways to enslave a woman completely.' He really fell for it when I told him that I had been longing to see him. As I was the one in need and had nothing to lose, I submitted to all his perversions and made him happy. I benefited from that. In the morning, he complimented me by saying that my looks had improved since childbirth and told me to get in touch with him if I needed anything.

'Are you going to start your activism again?'

'No, never. I like archaeology. I want to complete my work in that area.'

'Let me see. But if you tell anyone, including your son, about your punishment – remember, I will kill you and throw your body into the sea. And, pattavesi, come back if you need sex.'

He kissed me on both cheeks before he left. He gave me a large sum of money. A little while later, I was taken home in a chauffeur-driven car. I laughed at the irony of arriving in a tuk-tuk and leaving in style. The henchmen started *addressing me as 'madam'. I went to a supermarket and spent lavishly. I also visited a beauty parlour before going home. I bought gifts for Akka and the children. But she spat at me in disgust. She was an admirer of Rohana Wijeweera.*

Within a week, all the difficulties regarding my job disappeared. One of the Lion's men informed me that I could join duty the next day. He had also arranged a car and a flat for me. A driver was sent to keep an eye on all my activities. Akka refused to come with me. Lured by the thought of comfort, I left her and took my son with me to start a new life in the flat. At the office, I realized that my absence of one-and-a-half years had been treated as special leave, and that I had been transferred with promotion. That was how I became the assistant director of the Sigiriya Heritage Foundation at a very young age. I was slandered but, funnily enough, no one spoke about my association with the Lion. Nobody imagined that the military general would have any interest in the archaeological department. I went to meet the Lion three or four times after that. As he had found a new prey by then, his interest in me had waned. He called sometimes to threaten me with death if I dared to speak out. He would crack ribald jokes about his prey. When he called last week, he spoke about Poomani Selvanayagam.

You might be wondering why a stranger is telling you the story of her life. What I am about to say doesn't require a lengthy foreword. But the joy I feel at the Lion's death prompted me to write about all this. For thirteen years, I was silent. But I also have to tell you something else.

The colonel's wife, Anuradha, is a close friend of mine. We were neighbours in Colombo. She tried to protect me from the Lion's trap. But my foolishness led me to disaster.

She gave me your email address. She told me all about your movie project. She also told me that, while the white guy cavorts with his girl, you look at her with eyes full of longing. Her response when I asked why you didn't hire a female assistant prompted me to mail you. She said you are searching for a friend called Sugandhi or Andal Devanayaki. When she told me you had travelled centuries back in your hunt, I was amazed. The name Andal Devanayaki attracted me. I too have been looking for this Andal Devanayaki. She is said to have lived a century ago. In 2009, after the end of the civil war, the Sri Lankan government had entrusted the archaeology department with a top-secret project. We had been asked to scientifically establish that Sri Lankan history was exactly as narrated in the legends of the Mahavamsa, Culavamsa *and* Dipavamsa. *That is why the archaeological department started digging at certain locations. It is an effort to prove that Buddhist temples and Sinhalese culture have been in existence for over two thousand years. The search is easy, because we know beforehand what we are supposed to find. The archaeology department has a collection of artefacts found by European archaeologists from heritage sites like Anuradhapura and Sigiriya. Some of the minor artefacts from among these will be deposited in chosen sites and later discovered with great fanfare. We see it as political manipulation. As authorized Sri Lankan history itself is the product of great political manipulation, nobody considers this wrong.*

But certain positive developments have occurred. In the third month after rejoining work in 2002, I was able to retrieve an ancient palm-leaf manuscript written in the Pali language. I found it seven kilometres from Sigiriya, in

a village inhabited by the Vedar community. They conduct
some strange rituals based on this palm-leaf script. It is
said that these rituals allow you to communicate with
the dead and that they can be used to make spirits obey
your commands. A Tamil Buddhist monk, Sree Vallabha
Buddhanar, wrote this thousand-year-old text titled,
Susaana Supina or The Burial Ground of Dreams.
The heroine of this narrative is Andal Devanayaki. I am
familiar with the ancient Pali script, so I could understand
it easily. I wrote an article on that text. But further
research yielded no results. It was then that Anuradha
told me about you. If you are willing to cooperate, please
reply.

I replied immediately.

Dear Archaeologist,
Have you read the novel, Cemetery of Dreams, *by the*
Iranian writer, S. Mostofi? He lives in the US now. It's not
a work of great creativity. It's a thriller based on the US
hostage crisis in Iran. Quite readable. But there are certain
common points that the novel shares with the realities of your
country. I'm not an archaeologist like you, but it is possible
that we can be friends.

What your friend told you about me is not completely
true. I'm not sexually frustrated. She might have been
voicing her own desires.

I'm eager to know what you have discovered about Andal
Devanayaki. I am happy to tell you what I know about her.
But I don't like this game of hide-and-seek that you are
playing with me. As the Lion has been cremated, who do

*you fear now? Plan a trip to Jaffna. You can also meet your
friend.*

12

I was very eager to learn more about the *Susaana Supina* that the
archaeologist had told me about. But she never replied. Luckily, a
friend, Gayathri Perera, came to my rescue. Gayathri, who was the
daughter of the famous Sinhalese novelist, Karunaratne Perera,
had been my classmate at the Film Institute where I had learnt
to use the camera. She now worked in Colombo with an NGO
called HOPE. She also made documentaries for Al Jazeera. As
she was close to the murdered Lasantha Wickrematunge, editor
of *The Sunday Leader*, the Rajapaksa government kept a close
watch on her activities. She requested us to participate in a
campaign organized by human rights activists against the Galle
Literary Festival.

'Hi Peter! Are you still in Colombo?'

'No, I'm in Jaffna.'

'What for?'

'The same project, the movie on Rajini Thiranagama.'

'Aren't you ashamed of yourself? And you come from John
Abraham's land. Isn't it better to commit suicide rather than
produce a movie with Rajapaksa's alms?'

'This is not a government production. They are only
supporting us. A Hollywood company is producing the movie.'

'No, don't try to tell me that. Don't justify yourself. Anyway,
it's up to you. I know it's not something I should tell you now,
but I called thinking of my old buddy Peter. We have started
an online campaign against the Galle Literary Festival. We are

requesting writers around the world to not participate in it, as a protest against the terrible human rights violations and repression of self-expression in Sri Lanka. The campaign was started by HOPE and Reporters Sans Frontiers, an outfit based in France. Many eminent writers including Noam Chomsky, Arundhati Roy and Orhan Pamuk have declared their support. You too should support us.'

'Gayathri, in this situation? And I'm not a great writer either.'

'Come on. Don't you realize that if you get involved in such projects, you will have to sacrifice your individuality? When are you coming back to Colombo? I want to see you alone, without that casino girl.'

'Hopefully next week. I'll call you as soon as I get there. But tell me, have you heard of the *Susaana Supina?*'

'The what?'

'The *Susaana Supina.*'

'I've heard of it. But I can't remember where.'

'It's an old palm-leaf manuscript recently unearthed at Sigiriya.'

'Oh! I had read an article about it. But more interesting is the story written by Meenakshi Rajarathinam in *Bambarayak*, a Sinhalese magazine. It fills in some gaps in the history of the Sinhalese race. I can send you a link to the magazine's website. It is the Sinhalese translation of a Tamil story. You can also read the Tamil version online.'

She sent me the link immediately. When I clicked the Tamil page, a green-and-red top started spinning. The same top my mother had given me to stop my questions about my father. Unable to bear the painful memories that the spinning top was leading me to, I wondered whether I should shut my laptop. And then the inevitable happened.

The Story of Devanayaki – Part II
By Meenakshi Rajarathinam

It took me more than three months to read the *Susaana Supina* found in Sigiriya. Though I had to stay in Sigiriya, a friend working at the heritage site made arrangements for me to read the book in peace. I wish I could translate Sree Vallabha Buddhanar's entire book into English. But it will take a long time. For the time being, I think I should complete Devanayaki's story based on the available details.

The first part of the story ended when Rajaraja Chola conquered Kanthalur Salai. In many legends associated with Kanthalur, and in Poomani Pananaar's 'Kanthalur Pattu', Devanayaki does not commit suicide, nor does she escape from Kanthalur. She joyfully leads the victorious Rajaraja to her bedchamber. We might wonder how Devanayaki, who considered Mahendravarman to be her Lord Padmanabha, could do this. Sree Vallabha Buddhanar begins his *Susaana Supina* by raising this doubt. How could a woman forget the man she loved so easily and lead his enemy to her bedroom? How could she feel passion when the arms stained with her husband's blood encircled her? How could she open the windows of her mind and body to him? Buddhanar himself answers these questions in one sentence: 'A woman is like a river. A river that wants to flow.' I am not sure what he means by this.

When the Chola army marched into Kanthalur after having killed Mahendravarman and thrown his body into the sea, Devanayaki and Parvathy were the only women left in the palace. The rest of them had been captured while they were trying to escape through underground routes. Kanthalur tradition demanded that the victor, whoever he might be, should be greeted with respect. Those who do not have the strength of mind to do so, try to escape. 'Don't worry. The victor owns both the land and the women.' Though Queen Parvathy said that they would welcome the emperor in accordance to tradition, they didn't know anything about him. Devanayaki had wanted to meet the emperor ever since she had heard that his stern demeanour hid a loving heart. Though life at the palace was luxurious, Devanayaki had been getting tired of it. The main reason was that Mahendravarman had begun to tire of her when he realized that she too could not bear him a son. He was also much older than her.

It was Queen Parvathy who welcomed the emperor with ceremony. Devanayaki merely helped her. But the emperor had eyes only for Devanayaki. Realizing this, she tried her best to attract him. The Chola army beat drums and rejoiced. The emperor felt that it was all a joke. When he remembered that he had given orders to his lieutenants to stop the queens from leaping into the fire, he could not contain his laughter. He had expected a group of women pleading for their lives and their chastity.

'This is a surprise. This is the first time that I've been received like this in a palace I've conquered. Was your ruler that bad?'

'Well ... this is ... the tradition in ... Kanthalur...'

As Queen Parvathy fumbled for words, Devanayaki explained, 'It is because our ruler was such a good man that we receive you in this manner. He insisted that we should not break with tradition, come what may. That is the way of Kanthalur.'

'Then where are the others? I see only the queen mother and her daughter. Don't the rest of them believe in these traditions?'

Queen Parvathy's face fell when she heard herself being addressed as the queen mother. Devanayaki, on the other hand, felt happy. Now there was no need to compete with Parvathy. She smiled enticingly at the emperor. 'This is the tradition. Only the queens have the right to do this. Poomani Pananaar's song says that the winner owns the land and the women, and that he must be welcomed with lit lamps and a vermillion mark on his forehead. It is because this is your first military victory that you are surprised.'

The emperor was impressed by the sarcasm in her words. 'She knows that this is my first victory. She looks beautiful too. She must be Devanayaki, who was said to be helping Mahendravarman in administration and defence, or she would not speak so boldly.'

'Are you Devanayaki?'

'Yes, Your Highness.'

'I've heard a lot about you. You must join me for dinner, and afterwards too. Don't trouble the queen mother. Let her sleep early.'

The Chola military commanders celebrated all night with song and dance. Kantha flowed like a gushing river. They ravaged the beautiful women of Kanthalur. Those who resisted were killed and thrown into the sea, and those who obeyed helplessly were mocked and tortured. During this time, the second line of the military was looting and setting fire to the town. Lured by Devanayaki, the emperor hastened to the palace, spending only a little time with his commandants.

The army inspected every nook and corner of the palace carefully. They prepared the food. Realizing that she had nothing much to do, Queen Parvathy went to bed early, leaving Devanayaki to handle everything. Devanayaki respectfully invited the emperor inside.

'Can I trust you?'

'If you can trust the sun, you can trust me too.'

'My gurus have advised me not to trust the enemy's women, and not to eat the food they serve.'

'But I'm not the enemy now.'

'How can I trust you? I've heard that the women of the Chera empire are very clever and that they hide swords, knives and poison in their clothes.'

'Your cooks prepared the dinner. I have only love and respect for you. You can search me to see if I have any weapons or poison on me.'

Asking the soldiers to leave, the emperor approached Devanayaki. Devanayaki bowed her head coyly. The emperor stood still for a moment, lost in her mesmerizing beauty.

'Please don't misunderstand me, Your Highness. I don't have a sword or a knife.' She started removing her jewellery and garments. He stopped her. The emperor trusted her completely. She dressed and served him food.

'Your Highness, how do you govern the territories you conquer?'

'We don't carry any unnecessary burden. We take the gold, the precious stones and the weapons we seize back to Thanjavur. We also take elephants, horses and intelligent girls like you. Before we leave, we burn the city.'

'A good king like you should not do such things. People will consider you a thief.'

'But they are not my subjects.'

'After you won the war against Mahendravarman, you became our king. The people here are your subjects, including me. It is your responsibility to ensure our happiness.'

He felt that she was right. 'Why did I never think in this manner?' Most of her questions were related to governance and military affairs. He was pleased when he realized that she was quite knowledgeable in these matters. He felt that he could achieve a lot if he had someone like her by his side. The ministers he had appointed only agreed to everything he said and never asked any questions. 'You are asking many important questions. But first, let me ensure your well-being.'

After dinner, she led the king to the bedchamber. It was the best room in the palace and the emperor was impressed.

'Someone has said that in the bedchamber, there is no king and subject, only man and woman.'

'Not just someone, My Lord. It was Vatsyayana. But during Mahendravarman's time, we were king and subject in the bedchamber too. Not trusting his own queens, he locked us up in chastity belts.'

The emperor did not understand. But when Devanayaki explained, he burst into laughter. When he was convinced that the queen of Kanthalur was adept in matters other than administration, he put forward three demands. First, she should be his forever. Second, she should help him capture Mahinda's Anuradhapura, which boasted of the largest number of soldiers trained in Kanthalur. And third, she should come to Thanjavur and teach the young men the *Arthashastra* and politics.

She replied that, though she could not promise to fulfil the first request, she was happy to fulfil the other two.

'Why?'

'What if someone defeats you in war?'

13

Rajaraja had captured Kanthalur by manoeuvring his regiments skilfully. A few weeks before the cavalry reached Kanthalur, the elephant regiment and other sections of the military had crossed the Aruvamozhi. A section of the horsemen had come to Kanthalur disguised as merchants. They stayed with courtesans and bargained with traders over the price of pepper and weapons. They wandered all over the city, located the kalaris and weaponries, and figured out the best way to enter the fort. They passed all this information on to Rajaraja through spies. When they were able to identify some traitors in Mahendravarman's army, everything became easy. The Chola army began the battle only after having gathered information about the defence strategies of Kanthalur.

By creating the impression that the Chola army was weak during the first stage of the battle, Rajaraja was able to trounce the Kanthalur army. While Mahendravarman and his men rushed towards the southeast, a vast force that had arrived by ships from the west attacked them from behind. A huge section of the navy docked at the Kanthalur harbour. When the Cholas set fire to the houses and storehouses in the city, Mahendravarman was shocked. In the battle that followed, Kanthalur had to surrender before sunset. Rajaraja's victory was complete when he dragged Mahendravarman to the harbour, beheaded him and threw his body into the sea. Then, the Chola army entered the fort in triumph.

The reason for Rajaraja's victory was his ability to plan in minute detail and to effectively implement his strategies. His discipline, not only in military matters but also in his personal life, laid the foundation for his victory. He followed a strict regime. That is why he was able to wake up at the crack of dawn, even though he had celebrated the much-desired victory over Kanthalur until past midnight. Devanayaki was still fast asleep. She looked more beautiful when she slept, he thought, as he started his morning exercises taking care not to wake her.

She woke up to see him exercising with great vigour. The sight of his youth and strength excited her. She longed to be in his mighty arms once again. It was not yet dawn. But Rajaraja was not Mahendravarman, and she was not familiar with his likes and dislikes. It must be time for the Sree Padmanabhaswamy temple to open. She didn't know whether it would open at all in the midst of war. And even if it was open, how would she go there? Her father had once said that the Chola emperor, Arulmozhivarman Rajaraja, was an avatar of Lord Vishnu. She told herself that, from now on, the emperor was indeed her Lord Padmanabha. As he sat down to relax after exercising, she went up to him.

'Pardon me. I am not familiar with your routine,' she said.

He pulled her down beside him with a smile.

'You must know everything. Look and learn. My routine is not very complicated. For commanders of war like me, the military and the body are the same. We have to prepare ourselves through regular practice. It is said that a king should consider his body his country. The different parts must be carefully maintained.'

'This is not a mere country. It's an empire,' she said, running her fingers over his chest and resting her head on his shoulder.

'Devanayaki, this empire has many claimants.'

'I'm not bothered about the number of claimants. I just want a little space in your heart.'

'But you are interested in other matters.'

'Are you still thinking of the night that passed?'

'How can I forget? I had only heard about the beauteous women of the Chera empire.'

'You must have heard that they are shrewd and conniving.'

'I had also heard that they are nymphs who can transport you to the city of dreams.'

'And were you taken to the city of dreams?'

'I was. But I've not had enough, since I had to return in a hurry.'

'So what? You have the key to the city of dreams with you. It can be opened any time.'

'We don't need this lock and key. I believe that only love can open the gates to heaven. You will have a place not only in my heart but also in my royal court. You will be my seventh queen – Kantha Madevi.'

Devanayaki's eyes filled with tears of joy. She touched the emperor's feet. He pulled her up, wiped her tears away and kissed her. Then, he removed his signet ring and put it on her finger. The morning conch sounded in the fort. A breeze laden with the fragrance of the kadakapala from Agasthyakoodam blessed her lovingly. That was Devanayaki's second marriage.

'Don't weep, Kantha Madevi. Laugh. Forget your past. It was a bad dream.'

'I only have one request. I am a devotee of Lord Vishnu. I grew up singing Andal's songs in praise of Lord Padmanabha. The temple should not be harmed. Please tell the army not to cross the Thiruvaiga.'

'Agreed. They will not touch a thing beyond the Thiruvaiga. Anything else?'

'Just your love.'

'You are mischievous.'

'I am not merely a woman of the Chera dynasty. My mother hails from the dynasty of the divine nymphs of Kambuja. So I will be mischievous.'

When Rajaraja entered his first royal court in Kanthalur after his bath and breakfast, Devanayaki accompanied him. When the Chola army saw Devanayaki dressed in silk, with jasmine flowers in her hair and adorned with jewels, they thought that she was a perfect match for their emperor. They rose in unison to greet her when Rajaraja introduced her as 'Kantha Madeviyar'. She sat smiling, without interfering in matters of the court. Her smile did not falter when it was decided to behead four of Mahendravarman's most loyal lieutenants. She knew them well, but she pretended not to notice. Bound in chains, unable to contain their impotent rage, they shouted, 'You daughter of a whore.' She flinched. She felt as if she had been slapped across the face. It was as if she had been stripped bare in public. She left the court silently. The king ordered the four men to be beheaded immediately.

Devanayaki closed the door to her bedroom. She was not upset at having been openly insulted. Instead, she was pained as the emperor had been humiliated. When the servants announced that the emperor had arrived, she went down with red-rimmed eyes to serve him food.

'Your Highness, you were insulted because of me. Pardon me.'

'Devanayaki, all this is common in royal courts. The four men who humiliated you have been beheaded. Now sit down and eat.'

'But still, in front of all those people...'

'Forget it. Nobody will taunt you again.'

She forgot all her humiliation as, on that day, the journey was in the tantric style. He wanted to prove that he was not bad at satisfying her. The emperor stayed in Kanthalur for three weeks. What compelled him to stay was the conducive climate and the presence of Devanayaki. The specially brewed kantha, the delicious venison and Devanayaki's mischievousness made him more passionate. He never forgot to present something new to her each night. Though he was thirty-eight, Rajaraja had the vigour and strength of a youth.

Along with these celebrations, two important things were happening. Even as the Chola army was looting the houses and filling their royal coffers, Rajaraja was planning to attack King

Mahinda of Eelamandalam with his commander and trusted lieutenants. Devanayaki was a silent listener. On the day before they were to return to Thanjavur, as they were reviewing their plans to conquer Eelamandalam, Rajaraja gave Devanayaki an opportunity to speak. The commander was outlining the plan in detail.

'Your Highness, this is the best time to attack and conquer Eelamandalam. King Mahinda is not very strong. We must transport the first line of the navy to Kara Island, which lies close to Eelam. The island is sparsely populated. The second line of the navy must be positioned on the western shores of Eelam. The cavalry should be sent in from the north. I feel we should not use the elephant regiment. The northern part of Eelam is inhabited by the Tamils who support us. We will not face any opposition there. Moreover, as they are against the Sinhala rule, they might even join hands with us.'

'Commander, these are matters we have already discussed. Now let us listen to the three lieutenants and Kantha Madeviyar, if they have anything to say.'

'The three of us have spoken earlier. Now we must know Kantha Madeviyar's opinion.'

'What do you say, Devanayaki?'

'I fear that if I, who have not fought a single war, begin to speak about war, it will be presumptuous.'

'Don't worry. Speak.'

'The plan outlined would have been more than enough if we were preparing to capture a place like Kanthalur. But I feel this will not be sufficient in the case of Eelamandalam.'

'Then what should we do?'

'We have to know much more about Mahinda's Eelamandalam. This is the precious gem-studded necklace Mahinda presented me when he last visited Kanthalur. Do you see the box the necklace is in? The map of Anuradhapura, Mahinda's capital city, is engraved under it. It is not an ordinary map. It shows the routes that the queens can use to escape if the capital is captured by an enemy. Three of the routes are underground. Mahinda absent-mindedly gave me this box usually given to his queens. We should launch our attacks through these escape routes.'

'Madeviyar, what you have said is very important.'

'No, this is a small matter. How many spies do we have in Mahinda's capital?'

'Just two. They are Sinhalese merchants.'

'That's not enough. We need spies who will work for us around the clock. There must be women among the spies as Mahinda is a womanizer.'

'We don't use women as spies, Madeviyar. They cannot be completely trusted.'

'The commander is being foolish, Your Highness. Women are often better than men at both keeping and extracting secrets.'

The lieutenants looked at one another.

'You are right. Let us recruit women to be our spies.'

'Yes, Your Highness.'

'They have to be especially trained. I have a small band of spies. According to them, Mahinda has a secret hideaway at some distance from his capital. I got this information when I made enquiries after coming to know that he was planning to attack Kanthalur. Mahinda reportedly spends a couple of weeks every month in this place with wine and women. I also hear that he has financial problems. It is not a small issue. As you know, many of his soldiers have been trained in Kanthalur, and they haven't been paid for months.'

'So this is the best time to attack.'

'Don't be in a hurry. Let us discuss this in detail after we reach Thanjavur.'

The next day, the Chola army left for Thanjavur. While the cavalry, the elephant regiment and the other regiments journeyed on land southwards via Aruvamozhi, the emperor and Devanayaki travelled with the navy. A luxurious ship was provided for their journey. When the last ship sailed, the Chola army did not forget to torch the harbour and the ships docked there.

By the time the ship crossed Kumari in the east, it was past twilight. Devanayaki lay looking at the stars, with her head resting on the emperor's lap. He stroked her curls and cheeks.

The gold and jewels looted from Kanthalur were stored in several ships. The weapons were transported over land. But the emperor felt that the most precious gem lay on his lap. When she sang 'Margazhi Thingal', he embraced her.

As she lay in his arms, she gave voice to something that had been troubling her.

'I feel that what Lord Padmanabha had predicted a year ago, when he appeared in my dreams, is about to come true.'

He looked at her questioningly.

'When twenty-eight is added to twenty-eight, what is the sum, My Lord? That is a calculation we women do. If I'm not wrong, I'll give birth to your baby eight months from today.'

14

It was during the eleven-day journey from Kanthalur to Nagapattinam that Rajaraja Chola finalized his plans to conquer Anuradhapura. Certain incidents that occurred during the course of the journey proved helpful. Though he was only modifying the plan he had prepared at Kanthalur based on new information, Devanayaki intervened at every phase. Devanayaki said that intelligence was more important than weapons to win a war, and if the military strategy was carefully planned, the battle was already half-won. But the emperor was not fully convinced. He knew from experience that the implementation of plans was far from easy. He firmly believed that the outcome of a war depended on the constant vigilance and presence of mind of the supreme commander.

On the third day of the journey, the fleet of ships dropped anchor at a small port called Kayalpattinam on the banks of the river Tamraparni. It was not merely to rest for a day that they had stopped there. This small place was inhabited only by Muslims. It had been captured by Rajaraja Chola from the Pandya king five years ago, but this was the first time he was visiting it.

An important harbour on the east coast, it was a major centre for horse-trading and shipbuilding. The carpenters of Kayalpattinam were adept at building ships, using the teakwood that flowed down the Tamraparni from Agasthyakoodam. They would make ships big enough to transport twenty-four Arab steeds. But ever since Rajaraja Chola captured the land, they made ships only for the royal navy. The ships from Kayalpattinam were bigger and sturdier than those made in Nagapattinam and Kodiakkarai.

Rajaraja had appointed a prominent horse-trader, Sultan Sayyed Muhammad, to govern the province in his absence. Sayyed Muhammad's father was a descendant of Muhammad Khalji, who had come from Egypt and settled here in the ninth century. His mother was from Chera Nadu. The sultan, who could speak six or seven languages, was not a mere horse-trader. He was a religious scholar and had a deep knowledge of Islamic medicine. He knew and practised the concepts of *Firdous al-Hikmah* and the methods of treatment used by Muhammad ibn Zakariya al-Razi. Being a merchant who had trade relations with more than fifty countries and a practitioner of medicine, he had close contacts with many rulers. His three wives and their children lived in a palace near the mosque on the beach. His younger brother, Abdul Qader, was a famous medical practitioner in Jaffna. As they practised medicine, the sultan and his brother were both called 'Vaidyar bhai'.

When the emperor's ships neared the harbour, Vaidyar bhai and his entourage were waiting to greet them with ceremonial splendour. The sultan embraced the emperor saying, 'As-salamu alaykum.' And when the emperor returned the salutation with, 'Wa alaykumu as-salam,' they were greatly pleased. They led the emperor and his beautiful queen to the city on a regally decorated elephant.

Rajaraja Chola first visited the Kadal Karai mosque established by the followers of Caliph Abu Bakr al-Siddiq, who had come to Kayalpattinam at the end of the seventh century to propagate Islam. Being a non-Muslim, the king prayed standing outside the mosque, but he gave a thousand gold coins for its renovation. After resting for a while in the sultan's palace, he visited the shipbuilding centre and the large stables. Devanayaki was surprised to see forty warships being built for the Chola army. The work on all forty ships was progressing simultaneously. The sultan's children, Suleiman and Razak, were supervising the hundred-odd carpenters and their assistants who were engaged in building the ships. Rajaraja instructed them about the work to be done on the interiors. He asked the Sultan to improve the facilities in the stables and to pay more attention to the health of the horses.

After a sumptuous dinner, when the emperor and Devanayaki were relaxing on the rooftop with the sultan, the conversation moved to important matters.

'Bhai, why aren't you happy? Do you have any problems in your business?'

'Your Highness, I do have some problems. I am caught in a big trap.'

'What happened?'

'It has been six months since I sold two hundred Arab steeds to Mahinda. He still hasn't paid me. In business, there needs to be a constant flow of money. If money gets blocked like this, everything becomes difficult. Mahinda has imprisoned my brother, Abdul Qader, who went to ask for the money.'

'Then why didn't you inform me?'

'I thought I shouldn't bother you.'

'Vaidyar bhai, who else will you ask for help but me when you are in trouble? Why doesn't Mahinda pay you?'

'He doesn't have the money, Your Highness. His extravagance and lack of administrative skills are the reason. His soldiers haven't been paid for over a year. Mahinda has a secret hideaway where he spends most of his time with beautiful women, drinking and gambling. All his money is flowing there. The country is in trouble.'

The sultan's words made Devanayaki very happy. This was what she had been longing to hear. But she kept silent in the presence of the sultan, feeling that it would be improper to speak about this.

'Don't worry about your money. Is there anyone we can trust in Mahinda's country?'

'There are many we can trust. More than half his warriors are from Chera. Even the Buddhist monks are against him.'

'We will decide on our course of action before I leave in the morning.'

Rajaraja said he was tired and retired early because he wanted to talk to Devanayaki about what they had just heard.

'What do you think?' he asked her.

'The sultan echoes my thoughts. This is the best time to attack Anuradhapura. The enemy is extremely weak. But we must not underestimate the strength of the Sinhalese.'

'Do any soldiers who were trained at Kanthalur occupy high positions in Mahinda's army?'

'My father's dear disciple, Iravipillai Nayanar, is second-in-command in Mahinda's army. He knows me personally. There are others too, like Kulachal Velukutty and Nesamani.'

'That is exactly what we need. We will send a small team on three ships to Sinhala. Let two or three expert spies accompany them. You must send a message to Iravipillai Nayanar through them. You must write that the former queen of Kanthalur and the empress of the Chola empire, Devanayaki alias Kantha Madevi, gives assurance that the Sinhala soldiers will be paid and that they will be made part of the Chola army. We will use bhai's people to take care of the spies' needs.'

'That is a good move. But the spies must be trustworthy.'

'Absolutely. They will return to Thanjavur in three weeks with a reply.'

'We will prepare the message tomorrow. How can I thank you for permitting me to use the title "Empress of the Chola empire"?'

'Thank me through your actions, not words.'

'You are very clever.'

'This is my privilege, as emperor. But if what you say is right, we might not be able to go on such journeys.'

'I'm not sure. I merely voiced a doubt.'

He stroked her belly gently. Then he put his ear to her stomach, as if to listen to the throbbing of a new life. He raised his head and smiled.

'Can you hear anything?'

'Yes, I can. A young baby calling me "Appa".'

In the morning, everything proceeded according to plan. Three ships started for Sinhala with a letter from Devanayaki. Rajaraja and his entourage went to Nagapattinam. After three days of travel, they dropped anchor some distance from the harbour of Dhanushkodi and discussed how the military could proceed from there to Mannar. As Rameswaram was not under Chola rule, they did not stop there but proceeded to Kodiakkarai through the sea of Pamban. They reached Kodiakkarai after a three-day journey. The Chola army had an armoury and another shipbuilding unit there. But they did not make ships as big as the ones in Kayalpattinam. They made smaller but swifter ones that could launch fierce attacks.

Kodiakkarai was a beautiful place. Devanayaki, who was getting tired of the sea journey, was happy to stay there. It was a place like Kanthalur, full of greenery, small brooks and many-hued birds. A gentle, cool breeze wafted towards her. They ate delectable food prepared by the workers in the armoury, and drank a mild wine brewed from the jasmine flower. Added to it was Rajaraja's loving attention. She never wanted to leave. That night, she told him of a strange desire.

'Your Highness, you said that each of your queens has a separate palace. So won't you have to build one for me?'

'Don't worry about that. There are two vacant palaces in Thanjavur, another one is nearing completion on the banks of the Kaveri in Thiruvarur. You can choose the palace you want to live in.'

'I wish the palace was here.'

'If you are bewitched by Kodiakkarai, what will you say when you reach Nagapattinam, Thiruvarur or Thanjavur? If you don't like any of the palaces there, I'll build one for you here.'

They started the next morning, and a favourable wind hastened their arrival in Nagapattinam. The Chola empire welcomed the victorious king with pomp and splendour. Nagapattinam was grandly decorated, music played, and the people spilled out into the streets to celebrate the victory over Kanthalur. The ministers and other royals garlanded the emperor. They looked at the beautiful new queen in wonder. After the bustle of the welcoming ceremonies, Rajaraja astride his white horse and Devanayaki on a brown Arab steed rode through the streets. When they saw her sitting on the horse, the people realized that Kantha Madevi was unlike the other queens and well-versed in martial arts.

As the emperor and his retinue were about to leave for Thanjavur, a Buddhist monk arrived crying for help. It was Sree Vallabha Buddhanar who later wrote the *Susaana Supina*. The emperor alighted from his horse and bowed. Buddhanar said that he wanted to speak to the emperor in private. They moved away, towards the shade of a banyan tree.

'I am a Buddhist monk. I was born in Nagapattinam. I have been a resident of the Abhayagiri Vihara in Anuradhapura for the past eighteen years, but now the situation there is bad due to infighting between the monks of the Maha Vihara and the Abhayagiri Vihara. Mahinda's activities have further aggravated the situation. King Mahinda is an insult to his namesake, the great Buddhist monk. I came back with some merchants from Kambuja. Nagapattinam has a rich Buddhist tradition. You must recognize that and help us build a monastery here.'

The emperor listened carefully as the monk continued.

'King Maravijayattungavarman of Srivijaya was my disciple in the Abhayagiri Vihara. He has promised every aid required to build a monastery here if you give your consent.'

The monk bowed respectfully and bid farewell to the emperor. They reached the palace before twilight, accepting the hospitality of villages along the way. Six queens, including the emperor's senior queen, Loka Madevi, Vanathi Madevi who was Rajendra Chola's mother, Panchan Madevi, and the emperor's elder sister, Kundavai Pirattiyar, welcomed them. Kundavai liked the beautiful Devanayaki. She took off her diamond-studded bangle and put it around Devanayaki's wrist. Kundavai had arranged a special palace for Devanayaki. Rajendra Chola, who had matured into a handsome youth, addressed her as 'elder sister'.

The first thing Rajaraja did after his return was to promise aid to Sree Vallabha Buddhanar for building a Buddhist vihara. He spoke to Buddhanar privately and gauged the situation. The emperor rejoiced when he was told that the monks were unhappy with Mahinda's rule.

The next order authorized Kantha Madevi to supervise the education system in the state. It was decided to establish an educational centre like the one in Kanthalur and to invite scholars from various places. Devanayaki was entrusted with the education of all the royal children, including Rajendra Chola. But she was not ready to assume all the responsibilities at once. She requested the king to give her time until the war against Mahinda was over. She also wanted to wait until the birth of her baby.

Devanayaki constituted a team of spies and personally trained them. She also wanted to train the royal prince herself. But Kundavai Pirattiyar dissuaded her, saying that horse-riding and martial training should not be done during pregnancy. Two months later, she was troubled by nausea. Loka Madevi,

Vanathi and Kundavai took care of her as if she were their own daughter.

The three ships sent to Anuradhapura from Kayalpattinam returned exactly three weeks after their departure. They came back with the message that Iravipillai Nayanar and his followers had decided to shift loyalties. They brought with them elaborately drawn plans of the city of Anuradhapura and its underground pathways. But they had been unable to get any information about Mahinda's personal life. The commander said that it would be best to attack after the severe summer had passed. By the next month, the western winds would start blowing.

But certain unforeseen circumstances led to a sudden declaration of war. Mahinda killed Sultan Sayyed Muhammad's brother without any provocation. The message he wanted to convey was that the sultan would suffer the same fate if he dared to demand the money he was owed. The sultan immediately approached the emperor for help. At the same time, enraged by the information that Devanayaki was the emperor's new queen, Mahinda set fire to the shipbuilding centre in Kodiakkarai. The emperor was forced to declare war even though the preparations were not complete.

So, when Devanayaki was four months pregnant, the war began.

15

Devanayaki wished to take part in the war. She had never experienced the thrill of rushing against the enemy on horseback, clad in armour. While in Kanthalur, she had requested the emperor to allow her to fight, but he didn't like the idea of women on the battlefield. Kundavai Pirattiyar also told her that ever since a Chola princess was killed in battle, none of the Chola women had fought in wars. As she was pregnant, it was futile to think about it now. But the night before the battle, she asked the emperor, 'Your Highness, can I come with you tomorrow?'

He was unable to contain his laughter.

'It will be a sight to see you get on a horse with your swollen stomach.'

'I'm not joking. We have not been able to proceed as planned and there is no time to fine-tune everything.'

'Yes, it would have been better if you could come along. But in your condition...'

'Well, I need not ride a horse.'

'No. It will be a problem for you as well as for me.'

'I agree. I will try to help you from here with my spies. But how will you conduct the war?'

'The Chola army always bathes in the holy waters of the Keerimalai and prays to Lord Naguleswaram before going into battle. As the temple at Keerimalai is controlled by the Chola empire, no one will impede our progress. Moreover, Kuthiramukhi Madeviyar's blessings are with us.'

'Who is Kuthiramukhi Madeviyar?'

'A Chola princess who lived four hundred years ago. Her real name was Maruthapura Veeravalli. Legend has it that she had a face like that of a horse, but when she battled in Keerimalai she regained her human form. There is another story that says she was a courageous soldier in the Chola army and that a Sinhala commander trapped her in Keerimalai and killed her after violating her. It is said that when the Sinhalese soldiers cast her dead body into the sea, it walked over water, bathed and purified itself in the Keerimalai springs and then flew heavenwards. It is believed that if you pray to Kuthiramukhi Madeviyar before going into battle, victory is certain.'

'Your Highness, I am not questioning your beliefs. But this time, victory can be ensured only if the army bathes in the Keerimalai springs after the battle.'

'How can I break with tradition?'

'There is no other way to capture Anuradhapura. The Sinhalese set fire to the shipbuilding centre in Kodiakkarai knowing about your belief. They have surrounded Keerimalai in preparation to fight. We can defeat them, but the war will be fought at our doorstep. Anuradhapura is a long way away, and many obstacles lie ahead of us. It will not be easy.'

'Then?'

'The war should begin on their home ground. Only a small segment of the Chola army should proceed to Keerimalai. They should not be overly aggressive. What they should do is provoke the Sinhala army by attacking and then retreating. At the same time, fleets of ships should move from Kayalpattinam to Manthai and from Kanthalur to Puttalam. From Manthai, our smaller ships can sail without difficulty along the river Aruvi to Anuradhapura. You have to be careful until you reach Lake Puttalam. Never take the ships to the left bank of the river. Those are marshlands. You have to alight on the sandy banks to the right, circumnavigate around the lake and then dock. When Mahinda's men move north to attack the Cholas, the ships coming over the Aruvi river with the men from Puttalam must attack his fortress. At that point, Iravipillai Nayanar and his men will shift loyalties and join us.'

'Devanayaki! Getting you as my queen is the greatest blessing I have received.'

'It is all due to your grace. The newly appointed team of spies is very efficient. I formulated this plan based on the information they gave me.'

But neither the emperor nor his commanders were willing to accept her plan in its entirety. The Chola army embarked only after bathing in Keerimalai and offering prayers to Kuthiramukhi Madeviyar. They had to pay a heavy price for that. Just as Devanayaki had predicted, the Sinhala army had already surrounded Keerimalai. It was only after a terrible battle that lasted for seventeen days that Rajaraja was able to defeat them and enter Yalpanam. By then, one-fourth of the army was lost. It was when the emperor was considering retreat that Devanayaki's messengers came to meet him. They respectfully handed over the palm leaf Kantha Madeviyar had entrusted them with.

> Don't be perturbed, Your Highness. After coming to know that your entire army has moved to Keerimalai, I ordered Sultan Sayyed Muhammad's men to go to Manthai. His ships, masquerading as trading ships, must now be proceeding there. They will reach Anuradhapura along the river and hand over the message to Iravipillai Nayanar. Your Highness should not go there by land. Take the sea route from Yalpanam to Manthai instead. I have ordered the commander at Kanthalur to move to Anuradhapura via Lake Puttalam. Pardon me for issuing these orders without your permission.
> Kantha Madeviyar

The emperor's eyes filled with tears. A young girl who probably had never even seen a warship was handling military operations brilliantly. Everything proceeded according to Devanayaki's directions. The only mistake was that the sultan's men reached earlier than planned. But this mistake proved costly as it helped Mahinda escape. Having received Kantha Madeviyar's message from the sultan, Iravipillai Nayanar and his group had begun rioting in the town. Realizing that all was lost, Mahinda escaped to his secret hideout, taking with him his queens, his children and as much gold and money as he could lay his hands on. When Rajaraja and his men reached Anuradhapura, the king and his family were not there.

Following the usual practice of the Chola army, Anuradhapura was completely destroyed. The prisoners were released. The streets were completely under the control of the Chola army. They searched for voluptuous Sinhalese women and raped them. They stole gold and precious gems. Those who resisted were killed. Following the emperor's directions, the Buddhist monasteries and places of worship were left unharmed. Within one month, the entire Sinhala army was completely routed. But lacking enough manpower, they could not move to the southern provinces, and so were unable to locate Mahinda's hideout. After capturing Anuradhapura, Rajaraja Chola assumed the title of 'Mummudi Chola'. It meant that he was the emperor of the Chola, the Chera and the Pandya empires. The only shortcoming in that dazzling victory was their inability to recover the royal crown and golden robes of the Pandya king which the Sinhalese had taken. Rajaraja renamed the territory of Sri Lanka that he had captured Mummudi Chola Mandalam, and shifted the capital to Polonnaruwa as it was more convenient. He made arrangements to construct temples and palaces there. He returned to Thanjavur only after establishing a strong administrative system in the country.

As always, the emperor got a new queen from Anuradhapura. Her name was Mangala, and she was the daughter of commander

Dattasena who had surrendered before the Chola army. Like Devanayaki, she too was extremely beautiful. But she did not have the delicate looks of a celestial nymph. She was like a voluptuous lotus bud in bloom. She was a couple of years older than Devanayaki. Unlike Devanayaki, she did not welcome the emperor. The Chola army caught her as she was attempting to escape through the underground tunnels. Some effort was needed to tame her. When she realized that escape was impossible, she stopped resisting. On the third day, she gave in and became Rajaraja Chola's eighth queen.

She obeyed every order silently. The emperor began to suspect that she couldn't speak. Finally, when she lay in his long, strong arms, she spoke for the first time. Very respectfully, in subdued tones, she asked, 'Do you love me?' Hearing the tinkle of her Sinhalese voice, the emperor was pleased: Oh, this beauty can talk!

'I love you very much,' he said, and hugged her.

Mangala was relieved. The emperor wasn't as tough as he appeared to be.

'O king, have you heard the story of Sinhabahu?'

'So you are a storyteller too? Good. Tell me.'

'I don't know how to tell stories. We Sinhalese descended from Sinhabahu nearly fifteen hundred years ago. When I saw your strong arms, I was reminded of him.'

'Well, tell me the story.'

'Sinhabahu's mother was a beautiful Vanga princess, Suppadevi. As a voice from heaven had predicted that she would marry a lion, the king and queen guarded their precious daughter fiercely. But once, as they were travelling to Magadha through a dense forest, a lion attacked them and carried Suppadevi into the forest. The lion took her to a cave. The king was never able to find her. The lion and the princess lived as husband and wife in the cave.'

'As husband and wife?'

'Yes. Somewhat like me and you. Though the princess tried to resist him, she stopped when she realized that escape was impossible. The lion liked her a lot, and slowly she started responding to his love.'

'But they were still human and beast, were they not?'

'Our tradition holds that children can be born from the union of man and beast.'

'That is a terrible tradition.'

'If you love unconditionally then it does not matter, My Lord. I too came to you nervous and scared. Suppadevi gave birth to a son and a daughter – Sinhabahu and Sinhasivali. Sinhabahu's arms were like that of a lion's. When the lion went to hunt for prey, he would push a stone in front of the cave. When Sinhabahu was sixteen years of age, his mother told him everything. So one day, when the lion was out hunting, Sinhabahu pushed aside the stone covering the cave and escaped to the palace with his mother and sister. Her father, the Vanga king – I don't remember his name – was overjoyed.

'When the lion came back to the cave, he was very unhappy. Anger and sorrow drove him mad and he started attacking people in the town. The people complained to the king. The king spoke to Sinhabahu. He went to the forest with his bow and arrows. Seeing his son, the lion ran joyfully towards him. The lion thought that he had come back. But Sinhabahu shot the lion with a poisoned arrow. The lion roared in pain and died. That is the story.'

'What Sinhabahu did was wrong.'

'I felt the same way when I heard this story. Though the Vanga king promised to make him his heir, Sinhabahu established a new kingdom called Sinhapura. He married his own sister, Sinhasivali. They had sixteen pairs of twins. The eldest son, Vijaya, and his friends troubled the king with their misdeeds. Fed up with them, he half-tonsured the heads of his son and seven hundred of his friends and sent them all to Lanka on a ship. Vijaya married a Yaksha princess called Kuveni. We are all their descendants.'

'I liked the lion in your story better than Sinhabahu. Does your country still follow the tradition of men marrying their sisters?'

'Not among ordinary people. But the royals do as they please. There are those who even marry their own daughters. There are kings who have died early due to alcoholism. King Mahinda's misdeeds are endless.'

'Do you know where Mahinda is now?'

'I do. It is not easy to get there. I was taken there once.'

'Why?'

'Can the army chief's daughter disobey the king? I've heard that he doesn't sleep with the same woman twice. I was taken there blindfolded. After getting down from the palanquin, I had to climb more than a thousand steps. But when my blindfold was removed, I saw a heavenly place. A city of dreams where dance, music and liquor flowed like rivers. Thousands of women and gamblers from various corners of the earth were celebrating. This continued until dawn. I had to submit myself not just to the king but to his friends as well.

'I was ordered to forget everything when I was sent back. But I got a baby as a gift. The child had Mongoloid features, though, and was not the king's. Orders were issued to kill him before he turned one. The soldiers forcibly took him away. I did not ask what happened to him. Please, let's not talk about it.'

She sobbed into his chest. The emperor did not take Mangala to Thanjavur. He made her the Chola Madevi of Lanka. When he returned to Thanjavur after five months and eighteen days, Devanayaki was in the seventh day of her confinement.

16

The people in the city welcomed the victorious Rajaraja Chola with great celebrations. As Devanayaki had recently given birth, she did not actively participate in the festivities. It was twilight when the emperor came to meet her. Devanayaki was lying on a silken mattress, breastfeeding her baby daughter. Singing a lullaby, she joyfully placed the baby in the emperor's outstretched hands. In her hurry to get up, she forgot to cover her breasts. The king looked in wonder at Devanayaki who had become even more beautiful after giving birth. Then he looked carefully at the baby under the light of a lamp.

'Everyone says she has got your features.'

'That is natural, but she has inherited her golden complexion from you.'

'Well, let her inherit something from me. This is my humble gift to the emperor who defeated Mahinda.'

'Oh, is that so? We will name her Kuveni then.'

'What is the significance of this name?'

'When Vijaya, the first Sinhala prince, reached Lanka a thousand years ago, Kuveni was a princess there. Vijaya married her. Later, he abandoned Kuveni and her children to marry a Pandya princess. Distraught, she committed suicide after poisoning her children. It is believed that her curse brought about the downfall of the Sinhalese. It is in memory of my victory over the Sinhalese that I name her Kuveni.'

The emperor kissed the tender cheeks of the baby and murmured, 'My lovely baby, Kuveni,' in her ears. She burst out into a wail, stopping only when Devanayaki started to feed her again.

The emperor stayed for a while and explained each phase of the battle to Devanayaki in great detail. He apologized for proceeding to Keerimalai without paying heed to her warning. He thanked her for the directions she had sent through her spies. Her eyes filled with tears when he told her that victory would have been impossible but for her timely help. When he said that in return for their help, he had given the control of Puttalam to Sultan Sayyed Muhammad and had made Iravipillai the military chief of Anuradhapura, she wanted to ask what he planned to give her. But she contained herself.

To her surprise, though, he announced, 'Kantha Madevi, you are now the chief consort of Mummudi Chola. You have to sit on my left in the royal court and rule the country. When I leave the capital, you will be responsible for administration. Kundavai will apprise you of the details.'

Though initially she felt happy, Devanayaki quickly recognized the hidden danger in this command. The present consort was Loka Madevi. She thought to herself, 'If I replace her, immense problems will arise. As it is, they accuse me of not allowing the emperor to visit his other queens. Even Kundavai, who controls the queens as well as the emperor, is not favourably disposed towards me. So if I am made the chief consort, there will be a bitter power struggle inside the palace. That will finally result in weakening the emperor.'

'No, Your Highness. Let Loka Madevi continue to be your chief consort. I need not be present in court to help you with administration. You can give me some other gift in memory of the victory over Lanka.'

Mistaking her refusal for humility, the emperor was insistent. But when she explained, he understood and his respect for her increased. Anyone else would have accepted without bothering to think about the implications. He left her bedchamber wondering what would be an appropriate gift for her. That night, he stayed with Loka Madevi. Though dimmed by age, she was beautiful. She could never conceive and believed that to be the reason why the king was not interested in her. So she was very pleased when he came to her on his return from Sri Lanka.

As he had been away for five months, the emperor was fully occupied with matters of state and couldn't spend much time with Devanayaki and the baby. He had to travel within the country for several reasons: there were security threats from neighbouring countries, the emperor had to personally supervise the defence strategies, he also had to assess the skills of the newly recruited soldiers at various training centres and oversee the collection of taxes. It took him two months to set everything in order. By then, Devanayaki had recovered fully and Kuveni had begun to sit up and gurgle.

During the month of Margazhi, the season of festivals, the emperor took Devanayaki and Kuveni to the Ranganathaswamy temple in Srirangam. Their journey from Thanjavur to Uraiyur was in a beautifully decorated carriage drawn by four horses, accompanied by soldiers and music. They reached Uraiyur, the first capital of the Cholas, paid tribute at the tomb of Karikala Chola and went to the Ranganathaswamy temple in a decorated boat. The main priest of the temple and prominent citizens welcomed the emperor and Devanayaki with traditional rituals. The emperor gifted an elephant to the temple in Kuveni's name. Everyone stood spellbound when Devanayaki sang and danced in the temple.

That night, they stayed in the Uraiyur palace. It was then that the emperor told her in detail about his conquest of Sri Lanka. He told her how a group of crocodiles had attacked their boats while they were going to Anuradhapura from Manthai, and how one of the ships from Kanthalur had run aground in the swamps of Puttalam lake. He informed her that the underground labyrinths were exactly as inscribed under the jewellery box she had shown him. Devanayaki listened anxiously with Kuveni sucking at her breast. She interrupted him occasionally to clarify her doubts. After discussing the war, she wanted to know about the emperor's journey to the city of dreams in Sri Lanka. The emperor hesitated. Then he decided it was better to tell her everything, as she was extremely intelligent.

'I didn't get an opportunity to visit the city of dreams in royal style. Mahinda has made both the wife and daughter of his predecessor, King Sena, his queens. It is said that the daughter is very beautiful. By the time we reached there, Mahinda and his queens had escaped. Luckily, Mangala was there. She is the daughter of the army chief. Though she initially resisted, she later cooperated with us. She was with me until I left Anuradhapura.'

Feeling a twinge of jealousy, Devanayaki wanted to know more about Mangala. The emperor told her Mangala's story.

'Oh! Why didn't you bring her here?'

'She does not have the ability to assist me. Her language and culture are different. It will be difficult for her to adapt.'

'Is she beautiful?'

'Not as beautiful as you. But she is good enough to be the queen of a Chola emperor.'

'You are just saying this to please me.'

'No. If you are a frangipani bud, she is a lotus bud.'

Devanayaki burst into laughter. Fortunately, Kuveni did not wake up.

The next morning, they had a dip in the Kaveri and visited the Ranganathaswamy temple once more before returning to

Thanjavur. But before that, Rajaraja presented Devanayaki a special gift in the presence of Lord Ranganatha. It was a lock with seven keys that had been kept at the Lord's feet for a night.

'This is a gift for your help in the war against Sri Lanka. The new palace near the Thyagaraja temple in Thiruvarur on the banks of the river Kaveri now belongs to you. You must establish an intellectual centre there, like the one in Kanthalur. We must invite teachers from all over the country to stay. Our children must be trained in all subjects. We should also collect manuscripts and preserve them. Do you know how diligently all this has been done in the Buddhist monasteries in Anuradhapura? They carefully record history. The monks at Abhayagiri can tell you each and every incident that happened since the day the Buddha first came to Sri Lanka. Our ancestors were not as conscientious about recording history. We must teach our children history and not merely legends like that of Kuthiramukhi Madeviyar. We must inscribe on stone and copper sheets whatever we have achieved.'

Devanayaki was both surprised and proud at the changes that had come over the emperor after the Sri Lankan conquest. Was it due to Mangala's influence? Or that of the Buddhist monks? After the Kanthalur war, the emperor has realized that conquered territory must not be looted and destroyed, rather an effective administration system should be established there. Maybe Mangala, the lotus, had been able to influence him as well.

Devanayaki and her daughter shifted to the palace in Thiruvarur before long. It was a ploy to prevent Kundavai Pirattiyar from realizing that Devanayaki was advising the king on all matters of state. To keep Kundavai happy, the emperor made her his joint signatory on all royal commands. Kundavai and Rajaraja's queens were happy that Devanayaki was shifting to the new palace.

It was luxurious. The architecture of the palace at Thiruvarur made up for the lack of amenities in the emperor's other palaces. A tributary of the river Kaveri flowed through it. There was an underground pathway from the palace to the Thyagaraja temple. But most important of all was the mirror palace on the third floor, where the ceiling and walls were inlaid with mirrors. That was exclusively for the emperor.

The emperor invited all leading exponents of literature, music, dance, politics and logic to Thiruvarur. As they followed the gurukula system, arrangements were made for the students to stay there during the period of their studies. Apart from the education imparted by the gurus, Devanayaki especially trained each student in accordance with the position he was to assume in the administration of the country. For that reason, Rajendra Chola, though no longer an adolescent, was her most important disciple.

The three years that Devanayaki spent in Thiruvarur were the happiest in her life. During this period, Rajaraja never ventured overseas to wage wars. He used this time to devise plans to capture Kambuja and Srivijaya. When Devanayaki moved to Thiruvarur, the centre of the espionage team also shifted there. There were more than a thousand people, both men and women, in her team of spies. They informed her of developments all over the country and abroad. A special centre was established in Thiruvarur to train spies. Those who were selected had already completed their military training. Here, they were given training in psychology, taught different languages and given an insight into different cultures. Then, they were taught the skills of persuasion. Women were given special training in the art of seduction. The most important quality a spy needed was loyalty. They had several tricks to ensure this. The king would show great consideration towards them and their families, they would be trapped and later pardoned, traitors would be punished severely to set an example, or they would be tempted with offers of high positions.

Devanayaki lost the excess weight she had gained during pregnancy as she went horse-riding regularly. The emperor felt that she was growing more beautiful every day. Fortunately or unfortunately, she was never able to conceive again. But Kuveni's presence brightened their lives.

Life flowed smoothly, until an incident occurred that shocked the country. One night, when Devanayaki was offering her dance as tribute to Lord Thyagaraja, Sinhala spies disguised as theatre actors kidnapped Kuveni. The emperor was watching Devanayaki's dance when it happened. The child was drugged and taken away. The emperor was shocked as it had occurred in the capital of spies. In spite of searching through the night, the Chola army was unable to find the child. Some people reported seeing a small boat sailing down the Kaveri. Devanayaki lost consciousness. The next morning, a message in Sinhalese was found near the temple. It stated that the revenge for burning Anuradhapura had commenced. That was when they realized that Sinhala spies had kidnapped Kuveni and the actors had suddenly disappeared.

On the third day, Kuveni's corpse was found near the Chidambaram temple. Her body bore marks of sexual abuse. The word 'pattavesi' was gouged into her skin.

17

It seemed as though the pages containing information about the days that followed Kuveni's death were missing from the *Susaana Supina*. The book that was recovered in Sigiriya only mentions Devanayaki alighting from a Kambuja cargo ship at the Tirukonamalai harbour. What happened in the days immediately after Kuveni's death is not mentioned. It was after the Telugu Chola king, Bhima, was defeated and a vassal named Jatavarman was given power to rule over Kanchi, that Kuveni was killed. But the Chalukya's attack from the north was strong. In that situation, the emperor would not have been able to go back to Sri Lanka. Historical documents say that Rajaraja Chola had to spend months in Vengi to hold back the attacks of the Chalukyas. But the *Susaana Supina* says that when Kuveni was kidnapped, Rajaraja was in Thiruvarur. It is not clear how he reacted to the kidnapping. We do not know whether Mahinda's spies caused more trouble either. It is hoped that all will be known when the lost pages of the *Susaana Supina* are recovered.

In the first half of the *Susaana Supina*, it is mentioned that it took Devanayaki months to recover from the shock of losing her daughter, and so the administration of the intellectual centre was passed on to Rajendra Chola. She went to Sree Vallabha Buddhanar in the Chudamani Vihara to convert to Buddhism. But she was not in a mental state to be a sanyasin. Devanayaki was desperate for revenge against Mahinda. She had also not managed to free herself from worldly desires. Understanding this, Sree Vallabha Buddhanar sent her back, asking her to return only after she had freed herself from these bonds. Comforting herself with the thought that she would find solace in the verses of the Thiruppavai, Devanayaki returned to Thiruvarur. But when she returned, strange things began to happen in her life.

These later developments are recorded in an appendix to the *Susaana Supina* which was written by Chidambara Desikan about the legend of the statue of Gnana Saraswathi in Gangaikonda Cholapuram. When Devanayaki returned to Thiruvarur palace,

Rajendra Chola was busy creating an idol of Saraswathi for the stage. He worked on the black granite like an expert sculptor. Though the servants had been given strict instructions not to disturb him, they couldn't prevent Devanayaki from entering the room. She stood silently, looking at the sculptor and the idol. The work on the idol was nearly over. The goddess Saraswathi seated in padmasana on a lotus resembled Devanayaki. Saraswathi's lips, nose, beautiful eyes, long legs, voluptuous thighs, slim waist and broad lap were exactly like Devanayaki's, but the rest of the statue was incomplete. As he meditated on how to carve the upper half of the statue, Devanayaki entered the room. Sensing the presence of another person, Rajendra turned around in annoyance. But when he saw that it was Devanayaki, he folded his hands in respect. His hands that were used to carrying a sword were holding a chisel.

'Are you going to become a sculptor?'

'Forgive me. I was very upset when I heard that you were leaving. You are the person who opened the gates of knowledge to young people like me in Thanjavur. I carved this Saraswathi idol so that I would never forget you.'

'But your Saraswathi does not hold a veena.'

'This is not an ordinary Saraswathi idol. I have never seen you play a veena. This is a sensual Saraswathi who imparts all sorts of knowledge.'

'Then why are you lost in thought without completing the sculpture?'

'This is all I know.'

Devanayaki recognized the sparkle of love in his eyes. It was a complex situation.

Desikan discusses in detail the dilemma of a woman who has to romance both father and son. He justifies Devanayaki by observing that the father's relationship with her was merely the celebration of a victor and not love. She asked the young prince a question to provoke him.

'What if I permit you to know?'

'I should see you as a mother, as my teacher.'

'But you don't consider me so. I can see what you desire.'

'Then?'

'You are a prince. A king has the right to take everything he desires. So don't hesitate.'

Rajendra haltingly touched her hand. She too desired this. It was the crystallization of an anger that had been latent in her subconscious mind, towards the emperor who brought back a queen after every war. She conveniently forgot her promise to remain faithful to him until he was defeated in battle. Anyway, it was not just to have different rules for men and women. Devanayaki led the prince to her room. The youthful Rajendra was far more handsome than Rajaraja. The prince spent the first night internalizing the details he needed to complete the sculpture. It was almost dawn by the time he had finished measuring Devanayaki's features and recording it in his book. She was seated in padmasana and was amazed at his ability to control his passion in spite of his youth.

'Akka, can you sit in this manner in my workroom?'

'Not like this. I will tie my hair properly and wear my jewellery.'

'Don't wear too much. My Gnana Saraswathi is sensual.'

'I understand.'

Desikan gives a detailed explanation about why, in this sculpture, Gnana Saraswathi is portrayed in a sensual form. It is because this is the purest and most beautiful form of the Goddess. Knowledge in human beings works on three levels. The first level is that of basic information, which many mistake for knowledge. The second level is when information is processed to become knowledge. It is a consciousness about everything in this universe, which helps the evolution of mankind. But true knowledge is neither of these. It is the ability to use all of this information to make life more enjoyable. The limitless possibilities that knowledge offers is the ultimate aim of those who seek it. Man always hunts for pleasure. And lust is the greatest way to pleasure. All seekers of knowledge try to make sex more enjoyable. That is why Gnana Saraswathi is depicted as sensual.

After breakfast, Devanayaki arrived as promised. The only symbol of royalty she wore was the sacred thread that dangled beneath her navel. A raised platform was arranged for her near the idol. She sat on it in padmasana. Rajendra's glances and chisel moved in tandem. After completing the work, they discussed politics and administration. Rajendra clarified his doubts. But on the seventh day, he asked a difficult question.

'Is it right for a king to fulfil all his desires?'

In reply, she chanted a verse from the Mahabharata:

Sarvam balavatham prythyam
Sarvam balavatham ruche
Sarvam balavatham dharma
Sarvam balavatham swakam

'Vyasa says this to Kunti to comfort her. That is how he justifies the Sun God impregnating Kunti against her wishes. A strong man has an appetite for everything, has a taste for everything. Everything he does is dharma. Everything in this world belongs to him. Since you are a strong prince, it has been said that you have the right to possess everything you desire.'

'How did you decide that I was strong without experiencing my strength?'

'It is not just physical strength. It is connected to power. When I am encircled by your arms, it is as if I am within the Chola empire. I will not feel that way in anyone else's arms.'

'What is the might of a king?'

'That is not a question which can be answered in one sentence. There are hundreds of possible answers, like kingdom, wealth, military ... all these answers are correct. But they are not complete. The correct answer is that knowledge is the greatest strength of a king.'

The prince did not ask any further questions. He touched her feet respectfully. From that day onwards, he addressed Devanayaki as Gnana Saraswathi.

The idol was completed in less than a week. It was installed on the Thiruvathira of Margazhi, which was the emperor's birthday. It was followed by Devanayaki's dance recital. But, remembering Kuveni, she burst into tears at the end of the dance. That night, Devanayaki asked Rajendra for two things. She wanted another child to fill the void Kuveni's death had left, and she also desired Mahinda's death. The prince promised to grant both her requests. But, too impatient to wait, Devanayaki set forth on her Arab steed on the eighth day, accompanied by seven of her most trusted spies.

It is said that the news of Rajaraja's return after subduing the Chalukyas prompted Devanayaki to flee. Whatever the reason may have been, she couldn't face the emperor. According to Desikan's notes, she feared that he would murder her. Also, she did not want to live with him. Though he was in love with her, as the future emperor, Rajendra could not think of marrying his father's consort. There was no option for Devanayaki but to flee.

Prince Rajendra later became the emperor. After the death of Rajaraja, he too gained great victories. He defeated those who questioned the might of the Cholas and made the whole island of Lanka his own. He captured Mahinda and his queens and imprisoned them in Vellore. He always remembered his promise to Devanayaki. He kept Mahinda in prison until his death in the hope that Devanayaki would come back to him. As he had conquered territories up to the Ganga, he assumed the title 'Gangaikonda Chola'. He built a new capital called Gangaikonda Cholapuram. He installed the idol of Gnana Saraswathi in his new capital. Desikan doesn't say what happened to Devanayaki. We will have to depend on the available sections of the *Susaana Supina* for that information.

18

When Devanayaki alighted from the *Yasodhara*, a Kambuja cargo ship, at the Tirukonamalai harbour in Sri Lanka, nearly a year had elapsed since she had left Thanjavur. The *Susaana Supina* mentions that the ship sported a red Chinese silk flag with a yellow sun on it. It was the insignia of the Kambuja king, Jayavarman V. Devanayaki came to Tirukonamalai accompanied by Cham Prasidh, a rich diamond merchant who was a close friend of Jayavarman's. Cham Prasidh, who hailed from the Sapthadeva dynasty which had great influence on the administration in Yasodharapura, came to Anuradhapura as a representative of King Jayavarman. He had free access to Mahinda's secret hideaway, the city of dreams. It was to get there that Devanayaki had become Cham's mistress for a year. It was a nightmarish period for her, as Cham was a perverted sadist. Devanayaki had changed a lot in that year. To escape from pain, she found solace in liquor and opium, which drove her to the brink of insanity. By the time she got the opportunity to go to Mahinda's hideout, she had reached a state where she enjoyed everything. But Kuveni's face, which flashed before her eyes very often, fanned the fires of revenge.

Though the spring of youth had disappeared, Devanayaki's figure still held the people of Tirukonamalai spellbound. Like the heavenly nymphs of Kambuja, Devanayaki left the upper part of her body uncovered. She smeared sandalwood paste on her cheeks and breasts. Stepping on Sri Lankan soil for the first time in her life, Devanayaki bowed before Koneswara and to the soil of the country. Plump, balding Cham with a slight potbelly was in no way a suitable match for her. But he walked by her side, touching her as if to proclaim his ownership. Her Chinese maid stood close behind with a mirror, an array of cosmetics and a fan. Two other maids carried her jewellery and clothes. Anxious that age was casting a dark shadow on her glittering beauty, Devanayaki often looked into the mirror her maid carried and, every now and then, wiped her face with muslin dipped in rose water. There were two other maids who were her trusted servants. There were fifteen members in Cham's team, including his bodyguards and servants. Mahinda's men waited a short distance away from the harbour, with horse-drawn carriages. Though Tirukonamalai was under the control of Rajaraja Chola, there wasn't much evidence of the Chola army here. Rajaraja was more interested in adding territories to his empire rather than conquering the rest of Sri Lanka. So Cham could proceed to the city of dreams without much difficulty.

Sree Vallabha Buddhanar, who was in Tirukonamalai to establish a branch of the Chudamani Vihara, saw Devanayaki when he was on his way to an inn after offerings prayer at the Koneswara temple. Recognizing her as she was getting into a carriage, hanging on to Cham's arm, he joyfully went up to her. He asked her if she was well, but she pretended not to recognize him and handed him a silver coin as she would to any ordinary monk. Buddhanar politely refused. So she gave him a gold coin instead. He refused that too. Seeing this, Cham was unable to contain his anger. 'The monks on this island are never satisfied. Why don't you give him your necklace?'

Immediately, she took off her emerald-studded necklace. But Buddhanar refused that too, saying, 'I don't want anything that has been stained by sin. Give me something that is hard-earned.'

Devanayaki's face grew dark with rage. She wore the necklace again and jumped into the carriage. 'Let's go. What a nasty man. Is he a monk?' She sat close to Cham and comforted herself with the thought that he would not have understood what Buddhanar had said. But Cham knew Tamil. He liked the expression 'stained by sin'. When she turned to her maid to wipe her face with the muslin cloth, he mocked her in Tamil, saying, 'Will rose water clean the stains of sin?' Devanayaki was hurt.

Buddhanar does not find fault with Devanayaki. Instead, he launches into a story about Poornima, a female monkey. Poornima, a white monkey who belonged to the best of monkey species called Shipanga, lived on the Mahabodhi tree with her friends when the Buddha was meditating under it. When Sujatha came to offer kheer to the Buddha, the monkeys tried to snatch it away but failed. But the Buddha offered half the food to the monkeys before partaking of it himself. Poornima was surprised to see a good soul among human beings. So she plucked some berries for him from a nearby tree. Accepting the food, he stroked her gently. The berries Poornima brought him would be his only food until he attained enlightenment. In a short while, the Buddha went into a deep meditative state. Not realizing the importance of what he was doing, Poornima and her friends continued to live in the tree, fighting for food and sex. As she was the youngest, the male monkeys often fought over her. She always satisfied the victor. All this happened in the tree just above where Siddhartha Gautama sat in deep meditation. He was oblivious to it all. But on the forty-ninth day, when he found enlightenment, Poornima was lucky enough to witness it. Everyone else was sleeping. Poornima too received a ray of the divine light. Several births later, Poornima was reborn as Sanghamitra, the daughter of emperor Ashoka. She became a renowned Buddhist monk. Buddhanar prays that Devanayaki, who was immersed in lust, revenge and anger, would have a fate similar to Poornima's, at least in the next birth. After that, he asks a question: 'What do you call a creeper that easily winds itself around any tree?'

Cham, along with his entourage, proceeded to the city of dreams in horse-drawn carriages. They seemed to be ordinary, but the carriage in the middle was equipped with all sorts of luxuries. They reached a dense forest, one quite unlike any Devanayaki had seen before. There were trees taller than the towers of fortresses. Teak, rosewood and mahogany trees, more than six hundred years old. Beneath them were smaller trees and plants. One could barely see one's way through the dense foliage. The screeching of birds frightened by their presence and the chirping of crickets was deafening. No ray of sunlight could penetrate the forest even when the sun was at its peak. Devanayaki wondered how they would move forward. But plants had been cut away to create a path just wide enough for the carriages to pass. Mahinda's men walked in front of and behind the carriage, bearing lit torches. When the carriages entered the middle of the forest, everything became quiet. A frightening silence descended. Terrified, Devanayaki clutched Cham's hand.

'I'm scared, Bong.'

'Dev, don't fear. Do you want to hear a joke? Though this island is known as the country of Sinhala, or lions, there aren't any tigers or lions here. There are quite a few elephants, but not in such dense forests where they find it difficult to walk. There might be leopards, but they run away scared by all this noise. Here, we need fear only snakes.'

'How much further, Bong?'

'Three yojanas. After that, there is a mighty river. But as there are bamboo rafts strong enough to carry horse-carriages, we don't need to worry. Beyond this lie bamboo forests. There are plenty of elephants there. Six yojanas beyond that lie forests similar to this, but denser and more dangerous. But Mahinda has created green tunnels for us to pass. We don't need to go out of the forest.'

'Why?'

'Sinha Saila is in the middle of that forest. The people here call it Sigiriya. There are large towering rocks in the middle of the forest, nearly six hundred feet high. Mahinda's city of dreams is above that. We will reach there before twilight.'

'Why is it called the city of dreams?'

'You will know when we get there. It is a place of celebration for kings, queens, mistresses, diamond merchants, spice traders, iron manufacturers, shipowners and other wealthy people. The best of everything is available there, the best food, wine and women, the most enchanting dancers, melodious music. Once you enter the city of dreams, you enjoy ultimate freedom. There are no wrongs, only rights. Everyone can do what they want. The only condition is that what you want shouldn't go against anyone else's wishes. Everything has a price. Only those who can pay it come there. The identities of the visitors are kept secret.'

'How does this benefit Mahinda?'

'Dev, I have told you that Mahinda was the king of Anuradhapura. He lost his country in a war with Rajaraja Chola. Don't you know all this in spite of having been a dancer in Rajaraja's court?'

'I was a mere dancer. What do dancers and courtesans know about matters of state? We merely do what we're bid.'

'Though some land to the east of the island belongs to him, he cannot make use of it. He has possession only of this city. So, every man has to pay ten gold pieces to enter, but he can take a woman there without paying a fee. Whether man or woman, a tenth of the money you make belongs to Mahinda. His close associates always gift him something special.'

'Why don't you show me the gift you are giving him?'

He laughed.

'Look into the mirror. You will see the beauty I am going to offer him.'

She was shocked. She hadn't expected this. There was no escape. Though he had lost the war, Mahinda was about to win. She looked into the mirror. Her reflection seemed to mock her. 'You fool! You cannot escape.' She spoke after a while, her voice heavy with grief.

'Bong, are you tired of me?'

'Yes, Dev. I never stay with a woman for more than a year.'

Journeying over river and forest, they reached Sinha Saila by twilight. With the rays of the setting sun falling upon it, the place looked beautiful.

It was difficult to believe that such a magnificent place existed in the middle of the forest. A city perched atop boulders that were six hundred feet high. Sena and Anula, Mahinda's chief servants, were waiting to welcome them. They garlanded Cham and Devanayaki and escorted them to the beat of drums. They washed their feet in a lotus pond and ate fruits and drank tender coconut water. Cham gave Sena a hundred gold coins, which ensured their stay for ten days.

'Are you going back so soon? I thought you'd stay for a month.'

'No, Sena. I have work to attend to. Anula, this is my companion Devanayaki. You must take her around the city.'

Anula looked carefully at Devanayaki. Though she felt envious, she put her arms around her.

'Where will my servants stay?'

'All of that has been arranged. Devanayaki's maids too can stay here comfortably.'

'Oh! Can't I bring my maids upstairs?'

'Sorry, the rules don't allow that. They can only come up to the entrance.'

'But my clothes –'

'– will be brought upstairs. The maids of the city of dreams will fulfil all your wishes. Come, let's move on before it gets dark.'

The 'lion entrance' was halfway up the rocks. The eighteen-foot lion's statue looked more ferocious than a real beast. The entrance was through its mouth. Then, there were steps to climb. As they climbed up slowly, enjoying the scenic beauty on the way, Anula told them the story of Sinha Saila. The Sinhalese king, Kasyapa, had built this palace six years ago. Kasyapa, who had no claim to the throne, being the son of one of the king's mistresses who hailed from Pallava, usurped power by imprisoning and later killing his father Dhatusena. The legitimate heir to the throne was Moggallana, who escaped to the Pandya kingdom. Fearing that Moggallana would return seeking revenge, Kasyapa left Anuradhapura and established a more secure capital here. The fear that he would be punished for his sins haunted him constantly. He sought solace from guilt in women and wine. From then on, Sigiriya became the pleasure palace of the kings of Anuradhapura. Kasyapa ruled Lanka for eighteen years. Then, Moggallana returned with the help of the Pandya king. He wrested power from Kasyapa and killed him. He shifted the capital back to Anuradhapura.

'Mahinda is also trying to grab power from the Chola king who defeated him. We are sure to win if all of you help us.'

Devanayaki was silent. Sena continued talking to Cham. Anula changed the topic, feeling that Devanayaki did not have much interest in matters of state.

'Do you really belong to the apsara dynasty?'

'Yes, the Sapthadeva dynasty. The most powerful family in Yasodharapura.'

'The other two apsaras who came here resembled you, but they were very slender. Seeing your voluptuous face and striking features, I feel that you will become the queen of the city of dreams.'

'Don't tease me.'

By the time they reached the summit, night had fallen. The palace was bathed in the light of the full moon. There were hundreds of guests thronging the vast gardens. The palace resounded with laughter and music. Mahinda's family did not stay in the palace – it was filled only with guests. When she looked down from that great height, Devanayaki felt that she had reached the sky. She felt that the breeze would carry her away. Anula poured some toddy into a goblet and handed it to her.

'Drink. This is the beginning of your life here. After this, there is no difference between kings or mistresses. All are equal. Call them only by their names.'

'Dev!'

She was startled. Cham and Mahinda were just behind her.

'Mahinda, this is the gift I brought for you.'

He looked over her lazily. Then, as if receiving the gift with pleasure, he pulled her close and kissed her on both cheeks. Not wanting to look at him, Devanayaki closed her eyes tight.

19

The moment she spent in Mahinda's arms was the longest in Devanayaki's life. The man she most hated, the brain behind her baby daughter's murder – his arms were around her. She felt like a doe caught in a lion's cage. Thinking about the cruelties of the Sinhalese king, she felt fear creeping down her spine. At the same time, the memory of his mischievous eyes, which had gazed at her with longing when he was her father's student in Kanthalur, offered some solace. She remembered Shasthri's advice to defeat fear with intelligence. This was the time to act intelligently, to move carefully, controlling her emotions with her intellect. Mahinda would certainly look at her when he raised his head after the second kiss. As expected, after the formal kissing ritual, Mahinda looked carefully into Devanayaki's eyes as she slowly opened hers. Darkness had fallen and it was time for the lamps to be lit. The golden glow from the oil lamps flowed onto her face. She looked at Mahinda with an enticing smile that adeptly conveyed the promise of intoxication. He could not believe that the beauty he had longed for all his life was in his hands. With wonder in his voice, he said, 'Devanayaki!' Nodding, she fell on his chest. He led her into the palace. He only let go of her when he reached the main room that lay to northwest of the top storey.

It was a huge room. The Padmasambhava mandala was painted upon the western wall. She was glad that she had learnt the basics of tantric practice from Nissanka Vajran, who belonged to the dynasty of Vajrabodhi, while she had been in Jayavarman's court. She felt that it might help in exerting her influence on Mahinda. But she wondered whether Mahinda was even interested in tantric rituals. As far as she had heard, Mahinda wasn't into anything religious. But the Padmasambhava mandala indicated a possibility. She looked at him in surprise. He was wearing a white silk cloth around his waist and a length of silk around his shoulders. There were none of the trappings of royal attire. Though his youthful, mischievous glances had disappeared, he looked more handsome than ever. He did not bear the shadow of his age as Mahendravarman had. He was neither dark-complexioned like the Cholas, nor did he have Cham's slanting eyes. Fair, handsome, not very tall or overweight, he had an innocent smile playing upon his lips. Looking at him, she could not believe that the stories about his cruelties were true.

It was a beautiful room, with a green carpet spread over white marble. There were soft seats covered with leopard skin, an ornate rosewood cot, a silken mattress, and a huge wardrobe, also in rosewood, close to the cot. There were smaller rooms attached to the main room for bathing and changing. It had all the luxuries you could imagine. Two lamps with seven wicks shone their light upon a large mirror from the corners, creating an illusion of daylight. By this time her clothes and jewels had arrived. There were fragrant flowers and fruits and various beverages arranged on silver trays. The mattress was decorated with flowers as well. When the fragrance of camphor filled the room, it truly resembled paradise.

Mahinda pulled the wonderstruck Devanayaki towards him.

'Does the queen of Kanthalur like my city of dreams and my palace?'

'I haven't seen the whole city, but I really like the palace. I only regret the fact that I couldn't come here earlier.'

'I had invited you many times.'

'Why didn't you defeat Mahendravarman and bring me to Lanka? I used to dream about it when I lived with the aging king. I knew that jewel box, inscribed with the secret pathways of Anuradhapura and the Chinese word "huanying", was an invitation for me.'

'I wrote in Chinese so that the old man wouldn't understand. But it was an invitation you did not accept.'

'In Kanthalur, you remain faithful to the man you marry until he is defeated. Then you accept the victor. Why didn't you carry out your threat of humbling Kanthalur?'

'I had begun preparations for war. But Rajaraja's unexpected attack spoiled it all. I was extremely upset when the queen of Kanthalur became Chola Madevi. I entered into a war with Rajaraja Chola to get you. But, faced with his strength and intelligence, I failed. I attacked Kodiakkarai only because I knew that you were there. It saddened me that you had to become wife to both father and son. Tell me, why have you come looking for me, a king who has lost his country?'

'I did not come of my own volition. Cham Prasidh lured me into a trap when I was a guest in Jayavarman's palace. I have been his slave for the past year. He is a sadist who enjoys torturing me, mentally and physically. He is preparing an elaborate trap for both of us by offering me to you. Please don't ask me how Chola Madevi sank to such depths.'

She didn't say anything more. She put her jewels and clothes in the wardrobe. There was a sandalwood box covered in yellow silk, which was a special gift for Mahinda. Carved in the Angkor style, the sandalwood box held ten small, exquisite ivory Buddhas. Devanayaki removed the tenth Buddha by twisting it towards the left and respectfully offered the box to Mahinda.

'This is a humble gift from me.'

'What is it?'

'Nine Buddha statues. Open it.'

He opened the box. Devanayaki took a statuette out and explained.

'These are not mere Buddhas. They are Ratna Buddhas. Each Buddha is a jewel box. Look. If you turn the head towards the right, it opens. There are precious stones inside.'

Devanayaki took the gems out and gave them to Mahinda. He looked on with pleasure. 'Each Buddha contains a different kind of precious stone. This one is filled with rubies, the next with emeralds, then topaz. Each Buddha contains nine stones. What else can the mistress of a jewel merchant gift you? The Vajrayana of Kambuja says that if these Ratna Buddhas are kept in the bedroom, your life will be filled with pleasure.'

'We believe that Buddha statues shouldn't be kept in the bedroom.'

'That is according to Theravada Buddhism. According to Vajrayana, the bedroom is not an unclean place.' She smiled mischievously at Mahinda.

'Though I've installed the Padmasambhava mandala, I haven't formally accepted Vajrayana. The main reason is that I haven't found a suitable guru.'

'So you only need a good teacher?'

'Are you joking? You were a staunch devotee of Lord Padmanabha.'

'I was. I danced to Andal's Thiruppavai as an offering to the Lord. But in Kambuja, I accepted Padmasambhava instead of Padmanabha. There isn't a lot of difference between them.

For Padmanabha, the greatest pleasure is that of the soul. But Padmasambhava makes you realize that the body and the soul are one, and that the pleasure of the body is that of the mind too. He had experienced it through his rituals with Mandarava. Anyway, your queen shouldn't belong to a different religious sect.'

'Devanayaki, I am not intelligent enough to understand most of what you are telling me. But I am no longer the ruler of Lanka. I'm just an unfortunate man who, after having lost his kingdom, crown and throne, makes a living out of gambling.'

'If you want to, you can win back everything that you have lost.'

Mahinda did not reply. He sat in silence, gazing into nothingness. His face reflected his angst about his stillborn plan. He might have been able to command the loyalty of the Kanthalur army if he had succeeded in keeping Devanayaki by his side. Devanayaki moved closer to him and kissed his right hand.

'You are getting back everything that you had considered lost.'

'If you remain with me always...'

'Of course.'

'Not just you, but the army of Kanthalur too should be with me.'

'Don't doubt it. Everyone is fed up with the Chola rule. The military chief will stand by you if I command him. Anyway, the people of Kanthalur prefer the fair Sinhalese to the dark-skinned Cholas.'

'Why?'

'Who would dislike a handsome man like you?'

They only woke up when the cool breeze wafting from Sinha Saila roused them. He looked at Devanayaki, who was lying silently after she had woken up. He tried cracking a joke to make her laugh.

'Why do you look as if you have just delivered a baby?'

'It is as if a sea has flowed into me ... I am brimming over.'

'What do we call a child born of a lion and a tigress?'

'Siduva!'

They couldn't contain their laughter, and continued laughing and joking for a while. When Mahinda left just before day break for his daily exercise, she took the tenth Buddha in her hands and turned its head towards the right. There was a small bottle inside. She took it out, her face as bright as the sun with the thought of revenge. The bottle contained the poison of a king cobra. A drop was enough to kill a lion. But if she was careless, she would have to sacrifice her own life too. Comforting herself with the thought that this was the way out when all else failed, she closed the bottle and put the statue back in the box. Then, she stood gazing at her reflection in the mirror. She had never known that she could act so well. She had surprised herself with her expressions and her words. When had she ever used expressions like 'a sea has flowed into me'? Anyway, the lion had fallen for it. He was passionate. She decided to try and get him to allow her maids upstairs. She thought, 'If everything goes as planned, he might even entrust me with the keys to the city of dreams.' Her only fear was whether a Siduva would be born by then.

When she emerged after her bath in the lotus pond atop Sinha Saila, a thousand eyes were gazing at her. They murmured that Mahinda's new woman was not bad looking. Some of them consoled themselves with the thought that Mahinda would tire of her within a few days after which they could claim her. When she returned to the room after praying at the temple, Mahinda was waiting for her.

'It seems that you have finished your prayers. Now accept this gift.'

'A gift?'

'Yes. You gave me a gift last night. Now close your eyes and accept mine.'

She happily closed her eyes and stretched out her hands. He gave her a gold tray. It was heavy. Thinking that it might be an expensive gift, she held it tight.

'Open your eyes. You will jump for joy.'

By then, her hands were wet. Smiling, she slowly opened her eyes and was shocked. The tray fell from her hands. Cham's head, blood still flowing from it, fell at her feet.

'Aren't you happy? This is in return for pleasuring me last night. His body has been left on the death rock for vultures to eat. You can go and see it if you wish.'

Devanayaki fainted onto Mahinda's shoulder.

20

Several hours passed before Devanayaki regained consciousness. When she opened her eyes, she was lying with her head in Mahinda's lap. The maids were fanning her. Pungent oil was smeared on her forehead. For a while, she couldn't tell where she was or whose lap she was in. It took a few moments for realization to dawn. Seeing that she had woken up, the maids left the room. She looked at Mahinda with fear.

'You had a bad scare. Don't worry, the royal physician says that there is nothing to worry about. The maids are here to help you.'

Mahinda planted a kiss on her right hand. She sat up in bed. After she drank the grape juice and kantha the maid offered her in a crystal glass, she recovered completely. Her face lit up with a smile.

'I didn't expect the woman who advised me in matters of war to faint at the sight of blood.'

'It was not because I saw blood, but because it was Cham's blood. He was my man until yesterday, so I got flustered. I didn't imagine that you would take such a step trusting my words alone.'

'Are you upset?'

'I am not a fool to cry over Cham. From last night, he was nobody to me. But I was hurt when I realized that King Mahinda, whom I love, has such a cruel side to his nature.'

'Devanayaki, you have to understand that it is necessary to be cruel to the enemy. The enemy should not be treated as human. Do not show him the consideration that you would a fellow human being. Don't wait for an auspicious moment to kill someone who deserves to die. That is the tradition of the Sinhalese kings. You will understand all this when you live with me for a while. Come, get dressed. The guests of the city of dreams are waiting for me.'

She washed her face thoroughly and applied rose water to take away the pungent odour of the medicinal oils. The maids helped her to wear the sampot that Jayavarman had gifted her. She tied her hair in a half-moon and decorated it with jasmine and frangipani, then sprayed rose water and sandal paste on her face and breasts. Glancing at the mirror several times for reassurance, she stepped out of the room. Though her head did not sport an apsara crown, she looked like a divine nymph. When Devanayaki entered the main hall with Mahinda, the drums rolled. The people shouted, 'Long live Devanayaki, the queen of the city of dreams!' She sat next to Mahinda on the royal seat. He smiled with pride and began to speak.

'Dear guests! Welcome to the city of dreams. Today is a day of happiness for us. Devanayaki, the former queen of Kanthalur and the Madevi of the Cholas, is henceforth the queen of the city of dreams. I am breaking with tradition in Devanayaki's case. None of the women who have come here have slept with me for more than one night. That fortune belongs to Devanayaki alone. She will be mine forever. It is the fruition of a dream that has lasted for years, from the time I was a student in Kanthalur. That is why I decided to make her the queen of this city. She will join you in all the celebrations. She will be responsible for all the activities in this city.'

Mahinda looked around for approval. Anula and Sena looked at each other with displeasure writ large upon their faces. Many of the guests sported contemptuous smiles. Someone asked, 'Why would anyone buy a tired horse?' The reply was, 'If it is free, who will not accept it?'

Devanayaki pretended not to hear the insulting comments. She had developed a thick enough skin to remain unperturbed in the face of humiliation. Mahinda continued.

'Dear guests, the bell that signals the beginning of the games will be rung soon. Apart from chess and gambling, Go has been arranged for the Chinese. You can bet on birds and animals too. The best wine, women and food will brighten the celebrations. As usual, all games will come to an end when the sun sets. You can give a tenth of what you gain here to the city of dreams.'

The bell rang. Everyone moved towards the gaming centres. Mahinda escorted Devanayaki everywhere and explained the rules of gambling. She enjoyed the silence that surrounded the chess table and the noisy sounds of the cockfight. The taste of fried venison and kantha filled her with pleasure. Beauties from various countries eyed her with envy. In the afternoon, when she was accompanying Mahinda for a nap, Devanayaki voiced her anxiety.

'Most legends tell us of kings who lost their kingdoms while gambling. Do you think that you can win your kingdom back through it?'

'No. Lanka can only be won back through a war. This gambling centre is only a façade.'

'How far have the military arrangements proceeded?'

'I have brought together my fragmented army. Seven yojanas to the west of Sinha Saila, there is a camp that gives rigorous training to soldiers. A navy with more than a hundred ships has been readied in Gotavaya harbour in the south. The north coast is being watched by our warships masquerading as trade ships. Everything is progressing systematically. Efforts are on to forge alliances and to gather as many weapons as possible.'

'I am assured of the support of the rebels of Kanthalur. I can also arrange for weapons from there. But I will have to travel for that, or I must join the band of Sinhalese spies.'

'That is insane. I can't be separated from you.'

He looked askance at Devanayaki. She smiled provocatively. He understood what it meant. But he had to leave to resolve some problems that had arisen at the gambling tables.

The games ended when the sun set. The city of dreams received more than ten thousand gold coins as profit that night. Mahinda felt happy that the day of Devanayaki's arrival had brought such rich gains. He gifted Devanayaki a thousand gold coins. When she asked, 'Why should I accept money stained with sin?' Mahinda replied, 'These are the wages for the sin you committed yesterday. Accept it with joy.' Both of them laughed.

Soon, the lamps were lit. Bathed in the glow, the city of dreams resembled paradise. Music, dance and celebrations filled the palace. Beauties floated around like angels. Among them were young children who were barely eight or ten years old. Nobody spared an opportunity to hug or kiss one another. Some retreated into the corners with their partners. There were no skirmishes because everyone had chosen their partners earlier. As Devanayaki sauntered along with Mahinda, a woman from Kedar asked her, 'How did you get the beauty of a nymph with such a voluptuous body?'

'There is only one way. Your parents have to be like this.'

She laughed and ran away.

When they reached the main hall, people demanded that Devanayaki should dance and sing. She refused, saying that she didn't know songs suitable for such occasions. Yielding to Mahinda's insistence though, she sang 'Margazhi'. But once she started singing, she forgot her surroundings and started to dance. The city of dreams stood wonderstruck. The audience applauded. Ignoring the calls for more, she went back to Mahinda.

'I have heard you sing. But I never knew you danced so well.'

'This is the first time I've sung "Margazhi" after giving up Padmanabha for Padmasambhava. I was afraid of missing a step. But because it was before the man I adore, it was all right. It has been proven that there is no great difference between Padmanabha and Padmasambhava.'

As Mahinda lovingly pulled her towards him, she could see a man greedily kissing an eight-year-old girl. He held her mouth close even as she struggled to escape. Devanayaki remembered Kuveni. 'Why are small children being tortured?' she asked Mahinda. He replied that it was usual here. Her eyes filled with tears.

They returned to the palace soon after. Without waiting for any rituals, Mahinda burst upon her like a storm. After some initial hesitation, she expertly made her next move.

'Your Highness, new weapons are needed to win wars. As the enemy stands helpless before such weapons, other segments of the army can exploit the opportunity and advance. The Chinese have such weapons with them. They have started selling them at high prices. Do you have any Chinese merchants among your guests?'

Mahinda listened attentively to her advice. He felt bad because he hadn't thought of it before. There were many Chinese weapons traders among the guests.

'Shailendran from Kedar is their agent. We will speak to them.'

'Do you mind if I am there too?'

'No. Your presence will be helpful.'

Two Chinese men and Shailendran came to the meeting. Their expressions revealed the irritation they felt at the presence of a woman. Shailendran immediately expressed his displeasure.

'I've explained everything to them. They feel that Sinha Saila doesn't require new weapons for its security. There are thousands of soldiers on guard around the fortress. The moat is full of crocodiles. You have to walk up six hundred feet to the palace. You can't come here on elephant or horseback. The enemy cannot enter even if it wants to. But women are always nervous.'

'Shailendran, the security of the fort is not the only problem.'

'Then what is it? Is Mahinda going to war against the Cholas?'

Mahinda did not like the question and thought to himself, 'He does not even consider the fact that I was once a king.' But it was not wise to displease one of the most prominent guests of the city of dreams. Devanayaki was the one who replied.

'The weapons traders need not concern themselves with whether we are going to war or not. If you don't mind, Shailendran, I will talk to them in their language.'

Shailendran did not like her interference. He left the room saying, 'I am no longer needed here.' She tactfully presented her case before the Chinese traders. She wanted gunpowder, newly invented in China. Though they tried to be evasive, saying that they did not know anything about it, they agreed when she told them that they could name the price. They took a hundred gold coins as advance and agreed to deliver the goods by the first week of the next month. Mahinda had not even heard of gunpowder until then. Devanayaki did not explain its use to him either.

Devanayaki's hold on Mahinda and the city of dreams grew stronger with each passing day. With the help of certain rituals, she was able to tame a hurricane that lasted only for moments into a gentle breeze that lasted through the night. But she was unable to use the tenth Buddha in spite of staying there for a month. As each night passed, her suspicion that she had fallen in love with Mahinda grew stronger.

One day, Nakkeeran, a spy of Rajendra Chola, arrived in the guise of a Muslim trader. Devanayaki saw him as she sat in the royal hall with Mahinda. They recognized each other. When the crowds dispersed, she went to him after making sure that Mahinda had left.

'The prince commanded me to return only after finding Kantha Madeviyar. It troubles me to see you here. Shall I tell him?'

'Absolutely. Not only should you tell him, you should also carry my message to him. Just don't ask me how I got here.'

'Madeviyar, how can you live with the man who killed your daughter?'

'No more questions. Don't try to meet me in person.'

She prepared a message for the prince on palm leaves that very night. There were seven palm leaves on which she described the city of dreams, the military camps, and Mahinda's family which was living in Ruhuna on the east coast. In the letters, she addressed Rajendra as 'Sculptor' and signed it 'Gnana Saraswathi' in case Nakkeeran was intercepted. Everything was written in code.

Nakkeeran returned on the third day. He wandered around without participating in any gambling games, nor did he disrobe any woman. Sena wondered why he had come to the city of dreams. He informed Mahinda about this stranger but, intoxicated by Devanayaki, he paid no attention.

21

In those days, Sigiriya was more of a playground for the rich than a gamblers' den. The main attractions, of course, were the beauteous courtesans. There were women from Lanka, Vanga, Kalinga, and even from Greece. Unlike the slave girls the gamblers brought with them, most of the courtesans in Sigiriya were bold, free women. They were skilled in music and dance, and performed in separate places marked for them around the palace. There were stringent rules for how they should greet their visitors, how they should entertain them, and how much they could receive as gifts. All of this was recorded in a handbook titled *Swapnajalika* written by Vishakhadatta, a chief of the courtesans, five centuries ago when king Kasyapa founded the city of dreams. Mahinda made more money from the pleasure games played at night than from the gambling games during the day. A portrait of each and every beautiful woman in the city of dreams was etched upon the walls of the western entrance. These portraits were not mere decoration, but bait to lure visitors. A special type of paint – kanija – that did not fade in the rain or sun was used to paint them. As if to realize his dream, Mahinda had installed seven paintings of

Devanayaki. The court artist, Devatachan, and his disciples took great pains to paint these portraits, sitting on bamboo platforms suspended three hundred feet above the ground. Gladdened by the paintings that depicted Devanayaki's celestial beauty from varied perspectives, Mahinda asked the artist what reward he would like. He stood silent in all humility. When compelled, he said, 'If I speak of my desire, you will have me beheaded.' Unfortunately, the artist couldn't allow himself to lie. Though he didn't reveal his desire, Mahinda beheaded him anyway.

This hurt Devanayaki. She had posed for days for Devatachan before he started painting. He never made any advances towards her. He may have dreamt about it, but only dreamers can become good artists. She began to hate even the name of the city of dreams. But she did not tell Mahinda this. He was a man who did not hesitate to kill people for the most trivial reasons. She, on the other hand, found it a terrible task. She hadn't gathered the courage to use the tenth Buddha. To actually kill was much more difficult than to devise complex war strategies and advise kings on how to conduct wars. It is not difficult to kill if one is using weapons in an open fight. But the murder she had planned involved deceit. It was not enough to mix snake venom in his food. It must enter his bloodstream. The king's body did not bear the mark of a single wound, as he did not touch weapons. She chastised herself, 'You fool. Can't you bruise his lips if you want to? Then, as if applying salve to his wound ... But I will have to wait until either the city of dreams is completely in my control or Rajendra Chola's troops surround Sinha Saila.'

Rajendra's reply to the message sent through Nakkeeran arrived soon enough. A spy called Sumantran brought the reply on the twenty-first day. He too was disguised as a merchant.

Rajendra asked her to wait for a storm. He also wrote that she could contact Mangala in Polonnaruwa if she needed anything. But before Devanayaki could contact her, Mangala sent her messenger to Devanayaki. 'I know that seven of your portraits adorn Sinha Saila. My portrait is on the northern wall. Do not hesitate to ask me for help.' Devanayaki wanted to see Mangala's portrait. There were pictures of many beauties in the northern corner. Devanayaki could not be sure which one was Mangala. She couldn't ask anyone else about it, so she entrusted her maids with the job and they pointed out Mangala's portrait. She was happy when she saw it. Rajaraja's choice was, as always, faultless. Devanayaki was careful in her interaction with the spies. The messages were written in code and destroyed immediately after they were read. She ensured that she never met the same messenger twice.

Two weeks after she received Rajendra's message, the Chinese merchants brought the gunpowder. It came in four urns. Three big urns contained saltpetre and the smaller, fourth one had sulphur in it. The coal which had to be added was prepared after they reached Sinha Saila. In great secrecy, they demonstrated its preparation to Mahinda and Devanayaki. The Chinese traders used urine to mix the saltpetre, sulphur and coal. They taught them how to pack bamboo with gunpowder, how to make arrows of fire, and how to wrap the powder in palm leaves so that it would explode with great noise. Neither Mahinda nor his army chiefs were convinced about its efficacy during a war. They said they didn't need it because they had arrows, swords, spears, iron clubs and tridents. They joked that it could only be used to entertain children or scare elephants. But Devanayaki listened carefully and made arrangements to store the gunpowder in a cave near the palace.

After acquiring the gunpowder, Devanayaki's confidence soared. She thought about how to place it inside the palace at strategic points, when an idea came to her. Mahinda had once said to her, 'The diamond Buddhas in the bedchamber have proven lucky. Shall we install Buddha statues all over Sinha Saila?' There was a maid from China who was skilled in moulding clay idols. Devanayaki decided to stuff gunpowder in dry coconut shells after pouring away the water and to place them inside every statue. The wick would be under the statues' feet. Mahinda gladly agreed when she asked his permission to instal a hundred and one Buddhas cast in the mould of the diamond Buddhas all over the palace. He was happy to see her deepening interest in Buddhism. Within a week, one hundred and one black Buddhas were installed all over the palace. Twenty-one Buddhas were placed at the entrance. This upset several people. 'So the Buddha is to stand guard over gambling and prostitution,' they said mockingly. Anula said to Sena, 'After discarding Theravada and Mahayana, now Vajrayana is being practised. Nothing is forbidden anymore.' Both of them practised Theravada. As they were upset at losing their administrative powers in the city of dreams, they kept a close watch on Devanayaki's actions.

Devanayaki had learnt the basics of tantric knowledge at Kambuja. These practices became a blessing, as Mahinda desired novelty. Fortunately, at that point of time, Nissanka Vajran came to visit Sripada. On Devanayaki's request, Mahinda invited him to the city of dreams. Though he refused to visit Sinha Saila initially, he agreed to go after receiving Devanayaki's message. Nissanka Vajran was a sixty-year-old Buddhist monk. His body belied his age. A divine aura enveloped him. Mahinda and Devanayaki greeted him formally at the entrance, and led him in respectfully.

All arrangements were made for his stay. Seeing nothing but gambling dens and maids, the monk realized that he had come to the wrong place. The Buddha idols that lined the entrance gave him some solace.

Mahinda and Devanayaki met him as he was enjoying the beauty of the twilight in Sinha Saila after having finished his prayers. Devanayaki was worried that he would be angered by the activities in the city of dreams. But the monk was smiling. He greeted them with pleasure. Mahinda presented him with a diamond chain. Nissanka Vajran gave it to Devanayaki, saying that it would suit her better. The three of them sat on triangular seats. Sending the servants away, Devanayaki herself served food to the monk.

'Acharya, I hope that you are comfortable here.'

'It is indeed very comfortable. I have never seen such a beautiful place in my life. It is as beautiful as its name.'

'I was afraid that you would be displeased by the activities here.'

'Yes, there are things I disapprove of. But Amrapali was the Lord's disciple too. You cannot insist that only good things happen in this world. Tell me, why have you invited me here?'

'Devanayaki was your disciple in Yasodharapura.'

'I remember her, even though she was at the vihara for only a brief while. She was very intelligent.'

'In accordance with your teachings, I followed the path of Padmasambhava. But I could only learn the basic lessons of tantric practice. I want to complete my learning.'

'Learning is never complete. It is merely a journey towards completion. Only the state of nirvana is completion. Sometimes, it takes several births. It becomes possible only if you cleanse your life with noble actions. You have to be ready to make big sacrifices. Abjure violence and selfishness. Let me ask you, do you want happiness or nirvana?'

Devanayaki remained silent for a moment. Looking at Mahinda, she replied, 'Nirvana that is attained through happiness.'

'But before that, you must understand two things clearly. Your body and soul are not two entities but one. Not only that, each pore of your body yields pleasure. So the pleasure of the soul is that of the body too. The body and the universe are similar. As this universe is endless and deep, so is the human body. Attaining nirvana through happiness is the loftiest method by which one can celebrate the body. It is possible only through rigorous practice. Meditate on the Padmasambhava mantra for three days and focus your mind. Then come to me. Until then, we will spend the evenings discussing various types of knowledge.'

The following three evenings were devoted to discussion, in an effort to know the world from the perspectives of nature, man and power. Every day, the discussions would begin with seemingly light topics and move to abstruse philosophic complexities. They arrived at the realization that tantric rituals in Hinduism as well as Buddhism were merely two different routes which moved in parallel towards the ultimate truth. Apart from Padmasambhava, Kumarila Bhatta, Abhinavagupta and Sankara became the topics of conversation.

The discussion ended on the third day with a shloka from the *Soundarya Lahari*:

The earth placed in the muladhara, water in the manipura,
Fire in the svadhishthana, air in the heart, and space above.
Placing the mind between the brows and breaking through the
    kula-path,
You sport with your Lord secretly in the thousand-petalled
    lotus.

The guru placed his hands on his disciple's head, saying, 'I am lucky to have found such a dedicated and intelligent student.'

On the fourth night, the tantric practices began. A small anteroom near the bedchamber was chosen for this. Mahinda could see everything through his window. The guru and his disciple sat facing each other on either side of Padmasambhava mandalas that were drawn on the ground in green, yellow, white and red. They were both naked. In the light of the seven lamps, their bodies glowed like gold. The monk carried a bell and a small round metal stick, about a foot long. Flowers, honey, fruits, liquor, blood, a bowl from which smoke emanated, and a skull were placed on trays.

They bowed to each other and folded their hands before the Padmasambhava mandalas and lamps. They adorned each other with flowers. They tasted the honey, then poured liquor into the skulls and drank from it. They smoked datura. Then they broke a plantain into two and ate one half each. They dipped their fingers in blood and smeared it on each other's lips and tongues. They, thus, became nature and man.

The guru placed his left hand on his disciple's right shoulder, and her left hand on his right shoulder. They held their right hands to their chests in the anjali mudra and sat gazing into each other's eyes. The guru said, 'I am indeed lucky to have such an intelligent disciple.' It was a ritual that erased the outside world from their minds. It was the beginning of nature, focusing only on the man before her. After each stage, the guru tinkled the bell and performed some rituals. Then, shutting his eyes, meditating on Padmasambhava and Mandarava, he chanted the Padmasambhava mantra, 'Om ah hum vajra guru padma siddhi hum', one hundred and one times.

After this, the guru asked his disciple to open her eyes and look at the Padmasambhava mandala. After some time, she sat in vajrasana with her hands folded above her head. Then, the guru touched each point of her body with a diamond and chanted mantras that were unfamiliar to her. Finally, when their concentration was at its zenith and only the central point of the Padmasambhava mandala was visible, the guru drew her to him. Her mind was focussed on Padmasambhava and the guru's mind was filled with Mandarava.

Extinguishing one of the lamps, they moved to the next stage. Each part of Devanayaki's body obeyed the guru. Each embrace lasted for hours. When they reached the bed, she tried to extinguish the second lamp, but he stopped her, saying that everything should happen in the presence of fire. He said, 'Devanayaki, if you are lucky, you will acquire superhuman powers in fourteen days.' The guru's words surprised her. She felt her body change. For the first time, she slept without thoughts of killing Mahinda.

Nissanka Vajran taught her new practices every day. The mandalas drawn on the floor and the mantras they chanted changed accordingly. For Mahinda, who sat watching, it was a tremendous experience. He felt that, instead of the monk, it was he who was with Devanayaki and also in a similar state of mind. Often, he reached ecstasy before either of them did. He never felt any anger towards Devanayaki. A sense of shame filled her when she realized that the pleasure she had experienced thus far was nothing compared to what she was experiencing now. But she was happy at having discovered how to raise the power of the kundalini from the muladhara through the svadhishthana and manipura to the sahasrara.

There were great preparations for the fourteenth day, on which the karma mudra would be taught. The day began with a bath. She was taught to control her breathing while she was neck deep in water. The monk taught her how to control her muscles to increase and decrease the speed at which her body could move. The monk said that it was to teach her this that he had made all this effort. The preparations were complete by evening. A srichakra was drawn on the floor. The mantra being chanted was, 'Om hreem shreem Mahalakshmiye shreem hreem shreem namah'.

The srichakra was chosen instead of the vajravarahi or vajravahini, as it would be more familiar to Devanayaki who had been brought up Hindu. The rituals began with soft, slow, rhythmic chanting. The guru was very careful at each stage of the ritual. By the time she got to the stage of entering the srichakra, Devanayaki was in a state of extreme hysteria. It was the stage when the guru would share secret knowledge with his disciple.

'It's a secret known only to a guru and his disciple. Look at the srichakra. What do you see? This is the secret of the universe. The srichakra is the universe itself. The core of life. The centre of power.'

She listened in wonder. He blessed her. After several complex rituals, they reached the stage of the karma mudra. It was more difficult than any other mudra. They had to enter each other in a way that made it impossible to discern who was inside whom. That is why it is also known as the mata-pita mudra. She had surrendered herself to the guru. Both of them closed their eyes and brought the kundalini power to the manipura. At that moment, the guru gave all his powers to her and, assuming the form of a white-breasted eagle, flew away.

22

Devanayaki was transformed that night. It was an experience too divine to be described in words. At the moment when every pore of her body was in a state of ecstasy, the divine glow of knowledge enveloped her. The pure notes of the tantric mantras entered her soul. The fragrance of the divine parijat flower enveloped her. Someone held a glass filled with sweet nectar to her lips. She sipped it slowly. All the sorrows of the material world ended for her and, though she had yet to journey a long distance to attain the ultimate truth, she was free from thoughts of jealousy, revenge, selfhood, greed, fame and violence. Love for the universe filled her like a mesmerizing intoxication. She felt a new power enter her body and mind. That is how she found the strength of mind to carry her guru's body as he lay dead in her lap, and set him down on the death rock.

But the city of dreams was shocked by the death of Nissanka Vajran. Many suspected Devanayaki of killing him. People began to fear her. And Mahinda feared her the most. He was the only one who had seen her enveloped by the divine glow, grow as big as the sky, and sacrifice Nissanka Vajran's soul in the fire that emanated from her navel. Though the monk had pleaded for his life, she did not stop until she had taken his powers completely. Mahinda was aghast when he recalled that he had found pleasure in her arms. When she came to his room, Mahinda had already left. A naked Devanayaki, oblivious to everything, started meditating after lighting a lamp in front of the Padmasambhava mandala. Not even glancing at the food and drink her maids had kept for her, she meditated. Her mind contained only the srichakra. She came out of her trance on the seventh day, when the sun reached its zenith above Sinha Saila. The guru's disembodied voice guided her:

'A tantric's object of worship and place of worship is his or her body. The body is a holy temple with nine doors. The mind is the pure sanctum sanctorum. All doors lead to it. As you have practised the karma mudra from the srichakra, you can invoke any deity in your mind. It is best that you make Guru Padmasambhava your chosen deity. His superhuman powers will lead you to nirvana. Fire and water will be under your control. You can take any form and even travel through air. But remember this – without a proper guru, all this will be impossible. You cannot be prayed to unless you pray, you cannot experience pleasure without giving it. Without Siva, power is powerless. So find a suitable guru, or find a disciple and become a guru. It is my fortune that you became my disciple. That is the secret of my nirvana.'

Devanayaki had come out of her trance and was drinking milk when her chief maid, Neeli, came in looking upset.

'Kantha Madevi, I am scared. The whole city is talking ill about you.'

'That is all right. Isn't Mahinda happy?'

'He has also turned against us. Everyone says that the guru was killed for money. A meeting is being held in the central hall.'

She understood the gravity of the situation. They were fools who did not recognize the importance of nirvana.

A voice inside her murmured that she did not need to hide anything now. After being blessed by Padmasambhava, she did not need to fear anyone.

She walked towards the central hall.

By then, everyone in the city of dreams had turned against Devanayaki. Even the courtesans were voicing their displeasure in public. The chief courtesan, Sivalekha, accused Devanayaki of causing Nissanka Vajran's death by going against the rules outlined in the *Swapnajalika*. Sivalekha wanted to know why the city of dreams needed meditation and tantric practices. The majority felt that it was wrong to have statues of the Buddha in a place that sold pleasure, and they felt that it was a mistake to have invited a tantric guru to a gamblers' paradise. Many of the guests told Mahinda that they came to the city of dreams to enjoy themselves, not renounce the world. Sena and Anula used the opportunity to covertly spread rumours against Devanayaki. They exaggerated the truth and fabricated lies to spread all around the city.

When he could no longer ignore the accusations, Mahinda called a meeting. All the people in the city assembled and started speaking against Devanayaki. Sivalekha stood up first.

'Lord, all of us are here to sell pleasure and earn gold. But never before has a guest been killed here. No courtesan goes against the rules laid down by Vishakhadatta in the *Swapnajalika*. That is why the city has become popular among pleasure seekers. We do not want these secret rites that end in death.'

'That is what I too want to know. Why is the Buddha placed in a tavern, in a place where women pleasure men? The security guards saw the queen carrying the guru's dead body in her arms and walking out. The drops of blood that fell along the way can still be seen. Will anyone believe that the guru died of his own accord? If he had embraced samadhi, why is his death shrouded in mystery? Why wasn't the body given last rites?'

Mahinda sensed that things were going awry. But he did not have the courage to disturb Devanayaki's meditation and summon her to the court. As he thought about what to do, Devanayaki entered the hall. Her face was peaceful and glowing. A smile played upon her lips. People looked at the divine glow in her eyes with wonder. Everyone except those who had accused her became calm.

'Why has everyone gathered here? Is it because you saw the guru's dead body on the death rock? He attained samadhi last Friday. He entrusted me with feeding his body to the birds. His soul took the form of a white eagle and flew away. My seven-day meditation ended today. That is why I could not inform you earlier.'

Everyone looked at each other doubtfully. Mahinda too did not believe her. She explained, 'Lord, death comes to the wise sages when they will it. They discard their bodies like one discards old clothes when they become useless. Having finished the three stages of nirvana, the guru chose an appropriate time to enter samadhi through extreme joy. I doubt that the people assembled here are enlightened enough to understand all this.

'As for the accusations against me ... What has Vishakhadatta said in the *Swapnajalika*? A courtesan must obey every whim and fancy of the guest and give utmost pleasure. Though I'm not a courtesan, that is what I did. I did not hurt him physically, I merely gave him joy. It is something that tantrics have been doing for centuries.

'Now, for the question of what the Buddha is doing in Sinha Saila, this place of pleasure. Why did Mahinda and Sanghamitra come to Lanka? It was to lead the descendants of Sinhabahu, who had killed his father and married his sister, to the path of righteousness. It is an insult when gamblers and pimps like you take the name of that great man who renounced his kingdom and came here to spread love and peace. The greatness of Mahinda's name is lost when you do so.'

Mahinda trembled with rage at Devanayaki's words. Without waiting for his command, the guards tied Devanayaki to a pillar. Mahinda roared angrily, stunning all of Sinha Saila.

'You whore! How dare you speak to me about justice?'

He slapped her. Though she writhed in pain, she did not cry. The marks of his fingers were on her cheeks. At this, Sena got up feeling victorious.

'Lord, this is not all. There are other problems as well. This morning, Nakkeeran, a spy of the Chola King, came with a message for the queen. He came in after paying the entry fee. Acting on a hunch, we checked on him. We have been watching him for some time now. He comes every month and leaves after a day or two, never gambling or visiting courtesans.'

'Where is he? What is the message?'

'We have put him in the dungeon beneath the entrance. The message on the palm leaf says, "The storm is about to begin." The Chola king's tiger insignia is on the message.'

'Did you get any other information from him?'

'No. He refuses to speak in spite of being tortured. But he admitted that he had delivered such messages to the queen's maids before.'

'Is this true? You, who advised me to use the Kanthalur army to defeat the Chola king – you have been betraying me? Why have you come here? What does all this mean?'

Devanayaki knew that she was trapped. But she made no attempt to escape. She was no longer the Devanayaki who manipulated her enemies. Without losing composure, she said, 'If you had asked me this question yesterday, I wouldn't have answered, because until yesterday, I was burning for revenge against the brute who killed my daughter Kuveni. That is why I came here with a diamond-studded Buddha filled with the venom of a cobra. But it was not just my Kuveni you murdered. You killed hundreds of children and raped hundreds of women, so I didn't want to give you a punishment that would end quickly. I desired to take you prisoner when the Chola army attacked Lanka. But now my mind has no such thoughts. My guru taught me that I must counter violence with love, not more violence. Love is the only truth. It is only through love that we can make human lives joyful. Like the Buddha, like the great emperor Ashoka, Mahinda, you too should desist from violence. Try to love all the creatures of this earth.'

Though she was being held captive, there was a calm smile on Devanayaki's lips. Neither Mahinda nor anyone assembled there understood anything she said. They screamed, 'Kill her! She's a traitor!' Mahinda's sword fell upon her with lightning speed, cutting off her breasts. Blood splattered all around.

When Mahinda raised his sword again, someone stopped him. No one understood what happened after that. Gaining superhuman strength, Devanayaki towered over everyone. Placing one foot on Sigiriya and the next on Sripada, she walked across the sky. At the same moment, the Chola army surrounded Sinha Saila. Acting on information from the spies, they set fire to the black Buddhas at the entrance. Within seconds, Sinha Saila erupted with explosions. The main entrance was destroyed.

The army that climbed to the top had stronger gunpowder with them. They destroyed the palace and the maid's quarters. Hundreds of people were killed. Finally, they captured Mahinda who was trying to escape with his precious gems. The guards held him captive and brought him before Rajendra Chola. Rajendra Chola thought, 'Before returning to Thanjavur, Mahinda must be taken to Ruhuna where he has kept the Chola throne and crown. Then, like Akka has always desired, he must be put in prison until the end of his days.'

Rajendra Chola had only one question for Mahinda, 'Where is my Akka, Devanayaki?' Mahinda stood in silence, his head bowed. The spies told him everything. Rajendra was confused. Devanayaki had grown as tall as the sky. She had walked away, with one foot on Sigiriya and the next on Sripada. He was bewildered. He called Nakkeeran to find out what had really happened.

'It is true. After learning tantric rites from Nissanka Vajran, Madeviyar gained superhuman abilities. All emotions except love melted away from her. The last message that she gave me was to stop all preparations for war. If she had been the Madeviyar of yesteryear, she would have chopped his head off.'

'How can I see her?'

'I don't know, but I'm sure she will come to meet you.'

On the night that he returned from Ruhuna after retrieving the throne and the sword, Devanayaki came to Rajendra Chola's tent. She was dressed in Buddhist garb and had tonsured her head. Rajendra Chola didn't recognize her at first, but when he did, he couldn't control his feelings.

'Akka, can I place Mahinda's head at your feet?'

'My prince! Why do you behave like a small child? I am not in that frame of mind. I do not want to see blood.'

'Akka, all the lands between the Ganga and Lanka are now under the Chola empire. The construction of the capital city, Gangaikonda Cholapuram, is nearing completion. Akka, without you these victories would never have been possible.'

'No victory that is achieved by bloodshed is real victory. Real victory is won by love. Isn't that how your Akka was won?'

'Did he hurt you badly?'

'Yes, he did. But more than my body, it was my mind that was hurt. What I lost was what you adored the most. Padmasambhava returned it to me twofold. But I can only stay for this one night.'

'And then?'

'I have to return. My place is on the left of Padmasambhava's lap. Until dawn, I am your guru. How could I get a better disciple than you? Then, if I'm lucky enough, I will have another child like Kuveni.'

When Devanayaki said that, Rajendra Chola felt guilty. He took her to his tent. When he took off her saffron robes, he was surprised to see her more beautiful than ever. They became guru and disciple. She left before dawn. Before leaving, she kissed him on his forehead, saying, 'I don't think I'll be lucky this time.' Then she disappeared. Rajendra Chola rushed out to see if she had grown as tall as the sky, but he did not see anything.

In the morning, some distance from Sinha Saila, the villagers spotted a woman's corpse. As they were cannibals, they feasted on her body for three whole days.

23

Mahinda's city of dreams was devastated by the invading Chola army. Thousands of people including guests, courtesans, servants and soldiers were killed. The palace, the courtesan's quarters and the gambling halls were torched. The courtesans were the main target of the Chola army – hundreds, including Sivalekha, were tortured and killed. The Chola army descended the mountain with their loot without stopping to bury the dead. Sinha Saila was filled with vultures feeding on carcasses, and it was this Sinha Saila that Sree Vallabha Buddhanar called Susaana Supina.

On the seventh day after the war, Devanayaki appeared to Sree Vallabha Buddhanar in the evening as he was meditating in the Vihara at Tirukonamalai. He was aghast to see her bathed in blood. Thirsting for revenge, she resembled Kannaki in the *Silappadikaram*. She had the same fixity of purpose. Not wanting to scare the monk, Devanayaki assumed the form of a saffron-clad Buddhist monk. As he looked at her in bewilderment, she explained, 'Greetings, monk. I am Kanta Madevi, Devanayaki. You may know what has happened in Sinha Saila. I have come here in person since I need to repay a debt to you. Accept this pomegranate. I offer this after having cleansed my sins with blood.'

The realization that there were many ways to attain wisdom other than the one method he knew humbled him. He accepted the silver tray Devanayaki offered him. By then, Nissanka Vajran's samadhi and Devanayaki's attainment of nirvana had become a topic of discussion among the Buddhist monks. They considered it an example of the wondrous possibilities of Vajrayana. He led Devanayaki to his ashram with folded hands.

'Pardon me. Though I have strictly followed tradition, I have not been fortunate enough to attain nirvana even at the age of seventy-six. If in my ignorance I have said anything to hurt you, please forgive me.'

'Acharya, once you take the first step towards nirvana, there are no likes or dislikes, sorrows or pleasures, only ultimate joy. Even this body that you see is only a hallucination of your mind. Do you know why I came here with this pomegranate? I wanted to share the sweetness of pure love with the first monk I had ever met. These pomegranates were created when God restored my severed breasts.'

She broke the fruit in two and offered it to him. He took it with great respect and ate it. As she savoured the sweetness of divine joy, a beatific smile spread over Devanayaki's face. Buddhanar says that he saw Rupavati in that smile. Then, he starts telling the story of Rupavati from Haribatta's *Jatakamala*.

Rupavati lived in the city of Utpalavati in northern India. She was as beautiful as her name implied. This story takes place during a time when Utpalavati was reeling from drought and famine. Rupavati was born into a rich family, so she did not have to suffer. One day when she went out for a walk, she heard sounds of wailing from a house. A young woman had just given birth and, unable to control her hunger, was going to eat her newborn baby boy. Rupavati tried to dissuade her. 'This is madness. Can't you eat something else?' The woman replied, 'There is nothing else to eat in this house.' She started crying, saying that unless she ate something she would die. Rupavati knew that if she went to get something from her house, the woman would eat the baby by the time she came back. But if she took the baby with her, the woman would die by the time she returned. Either way, one life would be lost. Rupavati was in a dilemma. Then, coming to a decision, Rupavati asked the woman for a knife and she cut off her breasts and offered them as food.

The Buddha tells this story to demonstrate the value of sacrifice. Rupavati was an incarnation of the Buddha. When her husband praised Rupavati for her sacrifice, all that she had lost was restored. But Rupavati, who had gained freedom from her femininity, became a man and because the king of Utpalavati had no heir, Rupavati become the prince of the kingdom and ruled over the country for sixty years. Buddhanar said that he was happy that Devanayaki, like Rupavati, had attained freedom from material sorrows and gained wondrous powers.

Devanayaki listened to Rupavati's story with great attention. She had often wondered whether there had been a beautiful woman hidden inside the Buddha. She thought to herself, 'Unlike Rupavati, I did not donate my breasts. They were forcibly cut off.' She thought about Nissanka Vajran, who had said that just as lust had to be countered with lust, sometimes violence had to be countered with violence. Then, very gently, she reminded Buddhanar, 'I am not like Rupavati. If any woman's body or mind is wounded in Tamilakam, all this gentleness will disappear.'

'Don't think like that. As long as Rajendra Chola is on the throne, there is nothing to fear.'

'Somehow, I doubt it. In Sinha Saila, the Chola army did not win. They succumbed to violence and lust. Isn't violence always wrong, Acharya?'

'In war, sometimes...'

'At a very young age, I studied Kautilya's *Arthashastra* and other treatises on political science. Periya Koyikkan's daughter grew up listening to lessons of war and administration. None of those lessons taught me that innocent people could be murdered or that women could be raped. But the Chola and Sinhala armies always indulge in violence. No matter what level of nirvana I reach, I will not be able to tolerate violence. I will have to rush to that place where a woman's tears are shed. I will have to burn down the cities of sinners.'

Buddhanar was convinced that Devanayaki was an avatar of Kannaki. He prostrated himself at her feet. Initially, when he requested her permission to write her story, she refused saying that she was an ordinary woman. But when Buddhanar said that she had accomplished feats that no ordinary woman could, Devanayaki told him her story over three evenings. She told him to write not just what she had told him, but also to include what others had to say about her.

Sree Vallabha Buddhanar visited all the places that Devanayaki had lived in, beginning his journey from Kanthalur. He met several people. He learnt tantric rituals from the Thiruppavai onwards. As he stood in front of Sinha Saila, unable to climb the mountain, Devanayaki came from the skies and carried him in her arms to the mountaintop. By then, seven years had passed since the city of dreams had been devastated. Thousands of skeletons lay scattered all over the place, which now resembled a forest. The city of dreams had become a huge cemetery. Devanayaki built a small vihara there for Buddhanar, where he stayed and wrote her story. It took him forty-one days to complete it. He ends the work by telling us why he called Devanayaki's story the *Susaana Supina*: the cremation of dreams is the attainment of salvation – a stage when all desires that are the root of sorrow disappear from life.

It is believed that on completing the *Susaana Supina*, Buddhanar attained nirvana. The aborigines who came to hunt in Sinha Saila were the first to see it. They were cannibals, but they discarded Buddhanar's emaciated body and took only this palm-leaf script. Thinking that this work was magical, the illiterate tribe started praying to it. And in fact, many miracles began to occur in the village of Lahugala. The invasions of the occupying Sinhalese ceased, wild animals moved away respectfully, and nature began bowing to the wishes of the people. They had rains when they wanted. The sun shone when they desired. The fields were always ready for harvest. The hunters who had eaten Devanayaki's body were also of this tribe. They were considered to be the recipients of Devanayaki's special blessings, because it was to them that she had first appeared after attaining salvation. At that time, she was seething with anger at Mahinda who had cut off her breasts. She, who had destroyed the Arya Sinhala race, came to them like a goddess of revenge, and they accepted her. They believed that it was due to her power that the Chola army was able to wreak havoc on Sinha Saila. They started an annual festival in her name. Dancing in the form of Devanayaki Kolam became a part of the rituals. This Devanayaki Kolam later came to be known as Daivakolam. This ritual dance was performed only in Lahugala and some other adjacent villages near Sigiriya. Unlike in the other ritual dances in Sri Lanka, these people did not use masks. Very beautiful and healthy women assumed the guise of the goddess. They smeared coal, rice flour, lime and the flowers of the vaka tree on their faces. They wore garments made of palm leaves. There were other dancers who assumed the guise of demons, some of them wore the mask of a lion and others of kings. After several complex rituals that lasted for fourteen days, the grand finale occurred on the day of the new moon. The rituals ended at midnight when, to the rising crescendo of drums, the dancers wearing the guises of the king and the lion cut off the breasts of the goddess. This ritual was performed to protect the tribals from the Sinhalese and hence, was shrouded in great secrecy. As it was directed against the dominant Sinhalese community, it was not considered to be part of Sri Lankan tradition. In the beginning of the nineteenth century, the British banned it, calling it barbaric. But it is still performed in secret. It is believed that any woman whose breasts are cut off will attain superhuman powers, and that she will use these powers to kill the Sinhalese rulers.

Rajendra Chola thought Devanayaki was the Goddess Saraswathi and prayed to her. The centre of knowledge in Thiruvarur was named Deva Salai in her honour. Arrangements were made to teach tantric practices there. The day on which Devanayaki attained nirvana was celebrated with prayers and musical performances in Thiruvarur and Gangaikonda Cholapuram. This practice, called Devanayaki Aradhana, was conducted for centuries.

Rajendra Chola never missed any of these rituals. On the fourteenth day, he was shocked to see Devanayaki on the platform wearing anklets. The audience sat spellbound when she danced and sang her favourite song, 'Margazhi Thingal'. But it was a young girl who came down from the stage when the performance ended. That night, Devanayaki appeared in Rajendra Chola's dream. She told him, 'I am happy that you still remember me and are doing so much for me.' Hearing these words, Rajendra Chola looked around to see who had spoken. She felt pity for him and said, 'My prince, I am within you. At this stage of nirvana, I can accept anyone's body as my own.' Rajendra Chola thought that this was strange. 'Today is the last day of this phase. From tomorrow onwards, I will not be able to communicate with the people of this world. But it will take another thousand years to attain complete nirvana. Until then, my presence will be felt on this earth. During this time, it may cause divine births. Even now, there are many people in India and Sri Lanka who pray to me for favours. I will always be able to help them. I need to remind you of one thing – I will never forgive violence, no matter who commits it. You know that the Chola army doesn't have a very good reputation. Can't you, like the great emperor Ashoka, abjure wars and embrace non-violence?' He was not able to reply as Thribhuvana Madevi woke him up with a kiss.

As Devanayaki had desired, Mahinda lived for several years in prison before he succumbed to a painful death. Unfortunately, his family had to suffer the same fate. Since then, no Sinhala ruler has ruled from Anuradhapura. Though the Sinhalese, under Vijayabahu, regained control of Lanka after seventy-five years of Chola rule, they didn't dare make Anuradhapura or Sigiriya their capital. Vijayabahu ruled from Polonnaruwa which had been built by the Cholas. The Sinhalese kings were even afraid of assuming the name Mahinda. Mahinda VI, who killed Vijayabahu II at the end of the twelfth century, was able to rule only for five days. Nissanka Malla killed him and assumed power. It is believed that this Nissanka Malla was an avatar of Nissanka Vajran and that he killed Mahinda VI to avenge Devanayaki. Since then, no Sinhalese king has been named Mahinda.

After reading Devanayaki's story, Peter felt that he had travelled centuries back in time. As *Bambarayak*, unlike the magazine *Karupu*, did not carry readers' opinions, he could not read any criticism of the story. But he felt that a new world had opened before him. It was 2 a.m. but, eager to talk to Christie about this, he locked his room and went out.

24

Christie and Mary listened eagerly to the story of Devanayaki. We discussed the *Susaana Supina* until dawn. Mary liked Devanayaki. She said that it could not have been easy for a woman who lived centuries ago to think and behave the way she did. Christie was thinking about how he could use the myth in his movie. He said that, like Devanayaki's story, the lives of the women fighters in the Iyakkam exhibited the complex situation of female empowerment and misogynistic stances existing simultaneously. Mary did not agree with him at all. She felt that it was wrong to trivialize the life of a great woman like Devanayaki in this manner. Their argument hadn't ended even when I left. Christie asked me to rewrite the script of *The Woman Behind the Fall of the Tigers* to include Devanayaki's myth. I was happy because that is what I wanted to do, though I was not sure how.

When I said that I would need to go to Sigiriya, Christie joyfully agreed. Neither of them had seen Sigiriya before. Samaraveera and the colonel tried to dissuade us from travelling by road, saying that there were security problems. Samaraveera asked, 'Wouldn't it be better if you went back to Colombo and flew to Sigiriya?' But Christie insisted on driving down. He wanted to see Mullaitivu and other war memorials along the way. Samaraveera had no answer when Christie asked him how he could make a movie without seeing the places that were an integral part of the story. Reluctantly, he asked the colonel to help us with our trip. Anuradha Mendez called her friend in Sigiriya and made arrangements for our stay. I was glad to get a chance to meet the archaeologist who had evaded my mischievous questions.

The next morning, we set off in a black Mercedes Benz. Christie had insisted that the security guards not travel with us. I too felt that if they accompanied us, we would not be able to discuss anything. But the colonel had given our vehicle number to all the checkpoints en route to ensure a safe journey. Perhaps that is why our vehicle was not checked anywhere along the way. Sivapalan, a middle-aged man from Jaffna, was our chauffeur. Even while he was manoeuvring the vehicle with great difficulty on the Jaffna–Kandy A9 highway, which was in the process of being repaired, he continued to talk to me. His conversation centred on gossip about the Tamil film industry. From Rajnikant's and Kamal's new movies to the personal lives of actors, he had something to say about it all. When he heard that I had worked as Balu Mahendra's assistant, he was overjoyed. With pride, he said, 'Balu sir belongs to my country.' He wanted to know if any popular actor or director would be part of our movie. When I told him that it wasn't a commercial movie, he wanted to know what kind of film we were making. But he fell silent when he heard that the movie was about the murder of Rajini Thiranagama. His face fell.

'Why have you stopped talking, Sivapalan?'

'Because I'm scared.'

'Why do you fear Madam Rajini?'

'I'm not afraid of Madam. Doctor Madam was a nice lady. If Prabhakaran had taken her advice and become a leader of the people, the Iyakkam wouldn't have suffered this fate. But no one in Jaffna dares to speak about her murder.'

'Why?'

'Please don't ask me. Both my sons died in the freedom struggle. My only daughter was raped and killed by soldiers. They did not even leave my wife. She lost her leg in a bomb blast. I am her only support. Nobody talks about politics here. Let's talk about movies, about Ajit, Asin or Vikram. Let's leave politics alone.'

His words shocked me. I felt a deep sympathy for this man who was trying to drown his painful memories in movie trivia. Unable to continue my conversation with him, I sat silently looking out of the window. We were driving through the Elephant Pass with the sea on either side. Christie and Mary were recording the sights on their Handycams.

'Christie, we are passing through the area where decisive battles were fought by the Iyakkam.'

'I know, Peter. I have visited the places around Mullaitivu twice. I insisted on this journey for Mary's sake.'

'That's right. The person who is going to handle the camera must see these places.'

'Such wonderful landscapes! Perfect frames from every angle. This is great. But I'm fed up, Peter. There are war museums and war memorials everywhere, and ghoulish tourists gaping happily at them.'

'This is the time for war tourism in Sri Lanka. Hundreds of tourist buses come to Jaffna every day from the south. The word "war" has assumed the status of dignity in the Sinhalese community. Nobody talks of peace or democracy. That's why Rajini and what she stood for has become relevant.'

'But nobody here realizes it.'

'Well, there is a small group that does understand such matters. There are Sinhalese, Tamils and Muslims among them. I'm not talking only about intellectuals. Even among ordinary people, there are those who think differently. Our movie may become an inspiration for them.'

'But Peter, I don't understand how you can link Rajini's life with Devanayaki's myth in the way that Christie wants you to.'

'I'll tell you my idea. We can use the ritual performance at Lahugala. The *Susaana Supina* does say that if the mind or body of any woman is hurt, she will take divine birth.'

'That's not a bad idea. Christie, we can portray the scene where Devanayaki walks, towering above Lanka with one foot on Sigiriya and the other on Sripada, with the help of graphics.'

'Sorry, no graphics. I insist on making movies that are 100 per cent realistic.'

'Then what can we do? Peter, do you have any other ideas?'

'Devanayaki's story itself is unrealistic. I feel that most of it is Sree Vallabha Buddhanar's imagination. If we use that story, then how can we make realistic cinema? But I feel there is the possibility of exploring meta-reality.'

Immersed in these discussions, we did not realize how time flew. When we reached the city of Paranthan, the car turned from A9 to A35 towards Mullaitivu. At around 11.30, we arrived in Pudukuduirippu. My heart beat faster when we reached the place which had witnessed the last battle. Though I had several opportunities to come here after May 2001, when the freedom movement ended, I avoided it. There was an unknown fear in my mind. I could sense VP's presence here. Perhaps because they had no close ties with the Iyakkam, Christie and Mary were unperturbed. They were joking and laughing as they got out. I saw Sivapalan's eyes fill with tears. He did not get out of the car. I felt that this place too was a Susaana Supina – a burial ground where the dreams of an entire society were interred.

Major Pinto of the Sri Lankan army was waiting for us. He took us to the military camps. After meeting the senior officials there, we had lunch and went to visit the war memorials. Naturally, we went to VP's bunker first. It was built in the middle of several small bunkers in an extremely secure place. From outside, it looked like a single-storeyed building. But it was a four-storeyed building built forty feet deep, and it had served as the administrative centre of the Iyakkam. The bunker still showed signs of having been an extremely secure construction with many amenities. Mary was recording it all on her camera. In the operation rooms, we could see the stands on which maps would be placed when strategies were being planned. When Mary asked me, 'Isn't it here that VP would have taken many tough decisions,' I was shocked by the thought. It must have been the place where the decision to kill many people, like Rajiv Gandhi, Premadasa and Rajini Thiranagama, had been taken. But Major Pinto told us that all important decisions need not necessarily have been taken here as the Iyakkam had many such centres. The dimly lit room did not have much air. I felt suffocated and wanted to get out.

Our main purpose was to visit Sigiriya, so we did not spend much time here. The war museum displayed several weapons used by the Iyakkam. As in Divine Pearl, the military officers here also explained how they were used. The steel cage used to torture rebels in the Iyakkam looked horrifying. It had just enough space for one person, and was filled with sharp thorns. If the person inside moved, the thorns would wound him. This was the symbol of the Iyakkam. Unless one was extremely careful, anyone connected to the Iyakkam would be wounded mentally or physically. The destroyed tanks and abandoned vehicles seemed like absurdist art installations. The place where suicide boats and submarines were manufactured was similar. The pool made to train the Sea Tigers was the biggest in Sri Lanka, said the military officer. When the Jordanian ship, MV Farha III, had dropped anchor near Mullaitivu due to some mechanical fault, the Iyakkam captured it. They used its parts to make tanks and other weapons. It is said that they got fourteen thousand tonnes of food-grain from the ship. We saw their jail, which had more than sixty cells. But what remained etched in our minds were the words inscribed on the wall of the house that belonged to Soosai, the chief of the Sea Tigers:

'Our enemies are our best teachers.'

We left Mullaitivu in the evening and reached Sigiriya late at night. Perhaps we were fatigued by the journey, or drained emotionally by the sight of the war memorials, but none of us spoke much. Mary switched her camera off and dozed. Sivapalan drove carefully without disturbing our sleep. Though the road to Sigiriya was as well maintained as the A9 to Dambulla, we were delayed by traffic blocks and intermittent rain. I thought that the forests described in the *Susaana Supina* must have now become thickly populated urban spaces. We checked in at a hotel in Sigiriya at 11 p.m. and within minutes, I received the expected phone call. She said, 'I'm the archaeologist.' I felt quite happy. 'I waited at the hotel until eight for you people. When I heard that you would be arriving late, I decided to put off our meeting until tomorrow. You must have explored Mullaitivu very thoroughly. Was your journey comfortable?'

'Actually, we couldn't. But that disappointment has passed, now that I've heard your voice.'

'But we have never met.'

'Anuradha told me that heard melodies are sweet, but those unheard are sweeter.'

I felt that the archaeologist was confused. I disconnected, saying that we could meet the next day. But she rang back immediately. 'Don't forget to look at Sigiriya from the west, as the sun rises. It's a beautiful sight.'

As I sat on the balcony after a bath and dinner, I saw Sigiriya dimly lit by stars. It was a new-moon night. At midnight, I sent a text message to the archaeologist: 'Why are you not responding to my mails?' Her reply was immediate: 'Though the Lion is dead, his spirit still guards me.'

The journey had tired me out, and I fell into a deep sleep. I saw a dream that night after a long time.

Devanayaki from the *Susaana Supina* came to me, alighting from a white horse. She was dressed like a celestial nymph from Kambuja. She spoke to me as if she had known me for a long time. The first question she asked me was, 'Have you come to see my palace?'

I don't know what my reply was, but she took my right hand and kissed it. Then she pulled me onto the horse and rode up the steep mountain. I shook in fear when I saw that the horse was walking straight up the vertical rock face. Within seconds, we reached the top. She jumped off the horse, pulling me along with her. The horse suddenly disappeared. Sinha Saila still had the old gambling halls and courtesan's quarters. There were gamblers and beautiful women wherever we looked. Everyone was bowing respectfully to me and Devanayaki. Finally, we reached the main hall. Padmasambhava mandalas still adorned the walls. The lamps were lit and a map of Sri Lanka was drawn on the floor. Devanayaki came in after changing her clothes. Everything was arranged for tantric rituals. It was only then that I remembered I had been her disciple, learning these rituals for many days.

I woke up when I heard someone shouting, 'Stop, or you will meet Nissanka Vajran's fate!' Although I knew that it was all a dream, I could not go back to sleep. I finally fell asleep at dawn and missed the sunrise. The archaeologist came at eight to take us to Sigiriya. My hopes weren't misplaced. She was more beautiful than Anuradha. She wore a light blue Kandyan sari and blouse. During our journey, she gave us the official history of Sigiriya. We reached the top at around ten. Mary and Christie, now convinced that I had not been exaggerating about the scenic beauty of the place, started taking pictures.

25

Though the archaeologist had told me that she wanted to speak to me in private, it was only after a week that we got the opportunity to talk, as I was busy revising the script. We used to climb atop Sigiriya and spend the day discussing ideas and stretching our imaginations to the limit.

On the third day, we went to Lahugala in the evening to try and get some more information about the Devanayaki Kolam. It was there that the archaeologist had found the *Susaana Supina*. But the people there did not know anything about these rituals. A couple of old people said that some rituals were conducted here three or four generations ago.

After considering hundreds of options, Christie came to a decision on the afternoon of the fourth day. When I rewrote the script, intertwining the myth of Devanayaki with the murder of Rajini Thiranagama, albeit without any evidence to back it up, it became the story of every woman in Sri Lanka. They started resembling Devanayaki in her myriad moods. While Rajini countered violence with the message of peace, many other women were burning with the fire of revenge. Revenge against anyone who hurt the mind or body of a woman. The emotions of love, lust, sympathy, peace and revenge were all mixed up in it. My script attained a new dimension as it dealt with events that were believed to have happened centuries ago. The archaeologist's contribution to the new script was not negligible. She had to bear the brunt of our creative frenzy. It was because of her help that all our crazy desires – from my wanting to climb Sigiriya at midnight, to Christie's wish to fly over it in a helicopter – were easily achieved.

We became close during that time. Though we did not speak much, both of us felt that we could not stay away from each other for any length of time. Christie threw a party the night we completed the script. Naturally, the archaeologist was our chief guest. The party on the lawns of the hotel ended at midnight. Christie praised everyone to the skies, with special mention reserved for the archaeologist. Christie and I got drunk that night, but Mary merely sipped at her wine. The archaeologist drank only fruit juice. She wore a yellow sari and a sleeveless blouse. Like other Sinhalese women, she was a bit plump. I found the way she looked at me with her large eyes alluring. It was she who took me to my room after the party, as I was staggering. Mary smiled at me knowingly. I don't remember what happened afterwards. Did we speak?

Next morning, she groggily said, 'Good morning, Peter,' and went back to sleep. I realized then that I still did not know her name. So far, I had only addressed her as either 'archaeologist' or 'madam'. When we were having coffee after a bath, she told me her name without my asking. 'Now I will tell you what I wanted to say. You didn't have time for conversation last night. I am Devanayaki.' I was taken aback, and seeing that I was shocked, she paused. But I was able to regain my composure quickly.

'Were you sipping your fruit juice and waiting for the party to end?'

'You have been starving for a long time. Anuradha told me to offer you a feast.'

'I am not the only one who was starving.'

'Let's not argue about that. I'm Devanayaki, but unlike your friend, I'm not Andal Devanayaki. My grandmother called me Devanayaki. The women in my mother's house traditionally assumed this name. But my parents did not think it enough and named me Juliet D'Souza. Anyway, it is of other things that I wish to speak to you.

'Over the past few years, a group called Save Sri Lanka from Fascism, or SSF, has been gaining strength. After my son died last year, I joined them. It started as an online group on Facebook. As the political atmosphere is against us, all our operations are shrouded in secrecy. We create fake profiles to carry on our activities. Identities are created using historic icons. Iyakkam is referred to as the war in which Stalin was defeated by Hitler. We resist both Stalin who was killed and Hitler who killed.

'But I don't think this group is organized, or that it has any sort of leadership. Most of the active members are young. Their aim is to free this country from the fascist government and president. At the same time, they want to resist the return of the Iyakkam which is also fascist in nature. It is similar to the people's movement in Tunisia and Egypt. In Egypt, the struggle was against Hosseini Mubarak who was called the common enemy. Unfortunately, here we are up against two enemies. This country is caught not between the devil and the deep blue sea, but between two devils. Can you help us in our activities?'

'What exactly do you expect me to do, Juliet?'

'You artists would know better how art can be used to combat fascism. It would be nice if you could tell the government that you require my help until this movie is completed. Then I can be relieved from the burden of official duties.'

'I'll be happy to do it on one condition: your services will be required full time.'

'Of course. Juliet will be to Peter what Mary is to Christie.'

'But I doubt whether I can become Romeo.'

Juliet rose and came to me joyfully. Though I couldn't meet Andal Devanayaki, I was happy to have met another Devanayaki. She leaned on my shoulder like a weary traveller who had found her destination after years of wandering. I told her the story of my life. When I spoke about my mother, my eyes welled up with tears.

At breakfast, I spoke to Christie about Juliet. Both of them were happy. Christie immediately called Samaraveera. He was relieved to know that the script was complete and that we planned to start filming next month. Within hours, we received a fax permitting Juliet to work in our team until the movie was done. From then on, Juliet started living with me.

Meanwhile, far away in a slum in Colombo's Slave Island suburb, a group of young men were meeting in a dilapidated building. There were Tamils, Sinhalese and Muslims among them. When the doors and windows were closed and the room was lit only by a dim LED lamp, Gayathri Perera began speaking in a low voice.

'We are meeting today to discuss very important matters. Our biggest problem is to find a way to take SSF from Facebook campaigns to real activism. SSF has more than four hundred branches in this country, and a thousand-plus branches in Britain, Canada, Australia and Europe. For the first time in the history of Sri Lanka, the youth are coming together for the sake of democracy and freedom of expression, without caring about their Sinhalese, Tamil or Muslim identities. Fortunately, nowadays such movements are able to create an impact on society. The democratic movements that recently occurred in Tunisia, Egypt and Libya are examples. We saw the common people wresting power from dictators who had ruled for twenty or thirty years. In India too such movements are gathering momentum. But the situation in our country is different. In Egypt, Mubarak had to step down after a period of emergency that had lasted for thirty years. Gaddafi's rule in Libya had lasted longer than that. The people there agitated as they were fed up of misgovernance.

'The Sri Lankan situation is a far cry from this. The President, who emerged victorious in the twenty-five year struggle launched by the Iyakkam, enjoys the support of the masses. Most of the Sinhalese, even the youth, are in his favour. The Buddhist monks and Buddhist organizations see him as their saviour. A major faction of the army also supports him. The corporations love him. He is a close companion of the casino owners. Countries like Israel and China are extremely generous to him, as they want to safeguard their own interests. The anger that the peace-loving commoners have towards the inhuman practices of the Iyakkam is another reason for the support he enjoys. We must accept the reality that, unlike Mubarak or Gaddafi, the president is not hated by the people.

'Then why are we agitating against him? The answer is clear. He is the cleverest dictator in history. Behind his shining white clothes and wide smile, the fangs and claws of fascism are discernible. Voices of resistance and disagreement are manipulated into silence. Freedom of expression and creativity is completely denied. Honest journalism has become impossible. Many journalists, like Lasantha Wickrematunge, have been murdered in the past few years. He is also one of the worst war criminals in history. He is solely responsible for the murder of hundreds of innocent people. His actions left many destitute during the freedom movement. Though the international community criticized him, he justifies his stand by saying that it is an internal issue. He murdered his brother, sister-in-law and their children because they had wanted their share in the family property. He is an elder brother who will justify this act by saying that it is an internal issue. The fact that his younger brother was a stubborn ne'er-do-well was not reason enough to rape his sister-in-law and murder their children. The administration of the entire country is controlled by the president and a handful of his close relatives. Thirty-nine of his relatives occupy key posts, like Gota in military and urban development, and Basil in finance. The people in Slave Island who are being evacuated understand the deep connection between the military and the urban development ministry. During the freedom movement, Gota had complete control over the military. It is said that it was he – a former soldier – who gave orders to eradicate the leadership of the Iyakkam. The government has become imbalanced due to great victories. Things have reached a stage where the chief justice of the supreme court is facing impeachment. Justice Shirani Bandaranayake's crime was that she ruled against the government's decision to allow the urban development ministry the right to acquire any piece of land that it wanted. We also witnessed the military chief, General Fonseka, being thrown into prison when he turned against the president's decisions in the war against the Iyakkam.

'The government's policies on education and culture run parallel to this. Everything is planned meticulously. Great efforts are underway to rewrite history. Feeling that the great race myth is not strong enough, he uses his stooges in the archaeological department to fabricate history. The government is manipulating our art, music and cinema to achieve these ends. The prime example is this movie on Rajini Thiranagama called *The Woman Behind the Fall of the Tigers* that is being co-produced by the government. The president and his followers, who did not value any of the ideas put forward by Rajini, are now using her story to criticize the Iyakkam.

'We should realize that our country is heading towards a great disaster: the disaster of fascism. The fight for freedom was, in fact, a fight between two fascist groups. The only difference is that the fascist with more power and the authority of the state won. The victorious fascist becomes more dangerous than the defeated one when he gets the support of the majority. There might be those who think that democracy is the will of the majority. It is here that history shows us the truth. Hitler's Nazi party won the elections in Germany with a thumping majority. Ben Ali in Tunisia and Mubarak in Egypt garnered more than 90 per cent of the votes. There are also allegations that these statistics are fabricated. Whatever the case, it is our duty to correct the majority if they are on the wrong path. It is our responsibility.

'Though the country is facing such grave problems, SSF cannot act with impunity. If we criticize the president, we will be labelled supporters of the Iyakkam or JVP. It will be followed by arrests and murders. Our first challenge is to convince the people that SSF doesn't belong to any existing power structure. The best way to do that is to intensify our campaigns on Facebook. We also have to find the strength and courage to resist any sort of attack. In any case, we have to prepare ourselves for a mass movement against the government. We have seen how the Indian public took to the streets protesting against the rape of a young girl in Delhi. Such mass uprisings should happen in Colombo as well.

'We have an opportunity before us now. The next Commonwealth Summit will be held in Colombo in November. The president sees this as a chance to earn the approval of the international community. But we have decided to use this opportunity to react against fascism. Nearly ten thousand young men and women from different parts of Sri Lanka are with us. More than double this number are offering their support from foreign countries. Most of our supporters are based in Britain, Canada and Australia. The British prime minister is with us to a certain extent. Each of you must put forward your ideas to make this venture a success. I hope that will happen in today's discussion.'

For some time after Gayathri's speech, a silence descended upon the gathering. Though long discussions followed, nobody had any new ideas. The gathering began to disperse after deciding to hold another meeting a few days later.

Then Peer Mohammed, who had been sitting silently in the back row, stood up. 'If you don't mind, I have something to say.' Everyone listened eagerly. 'I feel that the greatest problem of our age is that Sri Lankan nationalism has sunk to unprecedented depths. The president's fascism is a part of this. The president is led not by Buddhist principles but by the fundamentalist ideologies of Dharmapala. Having repressed the Tamil Hindus, they have now turned against the Muslims. The activities of the Bodu Bala Sena prove this.'

Realizing that this was a new perspective, everyone sat up. When Gayathri intervened, asking, 'Have you forgotten being driven out of Jaffna when the Iyakkam was at its zenith?' Peer Mohammed replied:

'I can never forget it. I spoke about the BBS because I fear that this tragedy will recur in a different form in Colombo. It was when the activities of the Iyakkam drifted away from leftist ideology and moved towards Hindu fascism that they turned against the Muslims. If Sinhala fascism gains strength, their prime target will also be the Muslims. Karikalan, the leader of the Iyakkam in the eastern region, began the attacks. They turned against the Muslims in Jaffna after having driven away the Muslims in Batticaloa, Kilinochchi and Mullaitivu.

'I was then a student in the Osmania College. Most of the Muslim students in Jaffna studied there. Though it was called the Osmania College, it was really a higher secondary school with nearly 1,800 students. On 30 October 1990, the Iyakkam made an announcement asking all Muslims to gather in the college grounds at twelve noon. They went to streets where large Muslim populations lived and made this announcement on loudspeakers. As they knew and feared the way the Iyakkam functioned, everyone assembled on time. Anjaneyar, the Jaffna leader, addressed us. He angrily said that Muslims are traitors and that they act as informers for the government, that they tell tales of the activities of the Iyakkam when they travel to Colombo on business. "Therefore," he said, "for the safety of the Tamils in Jaffna, all Muslims must leave within two hours." When my father and a few young men questioned this decision, Anjaneyar fired a shot in the air and shouted that stern measures would be taken against those who refused to leave.

'As they were about to shoot my father and two others, everyone shouted, "Don't kill them. We will leave." Then they made us stand in line and robbed us of the valuables we had. They let us take only a pair of clothes and a hundred and fifty rupees with us. Then they looted our houses. The children of the Iyakkam activists sold our possessions in the market. The female freedom fighters did not have the patience to remove the gold ornaments from our women and they tore the jewellery off their bodies. My mother led me and my sister home with bleeding ears as they had forcefully taken her earrings. Nearly nine thousand Muslims left Jaffna that day. My grandmother died during the journey. My father worked at many jobs in Java Street in Colombo to take care of us. None of us have ever returned to Jaffna.'

Peer was openly weeping by the time he finished.

26

After we came back from Sigiriya, we got extremely busy. Tony Bernard had set up a temporary office of Transnational Pictures in Colombo. Christie's assistants from abroad had already started work on our project. In the following days, I came to realize how complex the process of making a Hollywood movie is. Their way of film-making was nothing like what I had been taught at the Film Institute. Juliet's presence was a great comfort. She helped answer the crew's questions about Sri Lankan culture and history. Each scene was finalized after in-depth discussions on the type of clothes worn by the people of Sri Lanka, their eating habits, their languages, and even the differences in the body language of the Tamils and the Sinhalese. The costume designer, Ursula Anderson, and the art director, Jan Lee, constantly came up with new questions. The director and scriptwriter were bound to answer their queries.

The casting director, David Smith, had shortlisted about a dozen artists for each role. The auditions were held at Hilton Hotel, so Christie and Mary had to be there often. Famous Sri Lankan actresses were considered for the roles of Rajini Thiranagama and Devanayaki. But a Khmer actress and a few Hollywood actresses were also in the running. The greatest challenge David faced was that no famous actor wanted to play VP. Though Christie wanted me to play myself in the movie, I refused. I wasn't sure if I could act out all that I had experienced.

Samaraveera had arranged a luxurious villa for us in Colombo Cinnamon Gardens, opposite Victoria Park. It had four air-conditioned bedrooms and other amenities. Christie was on the first floor with Mary, and Juliet and I occupied the second floor. A beautiful garden, a swimming pool on the terrace and respectful servants – life was comfortable. The star of the villa was Thambaiya, the chef. We enjoyed his cooking and did not even think of eating out. Two apartments were arranged for junior assistants, while the main assistants were with us at the villa.

Juliet and I enjoyed our honeymoon undisturbed. It was for the first time that I was experiencing the close company of a woman. Sugandhi and I had never stayed together, and women like Manju were merely a fleeting presence in my life. I realized that there was a happiness that lay beyond physical pleasure. Juliet's presence energized me mentally and physically. Her smile, her naughty glances and endearments, her touch – everything became dear to me. Though she was only a couple of years younger than me, she behaved like a girl.

Once, when she emerged dripping from the pool, I teased her, 'You should have taken part in the Miss Lanka beauty pageant when you were young.'

She laughed and said, 'This country became a killing field because of the actions of the husband of a former Miss Lanka.' I understood without needing any further explanation. 'Peter, as in any other culture, beauty is a curse for Sri Lankan women too. If she hadn't been beautiful, would the lion have kidnapped Suppadevi?'

I thought it a joke. Can lions have aesthetic sensibilities? After she came back wearing a sarong, she said, 'It is women who are most affected by dictatorship and fascism. It is the idea of power, not beauty, that influences dictators. The feeling that all beauty must submit to them is born out of this. It is said that the chief justice was impeached for being more beautiful than Miss Lanka. My beauty was the reason for my troubles. But I've decided to forget the past. After meeting you, I realized that life is to be celebrated.'

As we were going downstairs, Mary and Christie were coming up. 'Oh! Aunt Julia and the scriptwriter,' said Mary. Juliet and I enjoyed the joke as we loved Llosa's novel.

When Juliet started living with me, my life became more organized. She kept our room meticulously clean. She had a strict routine too. Work until five and then live, that was her style. It wasn't difficult, because Christie and Mary felt the same way. Though I tried telling her that writers and film-makers couldn't function like office workers, she ignored me. Her unwritten rule was that I spend all my time with her after sunset. Juliet enjoyed sitting on the balcony and talking to me while sipping whiskey.

She would tell me incidents from her life. She would also try to find out more about me. When I thought we knew each other very well, I asked her, 'What happened to your son?'

'I don't want to speak about it. Why should I think about painful things?'

'Sorry, you don't have to talk about it.'

'No. I will tell you. You must know the truth. Though I hated the Lion, I loved my son. His men kidnapped him from school when he was only three-and-a-half years old. I found his body on the beach in Colombo the next day. Later, I came to know that he was killed because it was feared that, one day, he would ask for his share in the Lion's vast property. Peter, I want a baby.'

'Do you?' I reflexively asked. She looked into my eyes. I could see the plea in hers. I couldn't control myself. I pulled her close and kissed her on the forehead. She understood that the kiss conveyed my consent. I don't know how long she remained in my arms. She was weeping and the words, 'thank you, thank you,' could be heard between her sobs.

It was dawn when I drifted into sleep. Then Manju called.

'Are you in Colombo?'

'Yes.'

'I got here yesterday. It's a new assignment. This time, I'll be here for a while.'

'What is this assignment?'

'You remember that I am now considered to be the lucky charm of gamblers, don't you? Have you heard of James Packer? The Bill Gates of the casino industry? Don't you know Kerry Packer, the Australian who invented one-day cricket matches? His son. A billionaire. The head of the casino group, Crown Resorts. He is planning to open a casino in Colombo. A thirty-six storey building, with four hundred and fifty rooms – Crown

Colombo. His partner here is the Lankan casino king, Ravi Wijeratne. Ravi is a good friend of mine. Ignoring the protests of the Buddhist monks, the president has given his clearance for the project. Fortunately, like other gamblers, Ravi too believes that I'm a lucky charm. I've been appointed the project coordinator in Colombo. Right now, I've nothing much to do. My brief is to influence the government in case any problems arise. My salary is huge, so I won't need to steal from you the next time I leave your bed in the morning. I live in a posh apartment in Park Tower.'

'Congrats, Manju! But sorry, there is no vacancy here.'

'What happened? Did you meet Devanayaki.'

'No. But I have a friend, Juliet, with me. She's an archaeologist in the government service. She is working with me on the movie. Anyway, you are in Colombo – let's meet.'

'Sure. If you give me a night or two, will Juliet get angry?'

'Not at all. We have a working arrangement.'

She laughed. 'Good luck. I'm busy this week. My boss is arriving, and I have to prepare his keynote address for the Commonwealth Summit. Let's meet next week. I'm throwing a party.'

'You are smart. You've really got Packer's key.'

'Well, I'm not a great artist like you. The government won't treat me as its guest.'

'All the best. And don't forget to demand sweat equity once the project is launched.'

'Absolutely. But these Buddhists are a problem. The boss has asked us to target the new generation of the president's family. Their weakness for Malayali women is well known.'

'Be careful. Someone from that generation might snap you up.'

'I wish they would. It would solve all our problems.'

She was laughing as she disconnected. Juliet was not able to understand our conversation in Malayalam, but she got the drift and looked at me accusingly.

'My friend, Manju Gopal. She has joined as a project coordinator in James Packer's casino project. I think Packer has appointed her to target the Indian middle-class who frequent casinos.'

'Are you friendly with the casino groups?'

'She is a failed actress. She only manages to survive with the help of these people.'

'Oh, what an escape route!' she said sarcastically and turned over to her side. I could see her face reflected in the mirror. Though she feigned anger, her eyes shone with happiness. I knew her anger would dissolve if I tickled her – once she started giggling, she couldn't stop. So that's what I did.

Soon, she was no longer angry, but she had a question for me.

'I felt jealous when you were talking to her. What did you mean by working arrangement?'

'What else could I say?'

'If you don't want to say, "she is my wife," at least you could say that we are living together.'

'I'm sorry, Juliet. I'll do that.'

'Thanks, my dear.'

She took my hand and placed it on her breast.

'We have to meet a friend this evening. She lives outside the city. So we will return only in the morning. Please tell Christie.'

'That's not a problem. We can come back early tomorrow.'

We left before it got dark. Because she knew the place, Juliet drove us there. Her friend lived in Gampaha, a small town nearly twenty-eight kilometres from the city. After leaving behind the city's traffic, we reached there in an hour.

She kept the identity of her friend a secret until we reached our destination. It was Gayathri Perera's house. A secret meeting of SSF was to be held there. They had begun the meeting in Gayathri's living room. Only women were present. A middle-aged woman, Kausuma Bandaranayake, was speaking when we entered. I later came to know that she was the secretary of the association, Sri Lankan War Widows. We sat silently, listening to her.

'Sri Lankan War Widows is a large organization. It is not only war widows who are with us now. The partners of terrorists who were killed are also part of the organization. The number of widows among civilians is far greater. There are more than one lakh war widows in Sri Lanka. Most of them are with us. All of them want to take revenge on the people who pushed them into their present condition. That is why we decided to join hands with the SSF. If you plan a protest at the Commonwealth Summit, we will join you.'

'Akka, our protest will not be sloganeering or marches. Though we have supporters from all over the world, we cannot organize a protest march in Colombo.'

'Why?'

'In spite of having committed genocide and suppressed freedom of expression, the president enjoys the support of the majority. Fascism does not merely affect an individual but a major chunk of society. So we have to be cautious or lives will be lost.'

Everyone fell silent. It was then that Gayathri noticed us. She introduced us to the gathering. Heated debates followed, and though no one had any clear-cut ideas, their determination surprised me. The meeting was followed by dinner, after which all the visitors left. When Gayathri had Juliet to herself, she asked, 'Juliet, what has happened to you?'

'Peter loves me. We are living together, that's all.'

'I'm not concerned about whom you sleep with. But this man makes movies by taking money from Rajapaksa. How can you collaborate on such a project?'

'Do you think I will take such a step for no reason?'

'What do you mean?'

'I want access to Temple Trees.'

Gayathri did not ask any more questions. We discussed a lot of other matters and engaged in heated debates. Finally, we started talking about the *Susaana Supina*.

'Peter, did you read the story in *Bambarayak*?'

'I did, but I felt that some parts were written too hurriedly.'

'Don't you want to meet its author, Meenakshi Rajarathinam?'

'Sure.'

'She is in Canada. We are Skyping at ten tonight.'

27

Like me, Juliet and Gayathri too were seeing Meenakshi for the first time. We were all anxious and shared what we knew about her, while we waited for the clock to strike ten. Gayathri spoke first, introducing us to Meenakshi.

'Meenakshi started the SSF movement. In 2009, the freedom struggle ended, and in August, Meenakshi's first post appeared on Facebook. It was titled "Black Widow". It was a cartoon depicting a cruelly raped half-naked woman called Sri Lanka and a victorious president in military uniform who stood with one leg on her chest. The caption below it said, "Don't you feel ashamed?" Her post went viral. It set off lengthy discussions amongst the activists in Lanka. But I found it hard to believe that the post was by a woman. I thought it must have been posted by a member of the Iyakkam. But I too participated eagerly in the discussions. Many people, including me, said that if this organization was anything like the Chechen Black Widows, we were against it.

'But later posts revealed that this group was different. The fact that Rajini Thiranagama, who critiqued the Iyakkam, the Lankan military and the Indian Peace Keeping Force, was repeatedly quoted in the blog proved that our suspicions were unfounded. It was decided to observe International Widows Day on 23 June 2010. That was when I received the first mail from Meenakshi. She said that the profile "Sri Lankan War Widows" had been created by her, and that she wished to observe this day in Sri Lanka too. She said that she wouldn't be here in person as she lived in Toronto. We made arrangements to observe International Widows Day in Sri Lanka as well. We called the meeting "Sri Lankan War Widows Day". Citing the name as problematic, the government refused us permission. But the truth was that the intelligence wing had sent a report saying that we were a group which always criticized the president. Another group that had the government's support observed Widows Day.

'It was during online discussions the same night that SSF was formed. It was a strong campaign. The discussion on war widows quickly moved on to other topics. The historical, racial, political and cultural aspects of war were debated upon. Those discussions helped us understand the fascist tendencies of the government and made us realize that it was our responsibility to act against it. Within a year, we had more than a hundred thousand followers. Meenakshi established a connection with each one of them by sending personal emails. But she never revealed her identity. We only knew her by her Gmail address: sww@gmail.com. But last week, I received an email that was quite personal in nature.'

Unable to contain my curiosity, I asked, 'What did the email say?'

'She introduced herself as a writer called Meenakshi Rajarathinam. Then she said, "I'm worried, Gayathri, by the trust and hope that the members of SSF have in me. I've never revealed my identity or anything else about myself. But you should know, because I feel that you will be able to lead this movement as I have some important personal matters to attend to." I expressed my desire to meet her in person. Initially, she was reluctant. But yesterday, she agreed to meet online.'

'Is this the Meenakshi Rajarathinam who wrote the story of Devanayaki?'

'Must be. Once, there was a post on SSF saying that Meenakshi Rajarathinam's story about Devanayaki attempts to read Sri Lankan history from a different perspective.'

'But in *Bambarayak*, Meenakshi says that an archaeologist started reading the *Susaana Supina*. Has anything like that happened, Juliet?'

'Yes. Three or four years after the *Susaana Supina* was discovered, a young lady with a pronounced British accent came looking for me. I helped her. But no one came asking for that book afterwards. When the *Susaana Supina* was published on the *Bambarayak* website, the government took the copy to Colombo. I feel that the book might have been destroyed. They were not able to take any action against *Bambarayak* as it was published from abroad.'

'Juliet, was the young woman who met you Meenakshi Rajarathinam?'

'I'm not sure. She gave me some other name. She told me that she was a Keralite who was doing research at some university.'

We were confused. Meenakshi came on Skype at ten. She was in a dark room. She had covered half her face with a veil. We could only see her eyes and forehead. I thought her eyes looked familiar. Her low voice could be heard.

'Gayathri, this is a video recording. I am not in a situation where I can meet you personally. All the posts that have appeared in my name on Facebook and Twitter, the emails from me, everything was written by two girls called Arulmozhi Nangai and Yamuna Sridhar. They are singers who are part of the band SAD in Canada. I've written songs for them. They drew the cartoon for the first post by SSF. I only gave them the caption. As I don't have the use of my hands, I'm dependent on them. They type out my poems, stories and songs. It's been going on for three years now. Even this conversation was recorded by them. I agreed to this because Arulmozhi Nangai wants to record my life story in my own voice.

'I can sense your surprise at my appearance and my faltering voice. You might wonder if it is the same person who posts fiery messages. Yes, it is me. My face was disfigured by acid. My arms end at my elbows. In 2009, I was captured by the Sri Lankan military in Mullaitivu after the last battle, along with Isaipriya. As I was beautiful, they wanted to present me to the VIPs. So they took me to Colombo in a military boat. My husband, Major Stalin, had been killed just three days earlier in an encounter with the Sri Lankan navy. Stalin was a Sea Tiger under the command of Soosai. I don't know what happened to my three-year-old daughter, Kadalpura.

'I was repeatedly raped for three days in a secret room near Temple Trees. It was on my body that the high-ups in the government celebrated their victory over the freedom fighters. My cries were drowned in their roars of victory. When they realized I was exhausted, they took me in a military truck to Divine Pearl. I was confined there for another three weeks. As I was fairer than the other Tamil women fighters, the military leaders were greedy for my body. This body that you see now is my punishment for trying to escape from the high security area they had put me in. I was trying to escape at midnight, wearing a guard's uniform, when I was caught. The next day, I was questioned for three hours in the prayer room. It was rape using modern instruments. Unable to bear the pain, I confessed. When I admitted my guilt, the military chief ordered my hands to be cut off and my face disfigured with acid.

'The next morning, the first step of the punishment was carried out. They woke me up before dawn and led me to a room equipped for torture. Officer Robert Jayawardene warned me, "If you lie still, only your beauty will be harmed. We will merely brush your face with diluted acid. But if you struggle, the acid will burn your whole body." He had raped me two or three times before. But when he saw me, he wanted to kiss me before the torture began. "Let the last kiss you receive be mine," he said.

'He took a crystal bowl filled with acid. With the meticulous care of a beautician, he dipped the brush in acid and touched my left hand with it. I screamed with pain. "No, no, I won't hurt you," saying this, he came and sat by me, stroking my hair. "My beauty! I will save you from this punishment." I looked at him expectantly. "You must agree to rehabilitation." I nodded. To be honest, I was ready to do it. "Good. But to be worthy of it, you must do four things. You must speak to the media in support of the government's humanitarian operations. You must openly speak against VP and the Iyakkam. You must praise the president specifically, and commend his administrative skills. You must say that Mahinda's ideas are the only way through which Sri Lanka can achieve development. If you agree to all this, I will stop the punishment right now. Female Tigers stronger than you have escaped by agreeing to these demands. Now, most of them are docile wives to Sinhalese men. Isn't that more than enough for you women? You will be given a good job in Karuna Amman's department. You will be married off to a Sinhalese soldier. You can live peacefully."

'I was so furious that I wanted to slap him. But since I couldn't move, I spat on his face. "Mahinda's ideas, his..." The worst expletives flowed from my tongue. Surprisingly, Robert was unperturbed. He wiped his face and took up the brush again.

'I cannot forget the moment he painted my right cheek with acid. I felt that my face had caught fire. When I cried out, he taped my lips shut. The room was filled with the stench of burning flesh. I writhed in pain and every movement caused the acid to trickle down. Then he started brushing my left cheek with acid. Did it even cross his mind that he was destroying the same face he had once caressed? Not just him, many others had fondled these cheeks. From politicians to ordinary soldiers – they were all people I hated. I even hated Stalin, my husband. I had to marry him and bear his child as part of the Iyakkam's disciplinary action against me. An uncouth wretch, he would only address me as "whore". I had loved only one, but was not fortunate enough to be kissed by him. We can fall in love only once in a lifetime. All other relationships are merely glorified prostitutions.

'They waited for a week, perhaps for the acid burns to heal, to start on the next punishment – cutting off my hands. It happened in Divine Pearl, in the hall downstairs. All the prisoners and jail officials had gathered to watch. I was surprised, since no one had come to watch the acid brushing. As I was extremely conscious of my disfigured face, I did not look at anyone. I had partially lost vision in my left eye. The task of carrying out the punishment was given to the highest ranking military officer. As it is sinful to utter his name, I will call him General.

'The soldiers led me to a high platform. The implements to chop my hands off were arranged on a table nearby. I could see the glitter of the knife with my right eye. That was enough to send shivers down my spine. A military officer read out the list of crimes I was supposed to have committed. It was said that I had tried to escape by seducing the main security guard. It was also said that it was to prevent me from seducing anyone else that my face had been burnt with acid. And my hands were to be cut off to stop me from trying to escape. As I had not repented after the first phase of punishment, they were forced to carry out the second phase. The General came to the platform, smiling. Two soldiers held me to a pillar near the table and tied me to it with a smooth rope. Then I was asked to put my hands on the table, bow down and close my eyes. I obeyed like a machine. Someone marked a spot near my elbows with a marker pen. Then the General said in a sympathetic voice, "Poor thing. Don't cut off both her hands at once. Let's do it one by one, okay?" The soldiers tied my left hand to the pillar. I wanted to scream, "No! Cut off both my hands together." But punishments are not carried out according to the criminal's convenience. I put my right hand forward and shut my eyes. As I stood waiting for pain to claim my body, someone tapped me on my shoulder. It was the General. Calmly, he said, "I'll save you from this punishment. Can you speak to the TV channels in support of the president?"

'Was he repeating Robert's words? I thought I should act intelligently. Emotional outbursts would not help me. I looked at him and nodded in agreement. He asked the soldiers to free me. They did so, quickly. Robert too came up. I cried, "Please don't cut off my hands. Call the TV channels. I'll say whatever you want me to. Don't cut off my hands." I wept loudly. Robert looked at me in disbelief. The General and the other officers were happy at my change of heart. But they repeatedly questioned me to make sure my transformation was genuine. Eventually, they were convinced that the harsh punishment had had its effect and that I had realized the merits of the president and the military. When the General asked me if I wasn't upset at being raped, I shook my head with difficulty. An officer said, "Sir, that wasn't rape. She was really enjoying those moments." Everyone laughed and walked towards the officers' mess. Robert pulled my hand and asked me to come with him. I obeyed. He said, "You could have agreed before I hurt you." As I fumbled for an answer, he said, "Well, perhaps that's when you learnt your lesson."

'I had lunch with them. That night, they moved me from the cell to a guest room near the officers' quarters. A doctor came from Colombo to treat the acid burns. He wanted to admit me to a hospital in Colombo. I asked Robert whether it would be better if I went to the media after my wounds had healed. "I can tell them that I was hurt by the Iyakkam." He replied, "Though you are a Tiger, you are intelligent."

'The next day, I was admitted to the hospital. Everything was shrouded in secrecy. Robert was given the task of protecting as well as observing me. He was with me day and night. He trained me on how to behave before the media. He took me through the questions they were likely to ask and told me the right answers. After one week, a press conference was organized at the hospital itself. They presented me as a girl they had rescued from the

Tigers. Apart from the Sri Lankan media, the international media had also come to meet me.

'But I broke my promise. I answered their questions the way I wanted to. I repeated the expletives I had used to curse Robert when they asked me about Mahinda's ideas. Some members of the international media who had interacted with me in my capacity as a media coordinator for the Iyakkam in Kilinochchi understood what was happening. Though the military tried to move me to another hideout, it was impossible as the hospital was filled with the media, supporters of the opposition parties and human rights activists.

'Robert was suspended and another officer was entrusted with my security. Using that opportunity, a few foreign journalists along with HOPE, a human rights organization, rescued me. A member of HOPE pretended to be me and spent a week in the hospital. By the time the military realized that they had been duped, I had reached Canada by boat, ship and plane.

'But they carried out their punishment in the end. Three months after I reached Canada, it happened. Once when I was out, a hired criminal entered my apartment. When I returned, he attacked me. I thought he was a thief. But he did not want any money. Though the six-foot tall, well-built man could have raped me, he did not attempt to do so. He said, with no emotion, "I want your hands." He did not reply when I asked him who he was. He took out some very sophisticated instrument and cut off my hands, one by one, at exactly the same spots marked out in Divine Pearl. He put the severed limbs in a bag and took them away, making sure that no hospital could rejoin my limbs. Though I spent the entire night bathed in blood, I did not die.'

Meenakshi's story ended. In shock, we looked at our hands to make sure they were still there.

28

As we sat troubled, not knowing what had happened to Meenakshi after losing her hands, we received Arulmozhi Nangai's message: 'Same time tomorrow.'

I lost my peace of mind. I couldn't sleep at all. I didn't even notice that Juliet was beside me. If I shut my eyes, all I could see was Meenakshi's eyes. Her soft voice haunted me. I was sure that it was Sugandhi. I couldn't bring myself to tell Juliet. I was besieged by doubts. Who was Meenakshi Rajarathinam? Could Sugandhi write a story like 'Devanayaki', a story which had a historical background? Unable to sleep, I went to the balcony. Juliet came to me.

'What's the matter, Peter?'

'It's hot inside. I wanted some air.'

'No. Something is troubling you. Why don't you tell me?'

She kept a hand on my shoulder. To divert her attention, I asked, 'Why do you and Gayathri participate in this widow's meet?' She quickly moved away. I sensed that she was angry. I pulled her to me and said, 'My dear, please try to understand. You are no longer a widow. Forget the past.' I could see her eyes glitter even in the dim light of the room. Within no time, she had forgotten Meenakshi's story. But Juliet had something special to tell me. She guided my hand to her stomach and said, 'If you put your ear to my stomach, you will hear someone call you daddy.'

When I said that Gayathri may be able to hear us, she fell silent. She hugged me and drifted off to sleep. Meenakshi's half-covered face continued to haunt me. 'We can love only once in a lifetime.' I couldn't agree with her. I was falling in love with Juliet.

When we started for Colombo, Juliet said, 'Peter, look at Gayathri, look at the countless widows in Sri Lanka. We have to do something for them.' I could see Gayathri waving at us. I hadn't known that she was a war victim too. She never spoke about herself. Driving easily upon the empty roads, Juliet told me about her.

'Gayathri got married three months after she came back from the Film Institute. The groom was a smart journalist, Aniruddha Jayathilakan. Unfortunately, they could live together for only two weeks. He was an assistant editor with the *Sri Lanka Guardian*. His articles, which harshly criticized the human rights repression of the state, were a headache for the government. They decided to put an end to such writing by killing him. They had him murdered in the Maldives when he was on his honeymoon. They raped Gayathri before that. Then they pushed his body into the sea. It is rumoured that the assassins belonged to Gota's gang. The Maldives government protected the criminals.

'Gayathri's father, the novelist Karunarathna, couldn't bear it and died of shock. Gayathri's life was also threatened. But she remained unfazed and joined Vikrama's *Sunday Leader*. When Vikrama was killed, she started writing a column called "Witness" for *Al Jazeera*. Her mother, a lawyer, and her brother supported her in everything.'

I felt great respect for Gayathri, who had not let the tragedies in her life beat her down. When she said, 'Peter, almost all the women activists in Sri Lanka are rape victims,' I could feel tears welling up in my eyes. These words contained the answer to the question why Sri Lankan women chose to become suicide bombers.

It was a day when important decisions had to be taken in Colombo. I watched the screen test of the Khmer actress who had been shortlisted to play Devanayaki's role. I immediately told Christie that she wouldn't do. She was very slim, although her face bore some typical Kambuja features. 'Devanayaki was voluptuous,' I reminded him.

That night, we went back to Gayathri's house in Gampaha. At 10 p.m., Meenakshi came online. This time, the conversation was not recorded. There was a dignified sixty-year-old woman with her. Though Meenakshi had covered for face with a black veil, I recognized her voice with its pronounced British accent. It was Sugandhi. She admitted it herself.

'I might have confused you yesterday. So I decided to end this game of hide-and-seek. I am Sugandhi alias Andal Devanayaki. When I left the Iyakkam, I changed my name. Now I am Andal Devanayaki. This is my mother, Meenakshi Rajarathinam. If it wasn't for her, I wouldn't be alive now. As I lay in a pool of blood after my hands had been cut off, she saved me. She was my neighbour in Canada. She is from Trivandrum in Kerala. My birth mother, Dr Kanakavalli, had worked as a gynaecologist in Colombo Castle Street Hospital. Dr Rajarathinam, who was her colleague, married Meenakshi. In the massacre of 1983, Dr Rajarathinam, like my parents, was killed. Luckily, Mother escaped. During my last days with the Iyakkam, I used to secretly write poems under the pseudonym Eezhathachi. They were poems questioning the anti-democratic stance of the Sri Lankan government.

'It is this anti-democratic ideology that led to the downfall of the Iyakkam. The leadership was never ready to seriously consider criticism or rectify their mistakes. Instead, like fascists, they wiped out the people who criticized them. If it was a woman, they would get her married to somebody from the Tiger leadership and push her into the prison of marriage. The value system of the Iyakkam was extremely patriarchal. The marriage would be followed by pregnancies and children. All critical thinking would end with that. But swimming against the tide, I started writing under the pseudonym Eezhathachi. I emailed the poems to my father's friend, Nallur Sivachidambaram, who lived in Paris. He published them in an online magazine called *Karupu*. When the poems were well-received, we decided to publish my autobiography, *The Notes of a Female Fighter*. But Sivachidambaram was killed on the day it was advertised. It was around the same time that the last battle of Mullivaikkal took place. That put an end to my writing.

'I resumed after a few years. Some of my friends in Canada revived *Karupu*. For reasons of security, I used my mother's name while writing. My life was threatened both by the Iyakkam as well as by the government. But that is not the only reason why I decided to write under the name of Meenakshi Rajarathinam. It was Mother who brought me from the world of poetry to fiction. She told me the story of Devanayaki who had lived centuries ago in Kanthalur Salai. When we heard that a book called the *Susaana Supina* had been discovered in Sigiriya, Yamuna went there and scanned a copy for me. I read it with great difficulty and with a lot of help from Mother. I wrote a story exaggerating the information I found in that book. That is the reason why I'm known as Meenakshi Rajarathinam in SSF.'

When she stopped talking, the real Meenakshi Rajarathinam began to speak.

'I too would have been killed in the riots of 1983. A Sinhalese policeman rescued me when he came to know that I was from Kerala. He took pity on me. But I wasn't in a position to go back home as I was known as the woman who had married a Sinhalese. They didn't know I was married to a Tamilian. I was three months pregnant with Arul then. I gave birth to her in a refugee camp. I lived there for three years. One day, Dr Sridhar, who was practising in Canada, came to our camp. He was involved with an organization that rehabilitated refugees. His family had been killed in the riots of 1983 when they had come to Sri Lanka on vacation.

'He thought that I was his dead wife Manimekhala and hugged me tight. I was astounded. He was weeping, calling out, "Mani! Mani!" When he realized his mistake, he fell at my feet begging forgiveness. I too started weeping. He asked me whether I would go with him and I agreed. Anyone in my situation would have. I flew to Canada with my two-year-old daughter. The next year, I gave birth to Yamuna. Dr Sridhar was working at Toronto General Hospital. I later joined the hospital as a nurse. Dr Sridhar was a very dignified man who did not hesitate to speak his mind. Naturally, he fell out with the Iyakkam. The cause for the quarrel was money. The unwritten rule was that every Sri Lankan Tamil in Canada should pay money to the Iyakkam in accordance with the salary they earned. They had deputed certain people to collect this money every month. We had to pay thirty dollars. When I started working, they raised it to forty. Apart from this, they would collect a couple of thousand dollars every year under some pretext or the other. If we refused to pay, they would threaten us by saying that we would not be allowed to return to our native land. When Arul was eight years old, she needed a major surgery. We had to spend a lot of money and could not afford to pay the Iyakkam. Dr Sridhar explained our position to the men who came to collect the money, but they refused to listen and threatened him. He told them that he wouldn't give money for them to buy guns and explosives.

'When he was coming back from work the next evening, the Iyakkam shot him in front of our apartment. I was on duty at the hospital. My children and a neighbour brought him there, but he was already dead. Nobody in our neighbourhood dared refuse the Iyakkam after that.'

Weeping openly, she continued, 'I lived alone in this country with my children. As I had a job, we did not face financial difficulties. Though I paid money to the Iyakkam regularly, I hated them. It was not just because they killed Dr Sridhar that I felt angry. Is this how freedom is obtained? Haven't you heard of Mahatma Gandhi? He won freedom for such a large country like India without using guns or bombs. What did these people gain after so much bloodshed?

'I was born into a family of musicians in Trivandrum. So I taught my daughters music and dance from a young age. When they grew up, they gravitated towards western music. Arulmozhi Nangai and Yamuna Sridhar are well-known singers now. Four years ago, they got a sister – Andal Devanayaki. They sing songs written by her. Their band is called SAD. For reasons of safety, we tell everyone that Sugandhi is dead.

'Devanayaki is like my eldest daughter. When I took her to the hospital, she was nearly dead because of the loss of blood. It took three months for her wounds to heal, and another month for her to be able to speak. She'd had a nervous breakdown. When I got to know that she was Dr Kanakavalli's daughter, my sense of responsibility doubled. I got expert doctors to treat her post-traumatic stress disorder. We treated her face as well. With music and love, I brought her back to life. Now she is all right. She can live, though she has lost her hands and vision in one eye.

'When I heard that the Iyakkam was planning a movie on Rajini Thiranagama with Devanayaki as the heroine, I was touched. Rajini was Dr Sridhar's student in Colombo Medical College. He was very proud of her. She had come to this house in Canada. Now I hear that it's a Hollywood production. My child can't take the role now, so someone else will have to do it.

'Even in her condition, Devanayaki is not idle. She is fighting the Lankan dictatorship with her stories and music. She is leading a huge youth movement. Though Arul and Yamuna handle her profile, she is the brain behind it. But she cannot continue with this. When millions of people protest against the president in Colombo, she cannot lead them. That is why it was decided to entrust Gayathri with the responsibility.'

When Meenakshi Rajarathinam stopped, Devanayaki bowed to us and removed her veil. I was shocked. Her face was a red mass. I could look at her only once. I ran out, crying uncontrollably. I got drunk that night, trying to drown out the memory of her face. I was not fully conscious even on the return journey to Colombo.

It took me three days to come out of my alcoholic haze, and even then I was weeping on Juliet's shoulders. Finally, she said, 'Please stop it, Peter. You have to decide – do you want Devanayaki who is disfigured and in Canada, or me?' I was struck by her question. Sugandhi was dear to me, but I had lost her ages ago. I couldn't think of a life without Juliet. She was carrying my baby. The selfish, practical man within me woke up. I hugged her and said, 'Juliet, you are the one I want.' I don't think she believed me.

The SSF activists, who had also seen Sugandhi on Skype, prepared for a mass uprising. They planned the protest against the Commonwealth Summit in three stages. The first stage was an online campaign with the slogan: 'Try the president as a war criminal. End his dictatorship.' Many other demands were also made. They wanted freedom of expression and the rehabilitation of widows and people maimed in the war. They also demanded putting a stop to the attacks on Muslims. The second stage envisaged a large number of discontented youth moving towards Colombo inspired by the online campaign. The city of Colombo was to be filled with people on the day of the Summit. Then the helpless dictator would have to surrender. We found this out from Juliet. The third stage was a heavily guarded secret. Only Gayathri knew about it.

Samaraveera informed us, with a great show of sympathy, of Gota's decision to halt any project that might create problems for the government until the Commonwealth Summit was over. But Christie was very happy about it. Everyone wanted a break. Christie went to New Zealand for a month with Mary. Though he invited us too, Juliet wasn't very interested. I made an excuse, saying that I had to work on the script and needed to stay in Colombo. We moved from the villa to an apartment close to where Manju was staying. Samaraveera made sure that we were comfortable. He also invited us to join in the activities connected with the summit. 'At this time, we need the help of creative artists like you. We are planning a dance based on Sri Lankan history for the opening ceremony. It will be followed by dances based on the cultures of all participating nations. Can't Juliet help us?'

That is what Juliet had desired all along. She wanted to gain access to the president's official residence, Temple Trees. Prashadi Ranasinghe was to choreograph the opening ceremony. She came to meet us because Samaraveera asked her to. She liked Juliet a lot. The Prashadi Dance Academy was glad to get a person like Juliet who had a deep knowledge of Sri Lankan history and culture. I told Samaraveera that we could include

Andal's 'Margazhi Thingal' as it would provide an opportunity for national integration. Samaraveera approved of the idea.

Juliet was given the responsibility of finding suitable dancers. She decided to utilize this opportunity. I told her to ask for Manju's help but, as expected, she said, 'I don't want these casino girls with me.' Gayathri and Juliet decided to stage the protest ahead of the opening ceremony. But they did not know how exactly to do it. As it involved music and dance, they called Arulmozhi Nangai. The next day, we received a message saying, 'We should grab this chance. We are devising a plan.'

Meanwhile, there was a huge campaign being carried on in the press and on social networking sites against the Commonwealth Summit. Protests against Sri Lanka were gaining momentum all over the world. Many heads of state declared that they wouldn't participate. Political parties in Tamil Nadu demanded that the Indian president not participate. The Sri Lankan Tamils living in Canada, Australia, UK, France and Mauritius also protested strongly.

29

The day of the Summit drew closer, but SSF could not create much of an impact in Sri Lanka, even though the online campaign continued and emigrants protested in front of Sri Lankan embassies in different countries. The Terrorist Investigation Division and the secret police were able to nip protests by small groups, like Sri Lankan War Widows, Families of the Disappeared and HOPE, in the bud. As SSF did not have an organized framework, they could not bring the smaller groups together.

The hope that people would join hands against the dictator was misplaced. The police arrested anyone they suspected of being involved in the agitation. The government implemented the Prevention of Terrorism Act, which permitted them to imprison suspects without trial for a period of eighteen months. Those whom they arrested were cruelly tortured. Fear spread like an epidemic. Everyone knew that the president's slogan – spring in the north and sunrise in the south – was merely a façade. The freedom the authorities granted was merely the charity of fascism and not a privilege of the citizens. It carried the stench of burnt flesh and was stained with blood. The majority was too afraid to react. Even those who spoke vociferously in private kept quiet out of fear.

The police did not arrest Gayathri or the other leaders of SSF. The plan was to undermine the support they had from the people and, thereby, make them objects of ridicule.

SSF had hoped that nearly a hundred thousand people would join the Save Sri Lanka from Fascism march from Jaffna to Colombo. But the numbers dwindled to ten thousand, and then five thousand. Gradually, even that seemed doubtful. Though many promised solidarity, they did not care to join the movement publicly. Yamuna and Arul, who had expected something akin to Tahrir Square, were disappointed. They, who from the beginning had been in disagreement with Meenakshi's idea of peaceful Gandhian resistance, shared their anxieties with Devanayaki.

'Akka, there is a huge gap between what Amma says and reality. I don't think Gandhian ideology is practical against Sri Lankan fascism. The possibility of a mass uprising like that in Tunisia or Egypt is very slim. A huge majority of the people trust and support the president who emerged successful after a twenty-five year war against terrorism. That is his strength. He knows how to manipulate Sri Lankan nationalism in his favour. This is the newest face of fascism. It is no longer what it used to be when Hitler and Mussolini were around. In the twenty-first century, fascism dons several masks: that of pseudo-democracy, development, and even that of peace. It is one of the strategies of power. It gives the majority the opportunity to ennoble their narrow racist feelings. It turns democracy, which we consider great, into something that is anti-people. The majority rapes, kills and silences the minority. I don't feel a peaceful, dignified resistance against this sort of power structure will suffice. But we cannot adopt the fascist ploys of the Iyakkam either. We have to forge a new path. Our enemy is not a person or the state, but the mindset of the majority.'

'But Arul, if we too resort to violence, what makes us different from them?'

'There is a difference. We are not making violence a weapon against the helpless. We are using it against those who have lost their humaneness to the insanity that power bequeaths. In the Iyakkam, a woman has the authority to kill a man who rapes or attempts to rape her. You wrote in Devanayaki's story, "I will come to the rescue whenever the tears of a woman fall." Don't you think Rajini Thiranagama was a reincarnation of Devanayaki? Aren't you also another reincarnation of Devanayaki? Isn't the same blood flowing through us?'

'Akka, there is something to what Arul says. I don't think peaceful protests will be effective. Violence should be countered with violence. Who is responsible for your plight? Who is responsible for the genocide and rapes in Sri Lanka? What is the use of speaking to them in the language of peace?'

'It's your youth that makes you respond in this way. I too felt the same when I was younger. Let's wait. When people see the real face of the government, they will take to the streets.'

'Akka, we cannot wait indefinitely. By the time realization dawns, tens of thousands will be massacred. Thousands of women will be raped.'

'Do as you wish. But try not to shed blood unless it is absolutely necessary.'

Arul was on her way back from Paris when Juliet rang. She heard Juliet's idea and felt that it might work. She discussed it with her friends in Toronto. The Canadian wing of SSF was happy with the plan. It was a great opportunity to take revenge to the enemy's doorstep. The plan had a greater chance of succeeding than any other that had been thought of. But who would execute it? And how? These were questions to which there were no easy answers.

'Shall we discuss it with Devanayaki?'

'No. She will only dissuade us. She says that we do not need to become like the Chechen Black Widows. Amma's Gandhian philosophy has had a deep impact on Akka. She feels that no one among us should sacrifice their life to take revenge. But there are many whose lives have been destroyed by the Sri Lankan military. There are many more who are waiting for just such an opportunity.'

Arul spoke to Devanayaki when Meenakshi was not present. She listened in silence, then, as was her wont, asked several questions.

'Yes, Arul, this is a good opportunity. But we will have to sacrifice lives. Many innocent people will also die. The heads of several states will be present at the inaugural session. We will have to kill many people to punish one war criminal. No, I cannot agree.'

'Suppose we have a plan that will not entail hurting anyone or getting hurt?'

'How is that possible?'

'The time of suicide bombers in the Iyakkam is over, Akka. This is the age of nano-weapons. Nano-weapon robotics is highly advanced now. There are weapons the size of insects that can be remote controlled. I intend an action using such weapons. We can hide a mosquito drone in the flowers adorning a dancer's hair. It can be operated from a distance. We can fill the mosquito with the venom of a cobra or cyanide. The victim will feel only a mosquito bite. Death won't be instantaneous. It will happen in a natural manner after a few hours.'

'Okay. It sounds good. But can the dancer operate the remote?'

'No. Someone in the audience has to do it. It will be easy to place someone in the audience.'

'But will fascism end with the death of one person? Lankan fascism is not centred upon an individual. It has affected the entire society. Someone else will take his place, or the military will assume power.'

'Then what can we do, Akka? Should we not use this opportunity?'

'I won't say that. I understand your feelings. But you know that my feelings about this issue are quite deep. I have devised some other plans with Yamuna. I couldn't discuss them with you as you were in Paris. We have people in Saint Lucia, a small Caribbean island. They are going to gift the president a gold Buddha. They will tell him that it brings luck if it is placed in the bedroom. As he is extremely superstitious, the Buddha will definitely get a place in his bedroom. We can detonate that Buddha from here with a phone. We have people in the Guyanese delegation as well. They will present fifty-three Buddha statues to adorn the dais, as an emblem of the unity of the Commonwealth countries. Some statues will be especially created for us. We will use the Buddha against those who commit violence in the name of the Buddha.'

'Akka, but will all this happen just as we plan it? Suppose these Buddhas are caught by security?'

'Yes, we might be caught. When it is known that the dancer is one of us, she might be killed. But one plan amongst the many might succeed. Tell me after you think about it properly.'

Arul and Yamuna decided on the operation after long discussions and enquiries. Only they knew the details. The mosquito drones were given to Yamuna by Donald Hume, an agent in the US military research wing. Their only interest was in using a weapon that hadn't yet been tested on people. They presented the final master-plan to Devanayaki.

'We did not think it fit to entrust others with this responsibility. Both of us are going to Colombo. Apart from us, only Juliet knows the final plan. Hume will get the mosquito drone to Sri Lanka. He will give us training for three days. We have been given seven minutes of stage time. Yamuna will dance to "Margazhi".'

'It will be followed by Buddha puja. I will sing a Sinhalese song and dance before Gnana Buddha, and Arul will do a Tamil song. The mosquito drone will be right in front of the statue. Juliet will operate the remote.'

'Make sure the plan is foolproof. Practise as much as you can. I am coming with you. I can't sit here and send you on such a dangerous mission.'

'But in your condition?'

'I want to see my Peter too.'

'If the government comes to know...'

'Can't you take me without their knowledge?'

Arul discussed matters with Gayathri and Juliet. She was glad to make arrangements for Devanayaki's visit. They made their travel plans.

'Akka will travel as Amina Peer Mohammed, I as Gloria Fernandes, and Yamuna will be Damayanthi Weerasinghe. That's what our documents will say. We will travel as if we are strangers to one another. Hume will send two US military officers for our protection. We will be staying in three different houses in Sri Lanka. Akka will be able to meet Peter in Peer Mohammed's house. Amma does not know of our plans. We have told her that we are going to the States for a programme, and Akka is coming along to consult with a cosmetic surgeon.'

Juliet became quite busy as the Commonwealth Heads of Government Meeting drew near. Apart from helping with the choreography, she was also engaged in arrangements for the inaugural session. Three days before the event, Gayathri came to meet her and finalize the SSF's projects. Gayathri had a mischievous smile on her face when she came back.

'Peter, Devanayaki arrived this morning. I have made her a promise.'

'What?'

'She wants to meet you. That is why she is here.'

'Okay.'

'She is here as Amina Peer Mohammed. She is staying in a slum near Slave Island in Peer's house. We must go there tonight.'

I agreed happily. Juliet couldn't come along as she was busy. I later realized that she did not want to trouble us with her presence. It was late evening by the time we reached Peer

Mohammed's house. It was just a shack. Peer gave us the only room in the house. It was very dimly lit. She stood up when I entered. She looked like a Muslim woman in her abaya. I was comforted when she said in her faltering voice, 'Ananda!'

No one else ever called me Ananda.

'Sugandhi…'

'No. I am Devanayaki now.'

I extended my hand towards her. I had forgotten that she had lost her hands. I sat down on the cot with her.

'I looked for you … for ages.'

'I know. I didn't want to disturb you – for your own sake. Why should you destroy your life for me? A tiger's stripes cannot be washed away, Peter.'

'Why didn't you escape with me, Devanayaki?'

'By that time, my fate had already been decided. The day before you went away, the Iyakkam had decided to get me married to Stalin. I had to obey them. Now you tell me, how is the movie coming along?'

'The shoot begins next month.'

'Is it shaping up the way we had planned it?'

'No, we have travelled further. This movie is about a movie that was being planned about Rajini during the heyday of the Iyakkam. But we are interweaving it with the myth of Andal Devanayaki. We had decided to cast you in Rajini's role, but in this movie we both are also characters. Hollywood actors are playing the roles.'

We spoke the whole night long. We realized it was dawn only when Peer woke up for his prayers.

'Do you know why I'm here? You used to say my cheeks and lips are more beautiful than anyone else's. I want to be kissed by you. If I remove my veil, you won't be able to do it. Kiss my forehead. My cheeks are just pieces of flesh.'

I held her close and removed her veil. Her disfigured face didn't scare me. I didn't see the burns. My mind still carried the image of her unblemished beauty. I hugged her and kissed her cheeks passionately.

'Ananda, I can't hug you back,' she wept. It was morning by then. We got up when we heard the voices of Peer Mohammed's children. Peer's wife gave us black tea with a piece of jaggery to sweeten it.

She asked with a smile, 'You were husband and wife?'

Devanayaki nodded.

She said, 'Don't go back. Stay here.'

Her words were sweeter than the piece of sugar she had given us.

30

A text message arrived from Juliet as I was saying goodbye to Devanayaki. It read: 'Enjoy ur old flame. Am busy. Can meet only after CHOGM. Bye.'

I knew what was keeping her busy. Devanayaki had told me the details of Operation Nano after swearing me to secrecy. She had also told me that the CIA was training Arul and Yamuna to use mosquito drones. But Juliet and Gayathri did not want to divulge the CIA's involvement. We could justify it by saying that the foe of a foe is a friend, but I felt that this decision taken in the aftermath of the failed mass uprising was wrong. I didn't know how to dissuade them. I was in mental turmoil when I left Peer's house.

Their right to take revenge was unquestionable. They had suffered greatly. But what good could this revenge do? The common man would desert SSF. Wasn't it the same mistake that the Iyakkam had made? They who had dreamt of a mass movement against fascism, how could they take such a step? How quickly the CIA had manipulated them into doing what it wanted. This is the problem that plagues all revolutions that lack a strong ideological background. I hoped Juliet wouldn't do anything rash.

Manju was stepping out of the lift when I got back to the apartment. She was in a black skirt suit and carried a Birkin bag. Very lightly made up, a pair of platinum-diamond earrings was her only jewellery. It was a corporate executive makeover. She was one of the lucky few who could enjoy life in the midst of war, revenge, blood and tears. It seemed absurd.

'Hi! How come you are alone? Where's your possessive girlfriend?'

'She is a government official busy with the CHOGM. Why are you dressed like this?'

'The Commonwealth Business Forum will be inaugurated today at 10 a.m. in Hotel Cinnamon Grand. My boss is speaking in a session titled "Sri Lanka: The Twenty-first Century Destination". Come along if you are bored. I am free as his high-profile secretaries have arrived from Australia.'

'Not today, maybe tomorrow. Thank you.'

I wasn't dressed for the Cinnamon Grand. After a bath and breakfast, I called Juliet. But her mobile was out of reach. Luckily, I got through to Peer Mohammed. He said that a white woman had come to fetch Devanayaki immediately after I left. On my table was the invite to the inauguration that Samaraveera had sent me. Juliet must have put it there. I opened my laptop and read the script. Then, I added a couple of scenes that revealed Devanayaki's plight. Rajini, who had died instantaneously, was so much more fortunate.

A little while later, Juliet called back. 'Why didn't you text? I am sorry for my message about enjoying your old flame. I meant it as a joke. I just met Devanayaki. It was a painful sight. But her strength of mind – wow! I cannot discuss anything more with you. The invite is on the table. I will be right up front. I'm also in charge of ushering in the guests.'

'I'll be there. I don't want to know your secrets. But don't take any risks. My baby is growing inside you.'

'I know. But one cannot shirk away from one's responsibilities.'

'You must move away if your safety is at stake.'

'I will try.'

'Bye. Take care.'

But her promise was weak, I knew.

Peter's words – 'My baby is growing inside you' – disturbed Juliet. She had desired access to Temple Trees. She had been willing to sacrifice her life for that. 'But ... Peter ... He too is right,' she thought. 'I have no right to put my baby's life in danger.'

They used Gayathri's home in Gampaha to plan Operation Nano. When Devanayaki reached there with Andrea, a CIA agent, Arulmozhi, Yamuna and Donald Hume were waiting for them. Juliet and Gayathri were right behind them in another car. There was a crystal bowl with mosquito drones on the table, and a one-foot high Buddha statue next to it. Hume had a huge hand-held lens with him. Once the doors were locked, he started talking.

'Operation Nano is not the first time we are using mosquito drones. We have experimented with them successfully several times. But this is the first time we are using them for a political purpose. We don't have the consent of the US government for this operation. We have not informed them about this. In such a situation, it is impossible to ask permission officially. So if this operation fails or we get caught, the US government will not take responsibility. They will only criticize us. I am saying this because I want to make it clear that this operation is planned with the full concurrence of SSF. But the US government is supporting us unofficially. They have only one intention: to curtail China's strong presence and influence in Lanka.'

'Mr Hume, we take complete responsibility for this operation. But we do have some differences of opinion. We do not support US policies completely. You're not very different from China as far as imperialist dreams are concerned. Anyway, show us how this works.'

Hearing Gayathri's words, Hume realized that they were indeed forces to contend with. He lifted a mosquito drone very carefully from the crystal bowl. Then, he gave the lens to Gayathri.

'Take a look, Miss Gayathri. For all purposes, this is a mosquito. Its wings will vibrate more than a thousand times per second. That's the antenna which receives our signals. There is a micro-camera at the end of it. The proboscis, you can call it the sting or thorn if you wish. This big part is the stomach. It contains cyanide. The microprocessor beneath it contains the brain of the mosquito. Unlike a natural mosquito that draws blood from humans, this metal mosquito injects poison. It weighs barely three grams.

'We'll place it above the Buddha statue. It is too small to be noticed. And even if it is seen, it will be mistaken for an ordinary mosquito. You said you have seven minutes of stage time. One minute after Yamuna's dance begins, the first mosquito must reach the target. With one or two bites, three milligrams of cyanide will be injected. You can use the second mosquito when the second dance performance is on. The target, immersed in the performance, will remain oblivious to all this. The two mosquitoes must reach the Buddha before the dances end. The success of the operation depends completely on the person who operates the remote control. You can do it from up to sixty feet away. We can watch its movements on the screen and control it.'

Hume stood to one side with the remote control that looked like a smartphone. He used it to control a drone and made it land on Gayathri's hand. She was horrified.

'Don't worry. It's empty.'

Hume gave a signal for the mosquito to inject. She didn't feel anything. 'As there is no itching, no one will feel its bite.' The drone returned to the Buddha's head.

'Now you try.' Everyone looked at Juliet, but Peter's words resounded in her head: My baby is growing inside you.

She took the remote from Hume and tried to operate it. But her hands were trembling. She couldn't do it properly. Hume said, 'We are moving a micro-object that weighs barely three grams.' He held her hands and tried to teach her. But she was unable to do it. It would either land on Devanayaki or on the floor.

'Sorry, she can't do it. Someone else, please.'

'No one else can enter the hall,' Gayathri told Hume. He smiled, as he had expected this answer.

'Okay. Then Andrea will do it. Our embassy can get her a pass. But it will cost you.' Gayathri agreed. The fair Andrea resembled a Bond heroine. She operated the drone deftly.

'Well done, Andrea,' said Hume. 'It's not surprising that an agent trained at the Farm is so skilled.'

Devanayaki was not satisfied with Operation Nano. Maybe it was because both attempts to use the Buddha statues had failed.

The airport officials had confiscated the Buddha statue brought by the Saint Lucia team. The Sri Lankan government refused the offer of Buddha statues from Guyana, citing security reasons. 'Maybe this Buddha will also let us down,' she thought. 'Even if the operation is successful, the death will be seen as a natural one and not create the desired impact. A cruel dictator does not deserve an easy death.'

When Hume and Andrea left, Devanayaki secretly conveyed her reservations to Gayathri. She also requested her not to share them with Arul as that would demoralize her.

'I too feel the same. Let them continue with this. We have planned something else.'

'What is that?'

'Fifty-five S-class Mercedes Benz cars have been imported for the CHOGM. Fifty-four cars are for the heads of state. As our president does not enjoy great support in the international community, most of the leaders are not participating in the meet. Mauritius has decided to boycott the meeting. Many countries like Canada and India are sending their foreign ministers or some other minister. They are the ones who will be using the new cars. These cars have been given special number plates. Cars bearing those number plates are permitted to cross security barriers. If there is a military jeep in front and behind, nobody will stop the car. We will drive a car filled with explosives, bearing the number plate CHOGM2L5. We will drive it to the venue as if the car belongs to a delegate who is late. We will have two military jeeps escorting us. Our people will be in those jeeps too. So we'll be able to reach the Rajapaksa Theatre – also called the Nelum Pokuna, or lotus pond – early.

'The event will begin with the national anthem, "Namo namo matha". Even the commanders shut their eyes when the national anthem is sung. That's when three people with explosives strapped to their body will jump up on the podium. Anyone who attempts to stop them will be shot down. Even if only one is able to reach the podium alive, the operation will succeed. We have estimated that it will take twenty-four seconds to reach the venue from the car. The car will explode. Yes, a lot of innocent lives will be lost, and we will also be among the victims. But we have a problem. The man who was supposed to drive the car was arrested by the TID yesterday.'

'So how do we proceed?'

'I don't know, but everything else is ready. We are looking for a new person.'

'Can I do it?'

'How will you drive without your hands?'

'I don't need hands to drive.'

The Commonwealth Business Forum was very grand. Though several industrial bigwigs like Rahul Bajaj were present, everyone was interested in what James Packer had to say. Packer did not disappoint. He began by praising the development policies of the Sri Lankan government to the skies. Analyzing the growth of the middle-class in countries like India, he pointed out opportunities for Sri Lanka to develop as a leisure destination. Sri Lanka, he said, is to India what Macau is to China. He also presented his project, Crown Colombo. Manju introduced me to him during lunch.

Weak protests were going on all over the country against the CHOGM. The opposition and the Buddhist monks had protested strongly against Packer. But neither the president nor his aides were troubled by all this. The people from Channel 4 were not allowed to go to Jaffna. When I told Manju all this on the way back, she laughed.

'Who is afraid of barking dogs on the street?'

'What if there are rabid dogs among them?'

'They must be beaten to death.'

I was taken aback. We didn't speak until we reached the apartment. Then she asked me, 'Can you give me this night?'

I had to agree, but I was not able to pleasure her in the way she desired. I was gripped by an unknown fear. I lay sleepless beside her. Then I fell into a nightmare.

Devanayaki came to the Nelum Pokuna from the skies, bathed in blood. Hearing her roar, everyone rose in fear. Her body moved in the forms of the Devanayaki Kolam. She asked, 'Where is the queen of this empire? Where are the judges? Where are they hiding, instead of beheading him who cut off my breasts? If you don't come here, I will take revenge for the tears and blood of millions of women. I'll burn the Nelum Pokuna and the casinos. Where ... where are you?'

Her voice echoed until the ends of the world. A sea of blood rose. I was sinking in it. As I woke up, I saw someone in bed next to me. It was Devanayaki, with her hands cut off. I was weeping, holding my head in my hands. She got up.

'Peter, what's wrong?' It was Manju. She was crying too.

31

They are fools who fight for freedom in a society where the majority are either religious fanatics or cowards or just plain selfish. But we cannot refrain from sacrificing our lives for that dream. We hold nothing dearer than freedom. We still dream of a day when the people will come marching to Colombo to wrest power from the dictator. We hope that our

*sacrifice will provide the impetus for an uprising. Goodbye
to all my friends.*
Meenakshi Rajarathinam

Seeing Meenakshi's Facebook post on 15 November 2013,
the day the CHOGM was to be inaugurated, many people –
including me – were shocked. Leaders like Gayathri had been
taken into custody, and the Sri Lankan military had tightened
security. The military and the Chinese espionage wing, the
MMS, who unofficially helped the government with security
for the CHOGM, started searching for Meenakshi. The cyber
wing of the TID made enquiries to find out the location from
where the Facebook post had been made. By 7 a.m., the post had
thousands of comments requesting Meenakshi to turn back.
But she didn't respond. When I rang her, she was unnaturally
emotionless.

'Ananda, we have nothing to lose.'

'Is your life of no value?'

'Our lives are not more valuable than the millions of lives
lost in the freedom movement. Our lives are not more precious
than those of Rajini Thiranagama or Lasantha Wickrematunge
who were killed in the resistance movements for freedom and
peace.'

'But you said that you would never be like the Black Widows
of Chechnya?'

'When I said that, I still had some expectations from the
people of this country. I dreamt of them rallying behind us with
the strength of a tornado.'

'Can't you sensitize the public through your writings? You are
a writer, after all.'

'I don't believe I can. Even the so-called intellectuals didn't react after reading the story of Devanayaki. That was a story potent enough to rewrite the history of Sri Lanka. Is it because there is a dearth of writers in the country? Of intellectuals? They are merely trumpet-blowers to the fascist overlord – greedy for pittances, like the titles of "Sri Lanka Sikhamani" and "Sri Lanka Thilaka", that are thrown to them. Writing is futile here.'

'Then why did you write the story of Devanayaki?'

'Because that was my story.'

'What do you mean?'

'That it is, indeed, my story. Devanayaki, who lived hundreds of years ago, continues to live through me. You have read it, haven't you? This is my last birth as a human being. This time, I will give up this body and attain nirvana. The soul of Nissanka Vajran has told me that it is time to return. To put one foot on Sinha Saila, the other on Sripada, and to fly to the skies. I desire to go to Kanthalur Salai and sing "Margazhi" before Lord Padmanabha. I wonder if the guru will allow me to do so.'

'How can you be radical and mystical at the same time?'

'Nothing is simple, Ananda.'

I hung up, not wanting to listen to her any more. Had she gone mad? Was the writer trapped in the last story she wrote? After a while, I received a text message: 'Plz chk ur mail'.

Dear Ananda,
I know that you are confused. But I spoke the truth. I received enlightenment the night I lost my hands, while I was writhing in pain at the hospital. It was Mother who awakened my memories. When she narrated Devanayaki's story, even she did not realize that it was my story. She still doesn't know.

*Devanayaki's story is repeated in different ways in her
different births. If her breasts were cut off then, now it is her
hands. Her line will not end with me. The fight for a woman's
honour and freedom will continue with others. I thank you
for giving me pleasure that enabled me to experience the
thousand-petalled lotus for at least one night in this birth. I
wish Juliet and your unborn child all happiness.
Devanayaki*

The Rajapaksa Theatre was a glowing tribute to contemporary
architecture. It was a replica of the lotus pond built in the twelfth
century by Parakramabahu in Polonnaruwa. It had the shape of
a lotus with eight petals. It had a main auditorium with a seating
capacity of 1,288 and an open-air auditorium on top. It was built
with funds the Chinese government had given in return for the
use of important strategic locations in Sri Lanka. Though it was
called the National Performing Arts Theatre previously, it was
renamed Nelum Pokuna Mahinda Rajapaksa Theatre for the
CHOGM.

As the invite had said that entry was only until nine, I reached
there before time with Manju. We were subjected to a thorough
security check a kilometre before the venue.

Juliet was in front, receiving guests. There was a long row
of hostesses clad in white, blue and yellow saris. I thought that
Juliet looked beautiful in her blue sari, worn low on the waist in
the Sri Lankan way. She led us to our seats. Though she didn't
approve of Manju's presence, she didn't show it as she was very
tense. I was also under great stress. Manju was oblivious to all
this. She was happy at having got the opportunity to participate
in such an important event. Christie and Mary were upset that

the Queen wasn't coming for the programme. Somehow, they didn't much care for Prince Charles. Mary kept saying that it was the first time in history that a meeting of Commonwealth heads was taking place in the Queen's absence.

As their names were announced, the heads of state came up on stage. There were hostesses to lead them to their seats. When she saw that it was the foreign affairs minister Salman Khurshid who was representing India, Manju got upset. She said that the prime minister or the president should have come. I ignored her. After the heads of state, Prince Charles and the president came on stage. Everyone stood up for the national anthem. 'Sri Lanka matha ... namo namo matha'. Selected students from various schools sang the anthem. When everyone sat down, Manju asked me. 'Who wrote this, Peter?' 'Ananda Samarakoon,' I whispered in her ear. I told her that, succumbing to superstition, the Lankan parliament had changed the song and Samarakoon had committed suicide, unable to bear this interference. Manju turned to me, 'What madness is this? Those mad people are responsible for the bloodshed in this nation.' I didn't say anything more as there were people all around.

After the welcome dance titled 'Ayubowan', the president got up to address the gathering. The audience welcomed him enthusiastically. He presented matters in a dignified manner. He stressed that we should worry not about wealth, but about poverty. It was a cleverly written speech. Each sentence conveyed his ability to project the development of the nation and to suppress any criticism against him. When Mary said, 'A wonderful man. Why do people criticize him unnecessarily,' Manju agreed with her. I sat in silence, looking at the stage.

Next was a dance showcasing Sri Lankan history. It used the
stage to the fullest extent. It utilized the three movable stages and
enhanced the performance with videos. It portrayed an oyster
rising out of the Indian Ocean. A beautiful dancer emerged from
the shell. Though I wanted to congratulate Juliet, she was nowhere
to be seen. After this was a fusion dance performance from all
the different countries present. I felt like slapping the Kathakali
dancer for performing badly and spoiling the entire experience.
But where was Arulmozhi Nangai? Yamuna? Margazhi Thingal?
The programme that had started at ten ended at twelve, but
there was no sign of Juliet.

Neither Peter nor Devanayaki knew that Arul and Yamuna had
been arrested. The TID had arrested them the previous night
from Hume's room. Xiang, a Chinese spy, had tipped them off.
She had been watching Andrea and Hume from the moment
they had landed in Sri Lanka. As they were US citizens, the
government asked them to leave without creating any fuss. The
US embassy put them on the first flight back home.

Though Arul and Yamuna were Canadians, they were not
given any preferential treatment and were taken to DP for
interrogation. They were tortured. It was a serious charge –
attempting to assassinate the president at the CHOGM. The
chief Wickrama Ranatunga ordered, 'First rape, then question.'
He had been an assistant at DP when Devanayaki had been
tortured with acid. Ranatunga felt that terrorists should not be
treated with kindness. As neither Arul nor Yamuna had been
trained by the Iyakkam, they would have broken down easily. But
the officers approached them as hardened terrorists who were
ready to take great risks in spite of tight security.

Arul was questioned by Lieutenant Caesar, a very tough
officer. The girl was still trembling from Ranatunga's commands.

Caesar saw her and just said, 'Take off your clothes.' Arul did not fight back. Scared, she pulled off her jeans quickly. She was too frightened by the stories she had heard to feel embarrassed by her nudity. She was praying for an escape route. The next command was to lie on the bed. Though she obeyed him meekly, he jumped on her like a lion on its prey. She shut her eyes in fear. When he finally stopped, there was not an inch of her body that did not bear the marks of his nails and teeth. She felt that she would die. He punched her in the stomach and asked, 'You whore, are you Gloria Fernandez?' She said, 'No … Sorry, I'm Arulmozhi Nangai.'

'Oh, so you do know how to speak the truth. Now get ready for the interrogation.'

He came back almost immediately. She was sobbing uncontrollably as she replied to his questions. When she told him she was a singer, he said, 'That's why your cries are melodious. I'll really make you sing.' Then he asked, 'Who is Meenakshi Rajarathinam?'

'My mother,' she said.

He was furious at her reply. 'Do you know what this is?' he asked. 'A pen?' she said. 'No. A torture pen. I'll push it inside you if you lie to me.' She looked at the pen in fear. It was three times as large as an ordinary pen. It had a sharp edge and metal thorns fixed to it. When Caesar pushed a button on it, a red light flashed in her face. As she stood in fear, not knowing what would happen next, two soldiers pushed her back onto the cot.

Caesar asked once more, 'Who is Meenakshi Rajarathinam?' The moment she replied, 'My mother,' the pen was pushed inside her vagina. She screamed at the electric current that shook her body. Finally, she broke down and said, 'It's Sugandhi, who was in the Iyakkam. Sugandhi is Meenakshi Rajarathinam.'

'Oh, now you are on track, you bitch.' He pulled the pen out. The thorns tore her flesh. She quickly replied to all his questions. If she delayed even for a little while, he would use the pen until she screamed for mercy.

Yamuna too was being interrogated in the same way in the next room. Colonel Rodriguez was more cruel than Caesar. He did not even give Yamuna the time to take her clothes off. He hit her until her breasts and nose bled, and burnt her around her navel and nipples with his cigarette. After that, he entered her. But the next stage was different. Instead of the torture pen, he used the 'raping robot'. The robot's hands were cold. She felt her ribs cracking under its strength. Its iron kiss was horrifying. When it entered her, she nearly collapsed with pain. She was sobbing as she answered the colonel's questions about Gayathri and Juliet. And when she refused to speak about Hume and Andrea, he brought out the torture pen as well.

When the interrogation ended, Yamuna's condition was worse than Arul's. Both of them were put in cells for further questioning. A gynaecologist from Colombo arrived to treat them.

Peter was tense when he left the Nelum Pokuna with Manju. Juliet had sent him a text message: 'Peter, they suspect me. You escape. I will never betray you.' The words were like a bullet flying towards his forehead. Peter was thinking about his baby. 'How can I escape and leave her to die?' Manju could sense Peter's anxiety. She poured him a glass of whiskey.

'What happened? Why are you worried?'

'We didn't see Juliet when we left.'

'Oh! Are you worried about that?'

'She is pregnant.'

'So you are worried about the baby.'

'Yes. She might have a miscarriage if she exerts herself like this.'

'Nothing will happen. Even if it does, just take another chance. If you want to be a father, I am ready.'

'Shut up,' Peter said, and showed her Juliet's message.

She was shocked. She immediately called Samaraveera and told him that she wanted to go back as her mother was ill. He arranged tickets for the evening flight.

My conscience accused me of betraying the woman I loved and abandoning my dream project on Rajini. But I quickly packed and left for the airport with Manju.

On the way, she showed me her iPhone. There was a video in it. An S-Class Benz with a CHOGM number plate was coming from Liberty Plaza car park minutes after the inaugural ceremony, and moving towards the venue. Acting on suspicion, the soldiers stopped the car near the Natural History Museum. Manju said, 'Peter, minutes after the driver got out, the car exploded. The security officers were killed. The government has hushed it up. It is said that a woman without hands was driving the car. There are pictures of her on WhatsApp. It is said that after the explosion, when the flames were rising, she flew into the sky. Facebook comments corroborate this story.'

I was shocked by the pictures. It was Devanayaki. I returned the phone to Manju.

'Anyway, we are safe,' she said.

'But how can a woman without hands drive a car? Then fly to the skies?'

'I'm sure she would have had people to help her. These are grossly exaggerated stories. Maybe she lost her hands in the explosion. Soldiers are known for making up such tales.'

When the aircraft took off, I saw Devanayaki. From a burning Lanka, she was coming to Kanthalur with me. She had placed one foot on Sigiriya and the other on Sripada. I could hear Arulmozhi Nangai's song:

I am sad sad sad
I am mad mad mad
Kill me kill me kill me
Fuck me fuck me fuck me
I am one who has lost her dreams
Forgotten poetry
Burnt love from her heart

···

Translator's Note
PRIYA K. NAIR

————◦∞◦————

A Conversation with T.D. Ramakrishnan

————◦∞◦————

Insights,
Interviews
and
More …

T.D. Ramakrishnan's novels have complex structures that offer plural perspectives, multiple modes of narration and a relentless revision of authorized history. Memories mingle with fables, blurring the boundaries of fact and fiction.

Malayalam literature written in the late fifties and sixties revealed the impact of modernism, but the criticism against such works was that the writers had never experienced the horrors of the World Wars or the existentialist angst that troubled the European writers, and that the modernist trends in these works were only copied from the west. In the late sixties, with O.V. Vijayan's *The Legends of Khasak*, postmodernism made its presence felt in Malayalam literature. Writers subverted the linear narrative structure and dealt with themes that had not been discussed before.

Malayalam literature of contemporary times displays disillusionment with the communist movement, the multiple effects of the gulf diaspora, the rise of consumerism and the increasing dependence on technology for entertainment and information. The youth displays a conscious ignorance of politics and is immersed in the extensive possibilities of state of the art technology.

T.D. Ramakrishnan has made a mark in Malayalam literature by using the extensive possibilities of alternative history. He has succeeded in mixing myth and history with impeccable ease. In Malayalam, C.V. Raman Pillai's *Marthandavarma* was the first novel to experiment with history. For years after that, history remained strictly an objective background against which plots played out. In an effort to problematize the discourse of accepted history, T.D. Ramakrishnan in his novel *Francis Itty Cora* explores the events of local history mixing it with myth and memory. In *Sugandhi Alias Andal Devanayaki*, the author uses the recorded history of the Eelam movement in Sri Lanka, but he universalizes the struggle for freedom by mixing it with the invented myth of Devanayaki who valiantly fought against the atrocities of King Mahinda using her brains as well as her body. He suggests that Devanayaki is reincarnated whenever women are exploited. Each woman has a Devanayaki within her who rebels against the cruelties of a patriarchal power structure. This very political novel provides an insight into the quest for identity that has become a mark of the contemporary world. Human beings marginalized because of gender, race, religion or politics strive for existence in a hostile world that is becoming increasingly fascist in its outlook. Though the novel is about the Eelam movement in Sri Lanka, the author understands that freedom of individuals is a highly contested issue everywhere in the contemporary world. He reiterates that women and children are always the most affected during times of violence – state sponsored or revolutionary. The fable of Devanayaki is a tale of resistance against the exploitation of women.

T.D. Ramakrishan's fictional narratives also display the characteristics of 'auto-modernity' as he uses the extensive possibilities of technology. The internet becomes a mode to express autonomy as characters slip into various identities with protean ease. Technology is used in unexpected ways, challenging traditional concepts of knowledge, culture and writing.

Most of the fiction written in Malayalam is located in Kerala. Very rarely are narratives placed outside this space. Local colour and flavour play a very important part in novels and poems. But T.D. Ramakrishnan's narrative spaces are never confined to the geographical terrain of Kerala. *Itty Cora* travels the world and *Sugandhi*, though set in Sri Lanka, brings the world into its ambit. The author uses a large canvas to depict his fictional narratives and, in so doing, he often challenges cartography, implying that borders are abstract and cannot be reduced to mere lines that exist to exclude. Travelling becomes a crucial feature in his texts, hinting at possibilities that have been overlooked by history.

The author is very conscious of the power of literature as something that can be used to resist fascist ideologies. His novel can be seen as a powerful articulation against authoritarian power structures. He firmly believes that the artist must question regimes that turn a blind eye towards stark realities.

Priya K. Nair: *Sugandhi Alias Andal Devanayaki* is set in Sri Lanka. What was your motivation in choosing this space?

T.D. Ramakrishnan: I have been keenly following the political and social changes in Sri Lanka for the past twenty-five years. Initially, I was inspired by the freedom movement in Sri Lanka. From my limited experience then, I'd assumed that this was a revolutionary movement, much like the movement led by Che Guevara. But after the assassination of Rajiv Gandhi, I grew suspicious about the modus operandi of this movement. A truly revolutionary movement would not use suicide bombers. They will not hire killers. Revolutions aim at removing the class of exploiters, but I cannot condone the murder of innocents. Any revolution needs to be democratic, otherwise its disintegration is inevitable. Sri Lanka is a lesson that teaches us the need for democracy within a revolt. A leader who makes undemocratic decisions will cause untold harm to the multitude.

I read Tamil literature, particularly Sri Lankan Tamil literature. I know that the political scenario in Sri Lanka is quite complex. There is state sponsored violence on one side, and the extremely violent Tamil movement on the other. I thought of finding out whether there was anyone who spoke of peace. I came to know that there was indeed a group of people who were against violence of any kind. There were writers, journalists, human rights activists – the intellectual elite, so to speak – but unfortunately, most of them were silenced. Some of them were deported, others killed. The violent movements preyed upon them. The genocide filled me with angst. Geographically, Sri Lanka is quite close to Kerala. I was born and brought up in Eyyal, in Thrissur. There were many people who went to Sri Lanka to look for work. Though there are many connections with this land, not much creative writing from India has focused on Sri Lanka. Most of the narratives produced have been partisan in nature. I wanted to write about the people who spoke for peace.

PKN: Your novels, quite unlike other Malayalam novels, choose locales other than Kerala for the stories to unfold. Why?

TDR: In the twenty-first century, literature has attained a global dimension. Not just literature, all discourses have acquired transnational characteristics. The contemporary age is marked by increased mobility. The movement of people across the globe has opened up multiple variations in the techniques of storytelling. The space in which a story unfolds is vast. One of the major problems that a writer faces today is to get people to read. They have many sources of entertainment, and so one way to capture their attention is to use literature to open new vistas of knowledge to them, to talk of new spaces. Literature is constantly reinventing itself.

I have tried to address the world in my fiction, I have attempted to speak to a global audience and hence, translation is vital.

PKN: In your fictional oeuvre, you often problematize myth and history. Could you speak about that?

TDR: A writer has to seek new strategies – one way is to problematize myth and history. In my novel, *Francis Itty Cora*, I have quoted Umberto Eco: 'Why write novels? To rewrite history.'

Accepted history is the voice of the power structure. This implies that the discourse of history is not objective or neutral. There are silences within the discourse of history. The marginalized have no space here and hence, history ought to be problematized. This opens up many possibilities for creative writers. So we have to explore the possibility of alternative histories, a discourse that challenges accepted notions that exist in the fields of sociology, anthropology and politics.

Myths have, from time immemorial, been the repository of human imagination. Myths travel from one person to another, and in the course of this travel, they change. This change is a clear indicator of the strength of human imagination. It has an aesthetics of its own. And a myth is a collaborative effort. It has political undercurrents. That is what makes it organic. When myth and history are used in a narrative, new dimensions open up before us. Myths have fascinated me, as have the silences in history – and my narratives blend myths and silences.

Myths should never be confused with events, or what can be called reality. Myths should be approached aesthetically. The pushpaka vimanam in the Ramayana is a brilliant example of heightened imagination – never to be confused with reality.

Some of the myths in north Kerala, like the Mappila Theyyam, are not very old. Myths can be generated even in contemporary society. In such a situation, myths become socio-political interventions. They open up infinite possibilities without any conclusion or end. I have created myths of my own which I have used in my novels. Andal Devanayaki is not an existing myth.

PKN: Your novels have been categorized as postmodern narratives. Was this a conscious attempt?

TDR: I have never tried consciously to write in a particular mode or use a specific technique. I can't write in that manner. For me, a particular idea or incident comes to mind and then I develop it into a story. I got the idea for this novel from Satchidanandan's poem 'Andal'.

Magical realism is a technique that most academics and critics have found in my novels. I believe that human imagination is magical. I indulge in wild fantasies that may appear absurd, but I attempt to take a quantum jump into meta-reality.

PKN: *Sugandhi* reflects stark reality too, doesn't it?

TDR: A work of fiction is not a photocopied image of social reality. It is a mixture of reality and meta-reality. This novel is a reaction to certain social issues that disturbed me. I was very close to several writers who belonged to Sri Lanka. I don't know where many of them are now; whether they survived the civil war or not. Shobasakthi (Antonythasan Jesuthasan) and V.I.S. Jayapalan have shared many experiences with me. I got a glimpse into the world of terror that they lived in by speaking to them. They just told me about the atrocities they were subjected to. War, whatever kind of war it may be, is a saga of violence and the worst affected are always women and children. But if I just put these events in my novel, I don't think that people would want to read it.

A writer is definitely a social activist, but not just a social activist. His social responsibility is rendered through his art. His creative output triggers thought. Writing is a political activity – it is a micro-level intervention, a rebellion against power structures.

A philosopher or a politician might suggest solutions to social crises, but a writer cannot put forward any answers. The human race has, at many stages and in many different spaces, made attempts to establish peace and to ensure the progress of humanity. Confucius, the Buddha and Marx have proposed ideologies to ensure peace and equality but, despite their interventions, violence and selfishness have only escalated.

I cannot categorically state what is right or wrong – that is relative. When joint families disintegrated and gave way to nuclear families, we bemoaned the loss of a tradition of communal living. Now we speak about polyamory, which is becoming increasingly common. It is the time-space framework that decides what is right or wrong.

Creative writing is a continuing revolt against oppression – not a riot, but a rebellion. It is rebellion to rejuvenate the system. It becomes the recreation of existence.

PKN: Could you comment on the current political scenario?

TDR: Fascism has many faces, and it has surfaced in many countries. The neo-Nazis and the radical left are gaining supporters. In some places the fascists are in power, in others they have a sizeable following.

In Germany, 12 per cent support the neo-Nazis. The Le Pens in France also have their supporters. It is frightening when we remember that these countries witnessed the bitter realities of the World War caused by fascism. They should never go back. But 12 per cent is the frightening reality.

In Sri Lanka and Burma too, such fascists have come to power. The ideology of fascism has been redefined. It uses new tactics. It comes in the guise of democracy or communism. It speaks of peace and development. It controls the corporate sector. Then, there is academic and intellectual fascism.

In India, it is now that we see the murder of writers.

What I say of Sri Lanka is applicable to the world at large. It can be about any country where the power structure turns against the people. In such places, women and children are the worst affected. That is why my novel focuses on the experiences of women in a country that is torn apart by internal strife. My fiction is an aesthetic rebellion against fascist structures.